MINE:
ORIGINS

MINE:
ORIGINS

A NOVEL BY

WILLIAM J. DAVIS

Special thanks to the professionals who made this novel possible.

Copyedited by Marcus Trower
Cover design by Dan Van Oss at CoverMint Design
Designed and typeset by Andrew Tennant

ISBN-13: ISBN: 978-0-578-46595-1

This novel is dedicated to all my readers, especially those who rate and review my work. Whether glowing or not, I value every comment, and you constantly drive me to tell a better story. Of course, none of this would be possible without the help of my family, friends, and Marcus Trower, a fantastic editor.

A special dedication and huge thank-you goes out to my best friend Dustin, who's always eager to share his opinion and who's spark set fire to the plot and transformed this book.

1
Brazil 1961

Terrified eyes watched from the darkness as footsteps approached through the dirt and leaves. The weathered green door panel of the tent flew open, and Cage stomped in.

"What the hell is it?"

Cage—a tall, muscular, thirty-eight-year-old army vet—took a crooked stance in the center of the operations tent and glared at Petrie, the young radio operator seated at a small desk across the room.

"Sorry, sir," Petrie, a young, thin, studious-looking man with no hair and reading glasses replied. "I don't know. He just ran in here and hid under my cot."

Cage pursed his lips in disgust and bent over. Sure enough, the grown man was tucked under Petrie's cot like a frightened child.

"Christ Almighty. Get out from under there!"

The man didn't budge or make a sound.

"Should I get help?" Petrie asked, and Cage scoffed. He stepped over to the cot, reached underneath, and grabbed the man's leg. The man screamed, then screamed again when Cage drug him to the middle of the room. He tried to crawl his way back, but Cage was too strong.

Cage flipped him over, saw who it was and that his shirt was covered in blood. "Damn, Jackson. What happened to you?"

Jackson rolled over on his belly and tried to crawl away again. "Don't let 'em get me. Don't let 'em get me. Don't let 'em—"

"Hey!" Cage shouted, and pinned him to the ground. "Hold still."

"Want me to get the doc?" Petrie asked.

"No. Just give me your chair."

Petrie got up, pushed the chair over, and Cage lifted Jackson by his collar and belt. Jackson—a gangly, long-haired redhead—struggled, but when Cage slammed his skinny body down into the chair, he was more afraid of Cage than what he'd just seen.

"Please, please, please, I have to go. I just want to go home."

"Sure," Cage replied. "I'll get you home as soon as you tell me what happened. Are you injured? You're covered in blood."

"Blood?"

"Yeah . . . blood," Cage said, and pulled Jackson's shirt out so he could see.

"Oh Jesus. Did it get me? Did it—?"

Cage slapped him in the face. "Don't start that again. Tell me what happened. Where's the rest of the survey team?"

Jackson spit, and blood dripped from his mouth down his chin. "Okay!" Jackson replied, then spit again. He hugged himself, leaned forward, and rocked back and forth. "Me, Todd, and Baxter finished surveying 103, and since it didn't take that long, Baxter wanted to get a jump on 104. We parked at the creek, grabbed our stuff, and headed in. Jackson's eyes strayed from Cage to the darkness under the cot.

"Hey!" Cage barked and snapped his fingers in Jackson's face. "Stay with me."

We crossed the creek, walked about fifty yards toward one of those giant kapok trees, but I forgot my tape and had to go back. Todd and Baxter kept going, and I started back to the Jeep." Jackson sighed, took a deep breath, then continued. "As soon as we lost sight of each other, I heard Baxter scream. I turned and looked but couldn't see what was going on. I dropped my gear and ran over to help, but then I heard Todd scream. There was something moving in the jungle, and I froze. Todd fell out of the sky and hit the ground right in front of me, but it was just his top half."

"What?"

"Just the top half . . . Jesus God . . . it was just his top half . . . blood and organs and . . . Oh Jesus. I ran. I heard them around me."

"Who?"

"I made it to the creek, and when I got to the other side, there was something hanging from a tree . . . It was Baxter."

"Somebody hung him?"

"No, no, no, no, no," Jackson replied, then covered his face and cried.

"Jackson! Goddamn it. Answer me," Cage shouted, and slapped his head.

Jackson sniveled, wiped the snot on his sleeve, and looked back at Cage.

"So, he was hanging, but he hadn't been hung . . . What the hell does that mean?"

"He was hung by the arms because he didn't have a head. His arms were pulled back around the limb, and he looked like he'd been crucified or something."

"Except his head was gone." Jackson grabbed Cage's collar with both hands and pulled him forward.

4

"No!" Jackson screamed, then muttered something under his breath.

"What?"

"His head wasn't missing. They gave it to me! They gave me his head. They gave it to me."

"They who?" Cage asked, and yanked Jackson's hands from his shirt.

Jackson sat silent for a moment and looked at the tent flap.

"Jackson! Who?"

"I was looking at Baxter, and I heard something. I turned around, and it was standing on the other side of the creek. It was standing right there!"

"What?"

"It! I don't know . . . It. It wasn't human. It was like a monkey, but it was big and stood up like a man."

Cage sighed and rubbed his eyes. "A big monkey. That's what you saw?" Cage shook his head. "A big monkey tore a man in half, lopped off another man's head, and crucified him on a tree branch?"

"It wasn't a monkey; it was something else. It stood there and looked at me, then pointed down along the bank."

"It drew a line in the sand? That's what you're

saying? That's just great," Cage said, and rubbed the back of his neck.

"Yes! It pointed at the creek and slapped itself on the chest! Then it pointed at the Jeep. I turned to run, but another one was standing right there. It was holding Baxter's head in its hands and shoved it into my chest. It made me take it. I ran to the Jeep and got back here as fast as I could."

Cage thought about it a moment, then stood up. "Let's go."

"What?" Jackson replied.

"There's still enough daylight left. You're gonna show me where all this happened. I want to see it for myself."

"Bullshit! I'm going home."

"You don't go anywhere without my approval, so get in the Jeep."

"No!" Jackson yelled, and tripped as he jumped out of his seat.

Cage walked out of the tent, got the attention of Mills and Parker, two security officers looking at something in Jackson's Jeep, and waved them over.

"Collect Mr. Jackson. The four of us are going for a little ride."

Cage slid into the driver's seat, and the two officers drug Jackson out of the tent. Mills and Parker were new hires. Two months ago they were MPs at Fort Bragg and still carried themselves with the same authority. They collected Jackson, threw him in the back seat, and Mills hopped in the back to keep Jackson from jumping out. The other guard hesitated to get in the front seat, and Cage looked at him. He noticed Baxter's head when he got in but looked back at the guard with a puzzled expression. The man just stood there.

Cage sighed, grabbed Baxter's head by the hair, and pitched it out of the car. "Can we go now?"

The man got in, and they drove into the jungle.

Survey sector 104 was at the westernmost end of the two-hundred-mile tract of jungle they were tasked to survey. As the project had just gotten started, base camp was twenty miles away, but in jungle terms, it took some time to get there.

As soon as they reached the creek, Jackson panicked, and the security officer couldn't hold him. He jumped out and ran toward camp.

"Let him go," Cage said as he drew his pistol. "We'll pick him up on the way back."

Cage found the tree where Baxter's body had been. There was blood on the branch and on the ground but no body. They crossed the creek, walked a hundred yards, but only found blood. On the way back to the Jeep, Cage stopped at the edge of the creek but motioned for the other two men to keep going.

There were two imprints in the dirt at the water's edge. Cage knelt down and took a closer look. They were big enough to be human. The spacing was wide enough to be someone standing there looking at the other side, but the shape was all wrong. The heel, toes, and arch were elongated and out of place. They were strange, but as Cage looked at the tracks, what bothered him most was there were only two. There were no tracks approaching or walking away, just two weird feet where something had stood.

His attention turned to the surface of the water, and he watched the reflections and ripples. Black, green, white, and brown twisted together in irregular patterns until the ripples smoothed. Cage made out the shape of the branches and leaves above. Among them, however, was a dark patch, and he saw it move.

Cage eased the safety off, moved his finger on the trigger, then raised the gun as quick as he could. He looked up but saw nothing. He scanned the trees. Whatever he thought he saw reflected in the water wasn't there. Cage flipped the safety back on, holstered his weapon, and walked back to the Jeep.

On their way to camp, they came across Jackson, who had run about a mile before exhaustion reduced his speed to a stroll. Cage stopped, and Jackson hopped in the back. They arrived at camp just before dark.

Cage went straight to the operations tent and had Petrie relay a message to their contact in Manaus. The regional agent passed it Stateside, and by the time Cage received a response he was on his way to bed.

Petrie delivered the decoded message, and Cage shook his head. *Collect live specimen for analysis, expert en route.*

"You've got to be kidding. Catch it with what?"

Cage woke before dawn, as he had done since childhood on the farm. He had a good night's sleep despite the events of the previous day. The army put him in enough terrifying situations over the years that a killer monkey attack wouldn't cause him to lose sleep. As he put on his boots, however, he thought about his orders and realized he didn't have many options to pull it off.

I don't even know what I'm trying to catch, Cage thought, and scratched his head. "Killer monkeys? Jesus Christ, I can't wait to write this field report."

Cage met with his security team over chow in the mess tent, the largest of the green canvas tents in camp. The key members of his team were already eating at one of the long folding tables, and Cage took a seat.

"I think Jackson saw a sniper team in a ghillie suit," Reese, a stocky black soldier, said.

"Amen, brother," Jones, the tallest man on the team, said. "That guy's a—"

"It doesn't matter," Cage said. "One man's missing and another lost his head. A sniper didn't do that, and Baxter didn't cut off his own head."

"I don't know," Pickett said from the other side of the table, then plucked a kernel of corn from his mustache and flicked it on the dirt floor. "If anyone was clumsy enough to do it, it'd be Baxter."

Cage sat there while the others laughed, then took a syringe from his shirt pocket and set it on the table.

"The bad news is . . . the lab wants one alive, but since we don't have a tranquilizer gun or any useful gear, we'll have to do it by hand."

"By hand?" Betts said, and Pickett scoffed.

"I know . . . but we've got our orders, so listen up. I got this from the doc, and he said there's enough in this syringe to knock out a horse."

"That's great," Pickett said, "but we have to get ahold of it first."

"Greased pig contest," London, the eldest man on the team, said, and scratched his salt-and-pepper hair. "I love it."

"I say we use Jackson for bait," Jones said, then stretched his long arm down the table and grabbed the salt. "He made friends with one already. All we have to do is tie him to a tree, and when the monkey comes down to give him a hug, you jab it in the arm, or is that shot administered in the buttocks?"

The whole team laughed, even Cage.

"You may not be too far off," Cage said. "But I don't think we'll need Jackson. He said the monkey men attacked right after they crossed the creek, so I think we're the bait."

"That's great," Silver said. "I hate long waits."

"Since we don't know exactly what we're catching, and we don't have anything to trap it with, I only see one way to do it. We let one of them grab one of us, and everyone dog-piles its hairy ass so I can knock it out. We get it back here before it wakes up and lock it in a Conex container until the lab rats get here."

"Lab rats?" Betts asked. "They're coming here?"

"I know. I feel the same way about it. Bottom line, we do our jobs, let them do theirs, and try to stay out of their way."

"Before I came down here, those sons of bitches tried to stick a—"

"Alright," Cage said. "That's enough BS. Gear up, and let's hit it."

Dawn offered just enough light to see, and the eight men set off in two Jeeps. When they reached the creek, the sun peeked below the clouds and shimmered off the damp leaves. Thin shafts of light fell through the canopy and disappeared in a fine mist that covered the jungle floor.

The men got out, slapped a clip in their rifles, and lined up along the bank.

"Set a line," Cage said. "If we get split up, ORP is that kapok tree, but keep the line tight."

Cage waved his arm, and everyone crossed. When he signaled again, Reese, Jones, and Silver went left; Pickett, Betts, and Landon went right; and Tombs backed up to Cage to watch everyone's six.

With fifteen feet between them, they moved forward toward the giant tree. Small animals scattered from the jungle in front of them, and most of the birds fluttered away.

The team came together at the base of the kapok tree, and Tombs lit a smoke.

"Reese is probably right," Tombs said. "Must have been Colombian military or MTT sniper." He leaned back against one of the enormous roots and took a long drag. As he exhaled, something hit the ground, shrieked, and raced through the undergrowth ahead of him. Tombs dropped the cigarette and leveled his rifle before the cigarette hit the ground. "Movement," Tombs said, but the others had heard it as well. They scanned the jungle down their rifle barrels but saw nothing.

Another thud, and something ran off around the tree.

"Circle up," Cage said. "Let's backtrack and see if it follows us."

More movement, but this time it ran straight for them. Reese tracked the shaking leaves and focused on the footsteps as it approached. His grip tightened on the trigger, but he stopped.

"What the fuck?"

A wild pig ran straight into his leg. He lowered his barrel as it entered their circle, and everyone turned to look. Reese laughed, and the jungle exploded with movement. The team opened fire. Gunshots, smoke, and shouting made it hard for them to see and impossible for them to hear. They felt a thump when something fell from the tree and hit the ground in the middle of the circle.

Silver saw the creature first and raised his barrel, but the creature grabbed it. Silver tried to pull the rifle away but only managed to pull the trigger. The short burst dropped Tombs and Pickett. Pickett fell into Betts, who turned to catch him, and the creature cut Pickett's throat. Two more creatures took advantage of the open flank and killed everyone except Cage.

The largest creature wrapped its arm around Cage's neck and grabbed the rifle with the other. Cage tried to pull free, but the creature was too strong.

The creature turned him around, and Cage saw his team. One of the creatures finished off London, then added London's body to the pile.

My turn to die, Cage thought, *but not without a fight*. He let the creature take his rifle, but just as he let go, he pulled a pistol with his free hand and pointed it blindly over his shoulder.

The creature let Cage twist free but held his wrist. Cage emptied the clip into the tree. The creature spun him back around and smiled.

Cage dropped the gun, but as the creature watched it fall, Cage sliced it across the chest with his knife. The creature roared, grabbed Cage's other arm, and threw him against the trunk of the tree. Cage managed to hold on to the knife, and the creature hissed as Cage got to his feet. Other creatures had gathered, but Cage kept his eyes on just the one.

The creature crouched, bared its teeth, and leapt for him. Cage stabbed, but the creature grabbed his wrist again. This time the creature lifted Cage off the ground with its left hand and pressed its right hand against his chest.

The creature's talon-like claws punctured his shirt and skin. Cage grabbed the creature's forearm and yelled. The creature stared at him, and Cage recognized the look. He wore it many times himself and knew he was done.

Another creature stepped in and put its hand on the attacker's shoulder. They looked at each other, and the second creature held up a finger and pointed toward the Jeeps.

The attacker's eyes rolled back to Cage. It scoffed and squeezed Cage's wrist until the knife dropped. The creature looked at the one that intervened, grinned, and raked its claws across Cage's chest, then let him go.

Cage screamed, dropped to his knees, and clutched his chest. All the creatures moved off into the jungle except the one that intervened, and Cage looked up at him. Without the slightest expression, it pointed at the ground, slapped itself on the chest, and pointed toward the Jeeps again.

Cage got to his feet and staggered away.

A week later, Cage was at Walter Reed National Military Medical Center in DC with more stitches than the surgeon wanted to count and another set of scars he couldn't talk about. It took six months of rehab for him to recover and six more months of training to be field ready again. The day after he passed his physical, he was on his way south.

2
Chemistry

The sun reached the summit of the slate roof across the quad and sparkled off Glen's half-empty glass of orange juice. He took a sip, set the glass back down, and watched the sweat slide into a puddle on the table. The light led his eye across the painted surface to the cover of a tattered Mead journal, where he read the title for the hundredth time, then crossed it out. The knuckle on his thumb cracked, and a sharp pain reminded him of his arthritis.

He didn't feel fifty last year, but as fifty-one approached, he felt himself falling apart. The tiny joints induced reflection, and he grinned. *If getting by was a career goal*, he thought, *I've achieved it*. Career wise, he hadn't made much of himself, even in zoological circles, but after he published a paper about the role of zoos in conservation, the *New Yorker* gave him a call.

Glen stared at the black-and-white splotches on the cover of the Mead journal. *I wonder if these damn things will always look this way*, Glen thought. *It's 1962. The world's changing. It always does.*

He thought about his last article, "Condemned to a Cage." *Zoo animals should live in a habitat, not a circus cage. Lucky that editor from the* New Yorker *heard someone talking about it at a party. I'm supposed to publish science but rarely do, and now I have to rewrite the damn thing for pedestrians.*

Glen rolled the overcooked sausage link out of the grease on his plate, cut it in half, and popped it in his mouth. As he chewed, he looked at the huge walnut tree where the main walk intersected the smaller sidewalk that connected the student union to the English building. His subject of the past two weeks made its descent, and Glen checked the time.

Squirrels sure are funny little things, he thought as he watched its jerky paranoid movements. It scurried a short distance, froze, changed course, then darted off again.

Every morning was the same. Glen opened his notebook to the next clean page, took a bite of his ham-and-cheese omelet, and readied his pen. The trash can closest to the cafeteria door filled up first, and the squirrel always found something good to take home, but for some unknown reason saved that can for last.

The creature moved toward the patio, scaled the farthest trash can, checked for people nearby, then dunked its head into the opening, as if bobbing for apples. It dangled inside by its hind feet, and the only sign the creature was there was the tail as it whipped round in excitement. Still, it emerged empty-handed, as was always the case with the first can. It hopped down, looked up at it with disgust, and scurried across the grass to the next one.

As the squirrel reached the second garbage can, Glen felt a sharp slap on his back and dropped his pen.

"Morning, Glen," a high-pitched voice said, and Frank Baldridge, a professor of chemistry, slid onto the bench on the other side of the table. He was a plump, pig-eyed man, and the whole picnic table shook as he wriggled in.

Glen smiled politely, then shifted left so Baldrige wouldn't block his view.

"I see you went with links," Baldridge said. "I prefer patties myself. Links look too much like cat turds, and I see enough of those at home. But to each his own, as they say."

19

"Morning, Frank," Glen replied, and slid a little further down the bench.

Frank held his arms out and shrugged. "Have I got bad breath or something?"

"No, no. I'm doing some research and need to keep an eye on that squirrel."

Frank twisted around and watched Glen's subject disappear into the second can.

"You're bullshitting me, right?" Frank asked, then shook his head with a laugh. "Animal science."

"Did you need something, Frank?"

Frank twisted back around, straightened his leather jacket over his stomach, and picked a ball of crust from the corner of his eye.

"Well, yeah. I didn't come down here to watch the squirrels. You know anything about dam construction?"

"Sorry, no. You should try the engineering department," Glen replied. "Why?"

"Yeah, I don't know anything about it either, but I've been working with a company that's doing some interesting things down in Brazil."

"Brazil. Is that right?"

"Yeah, and I need a little help from you."

"Me?"

"Well, companies used to be able to build whatever they wanted down there as long as they paid off the government first, but all the nature-lovin' hippies changed that. Companies have to do impact studies. You know, count the trees and monkeys and frogs."

"I get it, but what do you need with me?"

Glen watched the squirrel pop out of the trash with a half-eaten pancake in its mouth. It nibbled on the burned edge, and Glen picked up his pen.

"Quite a bit," Frank replied as Glen jotted down notes. "The government hired me to come up with a new way to remove vegetation on a massive scale."

After removing the blackest, crunchiest parts of the pancake, the squirrel dropped it, leapt down, and worked its way toward the hedgerow along the building.

It stopped twice and dug several small holes but eventually reached the trash can next to the cafeteria door. Glen made a note, then looked over at Frank, who was irritated by the lack of attention.

"Sorry, you lost me."

"Come on, Glen," Frank snapped, and scratched his dry scalp. "Think about it. The military needs to be able to get rid of trees so the enemy can't hide, and there's lots of trees in Southeast Asia."

"Hang on," Glen replied. "Weren't you talking about dams in Brazil? What's that got to do with the military or Asia?"

"There's a company building something called a micro-dam in the Amazon. They got permission from the Brazilian government to test my product in the valley they plan to flood. The US military wants to test the battlefield application as well. I'm telling you, it's exciting stuff."

The squirrel scaled the side of the can but paid close attention to the students near the cafeteria door. When it reached the top, it jumped in.

"So, what is it you need from me again?" Glen asked without taking his eye off the trash can.

"Like I said, the government wants someone to do an environmental impact study before they sign off on the test, and that's where you come in."

"Me? I can't go to Brazil!"

Just then the squirrel emerged from the trash can with an uncut peanut butter and jelly sandwich, and Glen noted it with a smile. The squirrel balanced the sandwich on the lid and eased over the edge. Once in position, it pulled the sandwich over as well. The creature's sharp claws tore through the soft bread, and the sandwich fell to the ground. The squirrel chattered, flicked its tail, and dove off the can to retrieve it.

"I don't need you, specifically, to go to Brazil. I checked the Study Abroad roster, and you've got two PhD students down there already."

"Yeah," Glen replied. "But they've got their own research to do. They can't spend three months on an environmental impact study for you."

"I'm not talking about three months. It's more like three days."

The squirrel sat at the base of the trash can with one paw on the sandwich and scanned the surroundings. Two students dumped their trays on the other side but didn't notice the squirrel or the sandwich. The squirrel tucked the sandwich under its chin and made a break for the walnut tree. Unfortunately for the squirrel, it failed to look up and hadn't noticed the crow perched on the gutter.

"You can't do an impact study in three days."

"No one's talking about a full-blown study here. All the Brazilians want is someone to take a peek at the valley, tell them it's not unique, and sign off on the project. Now, you've got one kid in Rio and another at the São Paulo zoo. Just lend me one of them for a couple of days. That's all I need."

23

The squirrel made it ten feet before the first attack. It dropped the sandwich and scurried a few feet away, and the crow grabbed the sandwich and took off. The soft white Wonder Bread tore almost instantly, and the prize fell back to earth. The squirrel reclaimed it, grabbed the edge with one paw, and reared up on its hind legs. It tucked as much of the sandwich as it could under its chin and staggered toward the tree with a clumsy, three-legged wobble.

"Three days?"

"Three days. That's all I need."

"But she won't be alone. Right?"

"God, no! The construction crew is already down there. They have a security team to look after everyone, and I hear it's a nice place to stay. It'll be just like living at home, except she'll have a great view of the jungle."

With each step, the sandwich slipped a little further down, and when the crow swooped back in, the squirrel stepped right in the middle of the sandwich. It tripped, and the squirrel tumbled forward. One paw was covered in peanut butter, dirt, and bits of grass, and it watched the crow walk all over its prize.

"How soon does this need to happen?" Glen asked, and tugged at the ponytail gathered at the back of his head.

"They can get her on a plane tomorrow."

"Tomorrow?"

"Yeah! Tomorrow. I'm telling you, they want to get this done."

With a light touch, the crow gripped the crust and took off toward the building. It cawed in victory as it banked into a turn, and the sandwich tore free. The prize landed five feet from the trash can from which its journey started, and the squirrel rushed for it. Thirty feet away the little squirrel raced, and the smell of peanut butter drove him on. Ten feet away, it was about to pounce, but the cafeteria door opened and a frightening gray bin rolled out. The squirrel slid to a stop and darted under the nearest bush.

"I'll call Katie as soon as I get back to the office and talk it over with her," Glen said as he tried to follow both the conversation and the drama played out on the lawn. "She was hoping to make a trip to the jungle while she was down there, so I'm sure she'll jump at the opportunity."

"Great! I'll get things rolling on my end. Just get a confirmation from her before noon." Frank stood up and looked down at Glen's half-eaten breakfast. "I'll let you get back to your squirrel study and cat shit. Oh, you should come by and see what I've been cooking up. It's not as exciting as watching squirrels rummage through the trash, but you might find it interesting."

"Sure. Just call the office, and my girl will set up a time."

Glen ate his sausage while the custodian scooped up the tattered sandwich and threw it in his bin. The squirrel barked and chattered at the man, then accepted defeat and licked the remains of the sandwich from its paw.

Sweat dripped off the glass of orange juice as Glen raised it to his lips, and the droplets pattered across the pages of his notebook. He shook off the water, dried the pages on his pant leg, and laid the journal back on the table. He stared at the cover a moment and wrote down a new title: *Home: The Place Where Everything Wants to Live.*

Katie Winston sat Indian-style with her back against a tree and a bowl of fruit in her lap. She gathered her long blond hair, gave it a twist, and stuffed it under her hat. Sturdy limbs crisscrossed above her, while a trickle of water tumbled over a rocky ledge below. The water gathered in a tiny creek that curved out of sight, but not before it pooled in a spot to get a drink.

Light provided an unnatural brightness, and even the shadows seemed somewhat lit. The sounds of the rainforest filled her ears. Birds chirped, thunder rumbled, and frogs croaked.

The whole place smelled of earth, dampness, and moss. The air was cool, but even with the dampness, the humidity was low. Katie watched the branches, heard the creatures moving and the faint sound of voices.

A strange hand covered in hair reached around the tree, and its long claws slipped around Katie's neck. In one fluid motion, the creature swung around and landed in Katie's lap.

"Gladys!" Katie said with a smile just inches from the young sloth's face. "You're sitting in your breakfast." She cupped the creature's bottom, as one might handle a child, lifted it up, and retrieved the bowl. "You're a mess, that's what you are."

With one arm around Katie's neck, Gladys turned and sat on her thigh, then perused the bowl for her favorite treat.

Marco, a male sloth not much older than Gladys, dangled from the branch above and retrieved a piece of melon for himself.

Katie took out a leather-bound journal and added their selection to her notes. She watched them interact with each other, but when they finished breakfast, Gladys was the only one that stayed.

Buttons fascinated the creature, and Gladys liked to hook her claw under them and hear the faint click when the nail slipped off. Gladys also liked to watch Katie write in her book, particularly if Katie was sketching. Katie looked up from her latest sketch of Gladys and wondered, *Does she know what I'm doing? Does she understand I'm drawing a picture of her? Does she recognize herself?* Katie was drawn to the creature's happy little face and smiled.

"Are you happy?"

Gladys twisted her head around and looked off over Katie's shoulder.

A sharp tap behind Katie made her turn as well, and she saw Lia, the zoo director's wife, and her four-year-old daughter, Gabriela, looking in. Katie smiled, and the little girl pressed her hands against the glass.

Gladys watched the child jump up and down, then looked a Katie. Katie rubbed her head, and Gladys climbed up into the tree.

Lia, a beautiful woman with long black hair, pulled a small piece of paper from her shirt pocket and waved it at Katie. Katie replied with a nod, got up, and made her way to the small door in the back of the exhibit.

Lia and Gabriela visited the zoo every day and knew all of the employees by name—at least Lia did. Gabriela didn't do too well with formal names, so she referred to them by whatever they happened to do.

Katie emerged from the employee entrance just down the hall and heard Gabriela call her name.

"Monkey lady! Monkey lady!"

Gabriela wrapped her arms around Katie's leg, and Lia handed Katie the note.

"Good morning," Lia said. "I hope we didn't interrupt something."

"Not at all," Katie replied. "They just finished their—"

"You smell funny," Gabriela interrupted.

"I do?" Katie answered with a childish tone. "What do I smell like?"

"You smell like a monkey!"

"Do I look like one too?" Katie asked, then puffed out her cheeks and pulled her ears out.

The little girl laughed, and Katie poked her in the stomach with a finger. Gabriela laughed, then returned to her mother's side.

"Murilo was going to come get you, but we were headed this way, so I saved him a trip," Lia said.

"I appreciate it. I hope it's nothing serious," Katie said, and unfolded the note.

Dr. Powel needs to speak with you. He will call back on my phone at noon.

Katie folded the note and tucked it in her breast pocket.

"We better let you get back to work," Lia said, and took Gabriela by the hand.

"So, where are you off to next?" Katie asked. "I bet you're going to visit the snake house."

"No!" Gabriela shouted. "No snakes!"

Katie smiled, and the three parted ways. She looked at her watch, and with two hours to spare she walked to the vet clinic to see her roommate.

Katie heard Amara barking orders before she opened the front door, and followed the voices to the exam room at the back of the building.

"Keep the mask over his nose! I've got two more shots, and I don't want him waking up on the table!"

Katie peered through the small window in the exam room door. An adult jaguar was laid out on the surgical table, and Amara was about to give it a shot.

Laura didn't recognize her assistant, but she recognized the look. The poor guy was terrified. Katie noticed the timid way he held the anesthetic muzzle with both hands, and both hands were shaking.

It's one thing to see an animal from a safe distance or through bars or glass, Katie thought. *But when you're up close, a cold sweat, trembling hands, and a constricted sphincter* is a common state.

Katie opened the door.

Amara looked up and smiled. "Thank Christ! Katie, get your ass over here and give me a hand!"

Katie hurried over to the table. "What do you need?"

"Hold this mask! Carlo, you hold the tail, if it's not too frightening, or go change your shorts. I don't care which, just get out of the way."

Katie took the young man's place, and Amara readied the last shot. With one hand stroking the animal's broad head, she made sure its muzzle stayed inside the clear plastic mask.

Amara lifted a tuft of its dense fur and pushed the needle in. The jaguar reared its head and growled. Katie held the mask, and Amara administered the shot, but she noticed the gauge on the tank of anesthesia. It was empty.

"Oh shit!" Amara yelled. "He's waking up. Get him back in the cage."

Katie dropped the mask and worked her arms under its head and shoulder. Amara wrapped her arms around its abdomen and back legs, and they lifted the jaguar off the table. Carlo opened the cage door, and

31

as they lowered the creature to put it in, its head rolled over and came to rest on Katie's shoulder.

Katie looked down at its teeth and laid her end in the cage. She cradled its head, and the jaguar opened its eyes. For an instant, Katie was mesmerized by the depth of color and the way its eyes were camouflaged like the rest of its body.

"Katie!"

Amara's voice snapped Katie out of it, but the animal blinked, then snapped at her arm. Its teeth locked down on Katie's sleeve, and Katie jerked back.

Amara stuck her finger in the jaguar's ear, and the sensation caused the cat to let go of Katie so it could turn its head. They pushed the animal inside, dropped the cage door, and locked it.

The two women stood up.

"Jesus Christ, Katie! What were you thinking? That thing could have bitten half your face off before you knew what was happening."

"I know," Katie replied. "I'm fine. I just got a little distracted."

Amara scoffed and shook her head, then turned her attention to her assistant, who was already working his way out the door.

"No. No. No! You get your ass back over here!"

"You can't talk to me like that," Carlo said. "You forget your place. I'm the man here."

"Man? You screw up like that again, and I'll neuter you myself. You're responsible for checking the equipment every morning, and if I can't trust you to do it, I've got no use for you."

Carlo stood there for a moment and couldn't come up with a believable excuse, so he pushed his glasses up the bridge of his nose, pulled a pack of cigarettes from his pocket, and went outside for a smoke.

Amara disassembled the syringes she'd just used and got them ready to be sterilized.

"We didn't get to talk before you left this morning," Amara said without looking up from her work. "Any change? It's been three days."

Katie sat down on the rolling stool next to her and rapped her fingers on the counter.

"I guess not," Amara said. "So . . . do you know what you want to do?"

"I have to tell him," Katie snapped.

"I'm not talking about Eric; I couldn't care less about him. I'm talking about you."

"I don't know," Katie replied. "The law down here is pretty strict—"

"I'll take care of it if you want me to."

"No. I just need some time to think. You're sure about this, right?"

"I can't say exactly how long you've been pregnant, but you are."

3

Merit

Cage stepped off the plane in Manaus, slipped his sunglasses on, and slung the heavy green duffel over his shoulder. *Whoever said "Time heals all wounds" was full of shit*, Cage thought as he walked across the tarmac. *It's been a year, but I feel the same way I did when I left.*

Cage rubbed his stomach. *That's not something I ate. You've never been scared of anything in your life.* It was a lie, but he hoped he'd start to believe it. Pull it together.

He walked through the terminal, stopped at the curb, and was about to throw his bag in the trunk of a seedy cab when a sedan double-parked next to it and the driver got out.

"Mr. Cage?"

"Yes, sir."

"I'm your ride. Throw your bag in the back and hop in."

The short, thin man popped the trunk, but Cage didn't leave the curb. He checked the surroundings, looked for anyone out of place, and looked back at the driver, who smiled.

"Mr. Sid sent me. He wanted to talk to you before you head upriver."

Cage walked over and threw his bag in the trunk, but before he let the driver close it, he pulled a small folded green towel out.

The driver looked at the towel, then at Cage, and slapped him on the back. "You won't need that, but if it makes you feel better, just try not to shoot me on the way to the dock."

"Dock?"

The driver shut the trunk and opened the back door. "Sid's Boat Sales and Salvage."

Cage got in, and the driver headed south through the city. At the waterfront, he turned east, passing boatyards, warehouses, and a commercial dock. He stopped in front of the only freshly painted warehouse, and Cage leaned over and looked up. The word *Sid's* was painted in giant Coca-Cola script, with *Boat Sales & Salvage* in three languages underneath.

The driver popped the trunk, and both men got out.

"Have a good day, Mr. Cage."

"Thanks, but aren't you taking me back to the airport?"

"No, sir. Mr. Sid only asked me to bring you here."

"Alright. Thanks for the ride."

"Yes, sir. You're most welcome."

Cage walked in the building and heard his name before the little bell over the door stopped ringing.

"Mr. Cage," Sid said from behind a shelf across the room.

"Yes, sir?"

"No need for that kind of formality down here. Just call me Sid."

Sid pitched the spool of fishing line back in the box, walked around the end of the isle, and stuck out his hand. Cage was surprised to see a local that spoke English without an accent, and he couldn't mask his expression.

"You made good time," Sid said, "and to answer your question, I was born and raised in the US of A. My family's Hispanic, so at least skin-deep I blend right in down here." He brushed the dust off the front of his short-sleeve shirt and led Cage down a short hallway beyond the sales counter. "You need to hit the head before we shove off?"

"I'm not flying to Ameia?"

"No. I need to deliver a boat up there, and I thought the ride would give us a chance to talk."

Sid opened another door, and they walked into a huge, brightly lit space with boats on jacks lined up along each wall. The smell of wood, paint, grease, and welding fumes was thick, and Cage was surprised Sid operated such a thriving place.

"This is quite a shop you got here," Cage said.

"Yeah, we're pretty proud of it. We mostly do maintenance and repair, but we've got the best radio, electronics, and navigation services on the continent."

"That's pretty impressive. Is that your sales pitch or is that actually true?"

"We're out this way," Sid said, then pointed at the sliding door at the river end of the building.

The place looked like an aircraft hangar, and teams of different specialties attacked each boat. The one boat that seemed out of place, however, was a sailboat with a long gash the length of the starboard side just above the waterline.

"What's the story with that one?"

Sid chuckled and shook his head. "That's what you get when someone who doesn't know the first thing about boats takes one out at night and mistakes a breakwater for a dock. The *cachaça* probably didn't help, but for some reason every politician thinks they can sail."

Once outside, Sid led him down a gangplank to a dock. It was substantial and extended about two hundred feet from shore. Larger boats were tied up here, and Cage looked up at each one as they passed by.

"Are we taking one of these?"

"Nah. The one we're delivering is right down there." Sid pointed at a forty-foot wooden boat called the *Uiara*.

Katie left the vet's office and walked around the São Paulo Zoo, lost in thought. She stopped at her favorite exhibits and watched all the families with small children. She studied the parents' faces and noticed both happiness and regret.

Katie watched and imagined herself as one of those parents and thought about what being one might mean. *What would Mom and Dad say? What about my career? Dad would be thrilled if I walked away from watching monkeys and shoveling shit. What about the wedding? We'd have to do it soon … Here, I guess.* Then she thought about Eric. *It's been seven months. We love each other, but what will he say? He's such a great guy. He'll be thrilled.*

Just before noon, Katie walked in the administration building and up the stairs to the director's office.

Rosalice Oliveira, Murilo's secretary, rifled through her purse, about to go to lunch. "*Olá*, Katie," Rosalice said with a smile. "Murilo is expecting you."

"*Olá*, Rosalice. How are you?" Katie replied.

"Fantastic. I leaving for lunch. Okay you go in. He expecting you."

"*Valeu.*"

"Ah, *muito bom*," Rosalice said. She stood up and gestured for Katie to go in.

Katie was always surprised by Dr. Ribeiro's uncluttered office. She was accustomed to the mess of professors, but being tidy allowed her to see the things that meant the most to him.

The chair rail along the length of the left-hand wall was a gallery of his four-year-old's work. Most were crude drawings of animals in the zoo, but there were portraits of family as well. Just out of Gabriela's reach were photos and mementos of Murilo's days at the zoo in Rio and his travels in Africa, Australia, and Europe. These weren't the standard photos of five guys in button-down shirts who pretended to be explorers every few years. Murilo jumped at the chance to get dirty. In a couple of photos he was covered in so much mud, Katie could barely tell him from the natives. Still, he didn't like for his wife to worry, so he often played down his role in the rescue of an injured animal or the capture of a predator in order to take samples.

Behind his desk was a large window with a great view of the park. Katie looked forward to visiting his office. She could see the arched entrance, and when the weather was nice, Dr. Ribeiro opened the window so he could listen to the animals and voices of his guests.

Pictures of his family were arranged along all three sides of his desk. Katie noticed they served a purpose; no matter how bad something got, he'd look at them and begin to smile.

The right half of his office was for informal meetings. There was a large framed map of the park over a couch and two high-backed chairs with an oval coffee table that anchored it all together.

Murilo stood up as soon as Katie walked in.

"Katie. Good afternoon. I hope you're doing well."

"I'm fine," Katie replied. "How are you?"

"Great. You just missed Lia and Gaby, but you received my message."

"Yes, though I was a little surprised Dr. Powel wanted to speak to me again. We just spoke last week."

"He didn't get into specifics with me, but it sounds like he has an opportunity for you to do some fieldwork."

"Wow, that would be great."

Murilo picked up the avocado-green phone from his desk, carried it to the coffee table, and checked his watch.

"Dr. Powel should be phoning any minute now, so please sit down, and I'll let you have some privacy."

Katie sat down, and Murilo walked over to the door and lifted his hat from the hook on the wall. "If you need time off to do this, take it. Just let me know how long you'll be gone."

"Thank you so mu— "

The phone rang, and Murilo left the office. Katie answered, and the international operator connected the call.

"Hello?" Katie said.

"Katie? Katie? Can you hear me?"

"Hello, Dr. Powel. I can hear you."

"I hate to interrupt your research down there, but how would you like to do some fieldwork in the Amazon for a few days?"

"I'd love it! What would I be doing?"

"You know there's a push to build hydroelectric dams in Brazil."

"They're not planning on damming up the Amazon, are they?"

"No. No. Nothing like that. There's a small area north of the Amazon River on the Rio Negro where the government is experimenting with something called a micro-dam. They want to build it at the end of a long, narrow valley, but they want a biologist to take a quick look first."

"An environmental impact study would take months. Is it just me?"

"That's what I told them, but they're not looking for anything formal. Mostly, they just want someone who knows what they're looking at to have a look around. It's such a small piece of the jungle that it won't have an impact, but they want someone to take a look anyway."

"Sounds simple enough," Katie replied. "When do I leave? Oh . . . do I need to figure out how to get there, or is that taken care of?"

"All the travel has been arranged. Unfortunately, you need to leave tomorrow."

"Tomorrow!"

"Sorry, Katie. They need it done quick, but they'll take care of everything. You'll have a nice place to stay, and they have all the gear you'll need, so you'll just need to take clothes and a few notebooks."

Katie sat there a moment.

"Katie? Are you still there, or did I lose you?"

"I'm still here. I'll do it."

"Perfect. I gave them your address, and a car will pick you up at 6 a.m. to take you to the airport. It'll take all day for you to get to the site, so be sure to pack some food. There aren't any phones up there, so we won't be able to communicate, but call me when you get back."

"Thanks for letting me get some fieldwork under my belt."

"You're welcome, Katie. I know you'll do a great job. Just be careful. Walking around in the jungle isn't like strolling around a zoo."

"I understand. I'll talk to you in a couple of days."

Katie hung up the phone, sat back in the chair, and smiled.

At the end of the day, Katie met Amara at the arched entrance to the zoo, and they caught the bus home.

Katie told her everything she knew about the trip, which wasn't much, but she was surprised Amara didn't have much to say.

When they reached their stop, a block from their fourth-floor walk-up, they got off the bus, crossed the street, and went in the small market next to the bakery.

Both shops were owned by the same family, and the doorway in the wall between them filled both sides with the smell of fresh bread. While Katie picked out food for the trip, Amara gathered just enough for one meal and tomorrow's lunch.

When they got home, Amara put the bags in the tiny kitchen and watched Katie pull back the curtains behind the couch. Katie cracked the window, and the city pushed its way in as an indiscernible blur of background noise. The two washed off the zoo and met in the cramped kitchen to fix dinner.

"You've been kind of quiet," Katie said as she rinsed off the vegetables and nudged Amara with her elbow.

"I'm just thinking."

Amara looked through the opening in the wall, over the couch, and out the window. A woman in the third-floor apartment across the street looked back while her husband yelled at her from the kitchen.

"Is there a problem with the jaguar?"

"Jaguar? No," Amara replied. "The circus it came from went bankrupt months ago, and the poor thing was in terrible health, but he'll be fine. What I'm worried about is you and this trip."

"Me? I'm fine. I'm excited to be going."

"Yeah."

"What? They're taking care of everything—the transportation, food, housing, and even the gear. Besides, I'll finally get to go someplace most people never get to see. It'll be an adventure. What's to worry about? I won't be alone."

Katie sat the colander of washed vegetables on the wooden countertop in front of Amara and handed her a towel from on the wall.

After a long pause, Amara said, "I just don't like it."

"You think an animal might get me?"

"You're damn right . . . the two-legged kind!"

"Aw, shit! It sounded like a bunch of suit-and-tie types, and Dr. Powel said they have security, so I'll be safe."

Katie turned around and opened the refrigerator door until it hit the counter next to the sink. She took out a bottle of juice, stepped aside to close the door, and looked over her shoulder at Amara.

"I keep telling you Brazil isn't the US, but you don't listen," Amara replied. She took a carrot from the colander and sliced it.

"It's not that bad."

"Yes, it is. You just put up with it. Did you forget about the custodian?"

"Come on! He left me alone eventually," Katie said, and poured a little olive oil in the skillet.

Amara scoffed and lopped the end off of a cucumber. "He sure did, right after I hit him in the nuts with a shovel!"

"Oh my God! Are you serious?" Katie asked, but Amara kept chopping. "I thought he finally got the hint. Huh . . . He always scurries away when I see him at work, and now I know why."

"You're too damn nice, and I don't want you to get hurt."

"Like I said, they have security, and I'll be working, so I expect everyone will leave me alone."

"Alright, I'll drop it. Just be careful," Amara added, then raked the chopped vegetables into the pan. "Speaking of being careful, you seeing Eric tonight?"

"Very funny. And yes, he's picking me up at eight."

"You going to tell him tonight or wait until you get back?"

"Probably tonight. That way he has a few days to think about it before we see each other again."

"Don't expect much. There's something off about him."

"Jesus, Amara, do you hate all men?"

"Not all of them, but most."

After waiting on the stoop for forty-five minutes, Eric pulled up to the curb and honked. The streetlight sparkled off the white paint and chrome of the little coupe, and Eric leaned across the passenger seat to yell out the window.

"Let's go, Katie!"

Katie brushed off the back of her dress, opened the door, and slid in. "Where's your car?"

"I left it at the plant so I could test-drive this. I love the Interlagos coupe, but I'm still sorting out production issues."

"Where are we going tonight?"

"I have to go in early, so I thought we'd just go to my place, and I can get you back before eleven."

"Straight to bed then?" Katie replied with a disgusted tone.

"I thought you enjoyed it, but if you'd rather not, I'll take you home right now."

"Don't bother. Pull over. I'll walk home."

"What the hell's wrong with you?"

"I thought we had a real relationship, but I guess I'm just someone to have sex with!"

"I've had a long day, so let's call it a night," Eric replied, then parked in the first spot he found.

"I'm pregnant," Katie said.

Eric stared with indifference out the windshield. "Well?"

"Well what? They have doctors down here who take care of that sort of thing, and I can chip in for some of the cost."

Katie looked at him and felt sick. She spent all afternoon wondering what he might say, and she imagined her future with him in it, the baby, the house they'd live in, and the life they'd lead. She clawed her purse. In a few little words, she felt like trash. She couldn't think. She felt dirty and wanted a shower.

"We talked about getting married, and you said you loved me!"

"I tell my wife the same thing," Eric said.

"Excuse me?"

"I've got a wife and two kids back in the States. You and I have had some fun, but that's all it was."

"You son of a bitch! How could you? You said—and the whole time you—oh my God. I was your girlfriend.

I only did things with you because I thought—and now—"

"I don't think I ever called you my girlfriend. We were just good friends who'd get together sometimes and screw. I mean, come on. I've got a family to support, so I can't spend a bunch of money on whores."

Katie slapped his face and yanked on the door handle, almost ripping it off. She opened the door, got out, and kicked a dent in the rear fender.

As she headed down the block, she could hear Eric screaming at her about the damage. Katie never turned around. She pulled her purse strap onto her shoulder, held up her right hand, and gave him the finger.

Amara was right, Katie thought to herself. He was one dick this world would be better off without.

It took Katie half an hour to get back to her block, and the whole way she was lost in thought. The smell of bread snapped her out of it, and she stopped outside the plate-glass window of the bakery.

From the sidewalk she watched the old couple inside. The heat of the kitchen wafted through an air vent above the door and carried with it a wonderful smell. Katie took a long, deep breath.

The old man sat at a small desk and shuffled through a stack of receipts while his wife decorated a cake in front of the window. She looked up at Katie, smiled, and waved for her to come in. Katie was horrible with names. She visited the bakery at least three times a week, but hard as she tried, their last name escaped her.

The German couple moved to São Paulo in the twenties, and while they spoke Portuguese fluently, they didn't speak English, so Katie prepared herself for a gesture-filled conversation. She gave up trying to remember their names and referred to them as the Bakers, which always made the Hagenmachers smile.

Katie walked in, and Mrs. Baker pulled a stool out from under the decorating table. She patted the seat, and Katie sat down. Mrs. Baker waved a finger at Katie to wait right there, then exchanged a few words in German with her husband. Mr. Baker emerged from the back with a small white plate and two undecorated cupcakes.

Mrs. Baker took the plate, smiled at Katie, and shooed the old man back to his desk. Katie watched the plump little couple. *They always seem to be happy, and even after working all day they can still smile.*

The old woman set the plate down on the table and settled on her stool. With icing already loaded in the bag, she iced the top of each cupcake and pushed them over to Katie. Mrs. Baker went back to work decorating the cake and talked to Katie the whole time. Whenever she reached an unbelievable detail, she'd stop and yell back at her husband to confirm it was true.

He'd answer "*Ja, Liebes*," and Katie smiled, even though she didn't understand a word. Still, just being there made her feel better.

Katie finished her treat right after Mrs. Baker finished her story, and Katie tried to pay. Mrs. Baker waved the money away, and they both got up. Katie started for the door, but the old woman wrapped her arms around and gave her a long, heartfelt hug. Katie returned the same.

Afterward, Mrs. Baker went to the counter, picked up a small picture next to the register, and showed it to Katie. It was a recent photo of the Bakers, taken in front of their shop, and they had their arms around a woman about Katie's age.

Mrs. Baker pointed at the woman, patted herself on the chest, then pointed at the woman again. She held up her finger to keep Katie's attention, then said, "Daughter, Germany. Today birthday."

Katie smiled and gave Mrs. Baker another hug. The old woman teared up and opened the door.

Amara was surprised to see Katie back so soon, and Katie was surprised to find Amara on the couch with the Dutch cotton exporter who lived down the hall. The two women exchanged half a smile, and Katie went to her room to pack.

Katie traveled light and started in the bathroom. She looked in the mirror, opened the medicine cabinet door, and took everything out: a comb, toothpaste, toothbrush, and deodorant.

She closed the cabinet door and looked at herself again. The mirror was never a place to put on her face; it was the place to see the worst parts of herself. She never liked to look, but whenever she did, she'd wonder why others found her beautiful. She noticed every imperfection and shook her head.

Katie went back to the bedroom, opened the closet door, and found her suitcase. The leather Schell Tripak was right where she left it when she moved in, and she tossed it on the bed. Katie came from a family of over-packers, and since it was a three-day trip, she gathered enough for six. Katie packed everything except what she'd need in the morning, then turned her attention to her field pack.

It was under the bed. She put it there so it would be handy, as she expected to use it a lot, and chuckled when she laid the pristine bag next to her suitcase. It was already packed. In fact, some of the items still had price tags attached.

Katie remembered the day her father bought it for her. He didn't want her to go, but he insisted on taking her shopping. Since neither he nor Katie knew what she needed, the salesman was all too happy to help.

The bag itself was a waterproof Swiss Army rucksack made of canvas and leather with two buckled straps that held the top flap down. She opened the flap and untied the cord that held the canvas bag closed. The gear inside was still neatly packed, and there was just enough room for the food she bought at the market.

The large pocket on the outside had a lid with leather straps as well and was the perfect place for journals. She took four fresh ones from her desk and a handful of pencils and tucked them in the pocket. She buckled the flap, tried to think of anything she might have forgotten to pack, and set the rucksack next to the door. She latched the suitcase, set it by the door as well, and looked at the clock. The sugar rush from the cupcakes had peaked, and she felt the crash.

4
Ash

Glen Powel hit the wipers and cringed at the squeak. One swipe pushed the drizzle away, and he turned them off. He had driven an hour, out of the city, through the suburbs, and into the farmland on the other side. Just when he thought he was lost, he reached the rural road toward the lake.

Five miles later, he saw a military checkpoint ahead. Glen rolled down the window and stopped at the gatehouse.

A young soldier walked over, but a second looked at him through the window.

"Can I help you, sir?" the young man asked.

"Hi," Glen replied with a smile. "I'm Dr. Powel. I have an appointment with Dr. Baldridge."

"Yes, sir. I just need to see your photo ID and check the list."

Glen pulled his wallet from the pocket of his sport

coat and handed the soldier his license. The soldier took it into the guard shack, showed it to the other soldier, and returned to the car.

"Thank you, sir," the soldier said as he handed it back to Glen and pointed ahead. "Follow this road for three clicks and park in front of the old office. You'll know it when you see it."

"Thanks," Glen replied, and the red-and-white barricade rose.

A mile in, the natural disorder of the forest around him turned into rows of different types of trees. Glen saw everything from evergreens to birch, but Bradford pears outnumbered them all. He passed row after row, but it wasn't long before he saw the facility in the distance. It looked like an old steel mill, and as he got closer, he could see he was right.

The road curved left, then back to the right, and stacks of rusty steel beams lay like fallen trees beyond the drainage ditch. The building itself was long and tall, with a steel framework that extend out into the lake.

The foundry office sign was propped up against a small white building, so he slowed to a crawl. The office was one story, but a large steel addition had been added behind. The addition was about eight stories tall and big enough to enclose a football field. As Glen pulled up and parked next to the other cars in the lot, he heard the roar of a diesel engine. Glen turned off the ignition and looked around for a source. The noise grew louder, and a huge front-end loader appeared around the corner of the building. It didn't have a bucket; it had a heavy two-prong fork with two chains dangling from the tips. Glen watched it drive off into the trees, past a stack of huge steel baskets six feet tall and twice as wide.

He got out of the car and noticed the nearest trees were sitting in baskets like giant houseplants.

Glen straightened the wrinkles out of his sport coat and checked his watch. He was early.

"Glen!" Frank shouted from the roof above the entrance. "Welcome to the fun house! I'll be right down."

A moment later, the main door opened and Frank came out to meet him.

Glen walked up the stairs, and Frank slapped him on the back. When they went inside, Glen was surprised the room was so small, given the size of the building. He wasn't surprised to see two more soldiers behind a counter near a steel door.

"Fellas," Frank said as he strutted toward the door, "this is Glen. I'm giving him a tour."

Without so much as a grin, both soldiers looked at Frank, and the older of the two slapped a clipboard on the counter.

"Picture ID, and sign here."

The soldier lifted the page and pointed at the signature line of the document beneath. The first line read *Penalty of Prosecution*, and Glen looked up at the soldier with a reluctant grin.

"Nutshell," the soldier said, "you talk about anything you see or hear, and you spend the rest of your life in prison."

"Sounds fair," Glen replied, then shook his head and signed the form.

The soldier took the clipboard, and the other soldier opened the door.

"Thanks, boys," Frank said with an excited smile. He slapped the soldier on the arm and gestured for Glen to come along.

The doorway opened at the midpoint of a long hallway with a door at each end. Frank led Glen to the right, unlocked it, and turned left. Unlike the previous hallway, this one had windows along the right-hand wall, and people in lab coats stood at workbenches.

Glen noticed the fluorescent lights and white walls. The whole place felt like a hospital, except for the chalkboards, covered in molecular diagrams, calculations, and words he couldn't pronounce.

"This is where we keep all the eggheads," Frank said, and knocked on the glass.

A few of the scientists looked up, but most ignored him.

As they reached the door at the end of the hall, Glen saw a huge room beyond, but Frank ushered him through a door to his left.

"This is my lab," Frank said, then pulled two lab coats from hooks on the wall and handed one to Glen. "Put this on."

No one else was in the room, and Glen thought, *He probably has his own room because no one can stand to work with him.* He smiled and followed Frank to the other side of the room.

"I set up a little demonstration before I show you the real thing. Have a seat."

Glen sat down on a stool, and Frank brought over three potted plants. He placed each one on the counter about three feet apart, then sat down as well.

"So here's the problem," Frank said. "How do you get rid of plants quickly?"

"Well—"

"You've got lots of choices. There are herbicides, but you have to wait for the plants to die. You could turn pests loose on them, but that would take time and be hard to control. You might try a blight or fungus, but weather conditions would be important. You could always set it on fire—that always works—but if you're talking about hundreds of acres, you couldn't easily contain it. Of course there's always chain saws and bulldozers, but again, that's a lot of time and effort, and you have to do something with all the debris. What they asked me to do is come up with a way to make a forest or jungle disappear in an instant, like a magic trick."

"Why would anyone want to do that?"

"Good question. Let's start with the civilian application. On a small scale, how about a homeowner who needs a tree removed? The only way to do it now is to start cutting and hope the tree doesn't fall on your house. On a larger scale, how about clearing land to build a school? Then again, what about clearing land to farm or to build a new road through the woods? Imagine the possibilities, right?"

"Okay," Glen replied. "It's an interesting idea, but what's with all the soldiers?"

"Obviously, the military application is endless. For example, the French spent ten years fighting in Southeast Asia. The jungle and tunnels made it impossible to win. We'll be there next, and the military needs an advantage the French didn't have. Glen, you know what kind of enemy is hard to kill? One that has something to hide behind! Tactically, imagine being able to fight a war in a jungle and having the ability to make all the vegetation from grass to trees go away in an instant. For that matter, you could clear a path for supply lines, an airstrip or landing zones for helicopters or paratroopers. You could even push the tree line back around a camp so you can see the enemy coming."

"Alright, Frank, I get it. So what am I looking at here?"

"Well, this is the magic trick," Frank replied, then opened a drawer and took out a box of long matches. He handed the box to Glen and said, "Let's start with victim number one. Strike a match and try to burn a leaf."

Glen chuckled, opened the container, and pulled out a match. He struck it and held the flame under the nearest leaf. The leaf sizzled, curled, and turned black, but the plant never caught fire.

"Okay, try it on this one," Frank said, and pointed at the second plant.

With the match still burning, Glen moved it over and held it under the tip of a leaf. It burned like a fuse down the leaf and stem to the trunk. From there, it burned in both directions, and the leaves fell off, but each one kept burning.

When the smoke cleared, ash was all that remained, and there was a crater in the pot like something had been dug up. Glen stared at the mess. Everything but the dirt was gone. The match started to burn his finger, and he blew it out.

"How about that?" Frank asked.

"That's crazy. Unbelievable."

"It's not over. Just you wait," Frank said, then pointed at the matches. "One more to go, and you're not going to believe what this plant does."

Glen struck another match and smiled.

"Alright, Glen. Light it up, but don't blink!"

Glen moved the match under the leaf, and there was a bright flash of white light and a loud pop. In a fraction of a second the plant became a cloud of ash.

"Holy shit!"

"That's what I said."

"How did you do that?"

"If I told you the details, you'd fall asleep, but essentially I developed a molecule that reacts with plant cells. It sits there until it gets the right amount of heat, and that starts a chain reaction. One cell ignites the ones next to it, but it happens so fast it looks instantaneous. Actually, coming up with the molecule was pretty easy. It took me a year to figure out how to propagate it throughout the cells. I ended up using a virus to move it from cell to cell. It's ingenious. All I have to do is spray a little on a plant, and in three days it's ready to pop."

"Okay, it works on a plant, but how do you know it works on something as big as a tree?" As soon as Glen said it, he remembered the trees outside in baskets and knew the answer.

"Once I got it to work, the government retrofit this old steel mill and set up large-scale testing and production. We've been making barrels of this stuff for months, and they insist we test each batch. Come on. You'll like this."

The two men left the lab, walked to the end of the hall, and entered the batch-testing facility. To the right, two technicians in blue coveralls and hard hats pushed opened a pair of tall metal doors.

The front-end loader Glen saw when he arrived was waiting on the other side. It had a tree, potted in a giant steel basket, suspended from chains. The loader pulled into the facility about twenty feet and lowered the basket to the ground. The two technicians unhooked it, and the loader backed out.

As the men closed the doors, Frank nudged Glen's arm and pointed at the ceiling, where a gantry rolled along two huge rails. A square steel frame was suspended from more chains, connected to the hook. Each of the four chains was attached to one of the four corners of the frame, then continued down forty feet. Once the rig was positioned over the tree, the hook lowered, and the technicians attached the chains to the basket. A whistle blew, and the tree was lifted off the floor. It stopped five feet off the ground.

The gantry rolled along the tracks. The tree floated past Glen and Frank toward another tall door to their left. The technicians pushed it open, and the tree passed through.

"Come on," Frank said. "You can see better from the observation deck."

They walked up a long metal staircase into a room atop a steel tower. Windows covered three walls, and there was a long bench close to the glass. Glen walked over and saw the entire facility below.

"Have a seat," Frank said. "You can see the whole process from here."

Close to the ceiling, Glen watched as the gantry squeaked to a stop and lowered the tree into position in the rightmost of three bays. Bright-yellow lines on the floor marked where it should go, and once it was in position, the technician unhooked the chains. He left the chamber, closed the doors, and pulled down a lever to seal it.

There was already a tree in the second and third bay, and after Frank's experiment with the three house-plants, Glen guessed what was going on. A light came on in the distance and illuminated stacks of black oil drums. Glen turned his head to ask, but Frank beat him to the question.

"Those barrels are full of product. The batch doesn't ship until it passes quality control; that's what we're doing now. We get about a hundred barrels per batch and run one batch per day, which is pretty good, but we pull one random barrel to test."

Down on the floor, a forklift plucked one of the barrels and drove it up to a pump and lowered it. The technician attached a hose and pressed a large green button on the panel next to him. A siren blared, and a moment later a fine mist drifted down on the first tree.

"That's it?" Glen asked. "That's all you need?"

"It doesn't take much," Frank replied. "Like I said, it multiplies as it invades the plant, so just like catching the flu, you only need to be on the receiving end of a sneeze. We treated the middle one yesterday, but the third one is ready to pop."

Glen stood up and walked to the glass. "They doing that now?"

"Any minute. You want a drink? They keep sodas in the fridge back here for guests. Want one?"

"No, thanks. I'm fine," Glen replied, unable to take his eyes of the tree. "Is it loud?"

"About like a gunshot, but the test chamber and glass muffle a lot of it."

A siren wailed, and a steel collar lowered from the ceiling like the vent over a stove. Louvers opened in the roof, and the gray light of the rainy day struck the tree with foreboding light.

"Ooh, here we go," Frank said, and hurried back over to the window from the fridge.

A long pole entered the chamber with a blue propane flame burning at the end. As it approached the branches, Glen's nose pressed against the glass. He couldn't blink. He couldn't breathe, and his mouth fell agape.

There was a blast of light and sound, and a plume of ash was sucked through the vent in the roof. The tree was gone. The dirt from the root ball was cast across the floor, and the entire chamber was dusted with ash.

"Unbelievable," Glen said, and Frank opened his bottle of Coke.

"I'm telling you, I can't wait to see the field test. It won't be long now. You sure you don't want a drink?"

"How soon is the test?" Glen asked as he realized Katie's trip might put her in danger.

"They're keeping the date and time a secret, but I'm guessing within the week. The ASH is in Belém by now, so it won't be long."

"The what?"

"ASH. It's what we call the stuff. I came up with the name myself."

Glen just stood there. An hour ago he was excited, but now he was concerned. *She'll get in, get out, and be back at the zoo before any of this happens*, he thought, but he felt his gut twist.

Katie set her bags next to the apartment door, put her hair up into a ponytail, and went over to the window to check the street. Amara came out of her room in the oversized T-shirt she always wore to bed and yawned as she walked down the hall.

"You sure you have everything?"

67

"I think so," Katie replied, and sat down on the windowsill.

"I know I've said this before, but please be careful. You don't speak the language yet, and there's all kinds of things going on out there."

"I got it," Katie replied with a smile. "I'll be careful, and if I have any trouble I'll just hit 'em with a shovel."

Amara smiled.

A black sedan pulled up in front of the building, and a man in a suit got out.

Katie raised the window. "Are you here for me?" she asked as she leaned out.

"Miss Winston?"

"Yes, I'll be right down."

"Do you need help with your bags?"

"No, no, I can get them."

Katie gave Amara a hug, opened the door, and picked up her bags. With her rucksack slung over her shoulder and suitcase in hand, she descended the narrow staircase to the street.

The trunk was open, and the driver met her at the door.

"Good morning, Miss Winston. You're getting an early start."

"Yes, but I think I'm in for a long day."

"Well then, we better get going."

The driver took her bags, loaded them in the trunk, and opened the door to the back seat. Katie slid in, and the driver walked around and sat down behind the wheel. He reached over and picked up a large envelope from the passenger seat and handed it to Katie.

"Here's your itinerary and a couple of forms TMV needs you to sign."

Katie took the envelope, and the driver pulled away.

"Thanks," Katie said as she unwound the string from the paper clasp. "I'm sorry, what's TMB?"

"TMV," the driver replied. "Tucker Metz Varela. It's a global construction and services company specializing in off-the-grid construction."

"Off the grid?"

"Yeah, you know, places without real roads or electricity. Difficult places to work."

"Of course," Katie replied, afraid she just looked stupid. "Off the grid. So what kind of difficult places have you worked?"

"Me? I grew up in Bertioga, on the coast. Moved to São Paulo after school, and I've been driving for TMV ever since. I don't do construction or go out to any of their sites. I just drive executives around. Where you headed?"

"The Amazon for a few days," Katie replied.

"Shit. Sorry, Miss Winston. Excuse my language."

Katie chuckled. "That's okay. I thought the same thing when I was asked to go."

"Well, just be careful."

"Good lord, not you too," Katie said with a smile.

The driver looked at her reflection in the rearview mirror, afraid he insulted her. "I hear that a lot."

The driver turned his attention back to the road, and Katie looked over the documents in the envelope.

5

Legs

When they reached the airport, the driver missed the turn to the main terminal.

"Wasn't that the road to the terminal?"

"Yes, ma'am, but you're not taking a commercial flight."

"Oh?"

"TMZ has their own fleet of passenger and cargo planes. Given some of the places they fly, commercial flights won't work."

A half mile later, he turned and parked in front of the largest of four hangars. The driver got out, opened Katie's door, and got her luggage from the trunk. As they walked toward the entrance, headlights passed along the wall.

A short blue bus parked, and a stream of people piled out. Katie's driver opened the office door, and everyone from the bus filed in. Half were in street clothes and the other half in suits. Every passenger walked inside without so much as a hello. Katie's driver, however, smiled, held the door, and followed her in.

The waiting room was empty except for a young woman sitting at a desk.

"This is Miss Winston," the driver said as he stepped up to the desk.

"Have you signed your waiver?" the woman replied, and looked at Katie.

"I haven't had a chance to rea— "

"Sign the form and get on the plane."

The driver pointed at the envelope tucked under Katie's arm, and she handed it to him.

The driver opened it, pulled out a packet of papers stapled together, and put them on the desk.

"Just sign the last page."

Katie didn't want to hold things up, so she grabbed a pen off the desk and signed.

"The plane's through there," the woman said, and waved her away with her hand. "I hope you brought a pillow."

The hangar was well lit, and though the aircraft was dirty, light sparkled off a few clean spots of the DC-3. The driver carried her bags to the steps near the rear of the fuselage and handed the suitcase up to the crewman, who flung it into the tail of the plane.

The driver started to hand him her rucksack, but Katie pulled it away.

"Sorry, I'll need to keep this one handy."

"Good luck, Miss Winston. I'll see you back here in a few days."

"Thanks, and thanks again for the ride." Katie lifted the rucksack over one shoulder and climbed up the stairs.

From the back of the plane, the aisle divided the seating into two seats on the left and one seat on the right. Most of the seats were taken, but she claimed the last single seat, two rows from the back. Katie stowed her rucksack in the overhead and sat down. Judging by the conversation and body language of the other passengers, everyone seemed to know each other, but none of them acknowledged Katie.

The plane sat in the hangar for ten minutes before another passenger climbed aboard. He was a tall, broad-shouldered man in his midthirties with blond hair and a buzz cut.

"Nice of you to join us, Russel," a pepper-haired passenger in a suit said, and Russel stopped beside him on his way to the front. He stood there a moment, then continued to the first row, where the crew had saved him a seat.

Another crewman closed the door at the back of the plane, and Katie looked outside. The ground crew removed the chocks, and the engines fired up one at a time. The plane rolled out of the hangar, made three sharp turns, and in ten minutes they were on their way.

Dawn broke over the horizon just as the plane turned north-northwest, so Katie had a perfect seat. The sky was cloudy in the east, but as the plane rose, the sunrise cast brilliant shades of orange and pink.

The aircraft buffeted until the crew found an altitude free of turbulence, and Katie decided to read. She opened the envelope and looked over the papers. One document was marketing copy regarding TMV Global. It talked about the company history, the countries in which they worked, and projects they'd completed. It was no surprise they were so involved in Brazil. Dam work was their specialty, and with so many rivers in the country, the government wanted to tap the resource.

One article in the packet described how the steel industry had grown in the south and manufacturing had grown with it. The cities in Brazil were growing as well, and collectively, modernization was sucking up all the power it could get.

Katie thought about Eric. She remembered him telling her all about the booming auto industry in Brazil.

74

Who knew so many manufacturers were making cars in South America?

Another document focused on TMV's three major divisions: construction, management, and security. It mentioned a close relationship with the US military, but that part was vague.

Katie looked up from the packet and took a closer look at the passengers around her. Four or five could have been soldiers. She looked across the aisle and saw a businessman looking at her legs. To her surprise, he didn't look away. Instead, he made a clicking sound with his mouth, tilted his head, and winked.

Katie turned more toward the window and returned to reading. Her itinerary started with the 6 a.m. pickup and departure from São Paulo. The next stop was Cuiabá. From there, she'd continue on to Porto Velho and stay in a hotel for the night. Early the next morning, she'd fly to Manaus, where she'd catch another plane to the construction site. The site was north of the Rio Negro, toward the border between Colombia and Venezuela.

When Katie reached the end of her itinerary, she returned the papers to the envelope and sat back in her seat. She sighed and felt exhausted just thinking about it, then smiled and thought, *I'm only an hour in.*

disembarked and gathered around the tail. The ground crew pulled out their bags and pitched them toward the crowd. Katie picked up hers and followed the others into the hangar.

Like the hangar in São Paulo, they walked through the bay, into a small office, and out the other side, where a small bus waited. Katie climbed up the steps, but the bus driver held out his hand.

"Miss Winston?"

"Yes."

"Welcome to Porto Velho. Take the seat right behind me, and I'll tell you when to get off."

"Thanks so much," Katie replied, and pushed her suitcase into the overhead. She sat down, stood her rucksack in front of her, and looked out the window.

The bus pulled away and stopped three times on its way downtown. By the time it reached Katie's hotel, only two other passengers were left: Russel, the ill-tempered, buzz-cut blond, and a thin Brazilian with a mustache and a pinstriped suit.

The driver opened the door, and both men pushed by as Katie tried to stand up. She reached for her suitcase, but the driver tapped her on the shoulder.

"Excuse me, ma'am. Let me give you a hand with that."

Katie stepped aside, and the driver wrestled it down. "Thank you."

"Happy to," the man replied. "Would you like a hand getting them in?"

"No. No, I've got it from here. They're not that heavy."

"Okay. I'll see you in the morning. I'll pick you up at seven. Oh, you might want to check your watch and make sure you have the right time."

Katie looked at hers and compared it with his. "Thanks. I forgot all about the time zone change."

She crossed the sidewalk, walked up to a long flight of concrete steps, and looked up at the hotel. The arches, pillars, and a terra-cotta roof made it look like a Spanish mission, and when she walked up, a bellman met her at the top and welcomed her inside. All Katie wanted to do was stop moving, so she checked in, had a meal in her room, and fell asleep reading a book.

The next morning her Westclox travel clock rang, and she picked it up from the nightstand. She turned off the alarm, counted the glow-in-the-dark dots, and tried not to fall back to sleep.

She stared at the curtains across the room and wanted to open them, but the urge to stay in a comfortable bed won out. Five minutes later, she yawned, stretched, and pulled back the covers. She crossed the room and peeked out the window. It was still dark, and she watched house lights come on all over the city. Daylight slowly turned black to gray, and buildings took shape.

She turned away, scratched the back of her knee, and slapped her butt cheeks.

"You ready for another long day?"

By six thirty, Katie had cleaned, packed, and checked out. The hotel offered guests bread and fruit for breakfast, so Katie fixed a small plate and took it outside. She sat on the top step of the entrance and watched people pass by.

The traffic on the boulevard picked up as more people went to work. When she finished, she returned the plate to the dining room and noticed a small sign that said *Toilet*. Probably not too many toilets in the Amazon, she thought, and made one last stop.

The little bus was parked in front of the hotel when she walked outside, and the driver smiled and waved. Katie carried her bags down the stairs and got on the bus.

"Good morning, Miss Winston," the driver said. "I hope the storm last night didn't keep you up. I heard today's weather is supposed to be beautiful."

79

"I must have slept right through it," Katie replied. "And good morning to you." Katie stowed her suitcase and noticed two men in the back of the bus. "Good morning, gentlemen," she said, and the two responded with a nod.

Katie sat down behind the driver, and at seven on the dot Russel Hendricks came out of the hotel with a young woman clinging to his arm. He handed her some cash, slung his duffel bag over his shoulder, and headed down the stairs from the hotel to the street.

"Good morning," Katie said as he got on the bus, but he walked past her without giving a reply.

"What are you two plotting back there?" Russel asked, then threw his duffel into a window seat and plopped down next to it.

The younger of the two men said something in Portuguese, and Russel grinned.

"I'm sure," Russel replied. "Which reminds me, your sister said to say hello."

The young man started to get up, but his friend held him down.

"Ready to go?" the driver asked, and with no reply, he shut the door and pulled away from the curb.

They stopped three times on the way to the airport, and after the last stop, the bus was packed. When they arrived, the parade of businessmen and laborers began again, through the office, into the hangar, and onto the plane.

For this leg, all the single seats were taken, so Kate slid into a double, next to the window. Several passengers stopped and looked at the empty seat but passed it by.

A young man in a dingy white T-shirt, however, gave Katie a thorough look and threw his small bag in the overhead.

"You mind?" he asked.

"Not at all. Have a seat."

He sat down, looked at her, and snapped his fingers. "You're Kathy . . . Karen . . . Ki— ?"

"Katie," Katie replied.

"Katie . . . Right. I knew it started with a *k*."

"I'm sorry, but do you know me?"

"You're the tree counter."

"I'm a zoologist. Who you are?"

"Oh . . . sorry . . . Chris Shackleford, heavy machinery operator. We're headed to the same place."

"Nice to meet you, Chris. You know, you're the first person I've met, other than the drivers, who's said hello."

"Not surprised; tree counters slow everything down."

"If it makes everyone feel better, I'm not actually counting trees. My PhD advisor just asked me to fly up and take a look around."

"Makes sense. We're on a pretty tight schedule. We didn't even get a full week between rotations this time."

"So, what kind of heavy machinery do you operate?"

"Aw, hell, I can drive anything. I grew up driving tractors. I dropped out of school to join a road crew, but I took this job for the travel and pay. Most of what I do down here is push trees and excavate."

"Push trees?"

"Yeah, clear the jungle."

"Oh."

"Driving a Cat is about all me and Grover do. You'll like him. He's a hell of a nice guy, but he looks like King Kong. He could probably knock down half the trees with his bare hands."

"He must be big."

"Big? He's big big! I asked him when I first met him, and he said he was six foot nine and three hundred and thirty pounds. He played tackle for the University of Alabama when he was a kid."

"Really?"

"Oh yeah."

The engines started, and Chris straightened up in the seat.

"Are you okay?" Katie asked, and Chris gave her a tense, troubled look.

"I hate flying. I try to sleep through it. I hope you don't mind."

"No. I'll try not to wake you."

Chris shut his eyes and gripped the armrests. He didn't make a sound during takeoff, groaned through the turbulence, and released the armrests when the plane leveled off.

Compared to yesterday, today will be easy, Katie thought. *Two short flights will be a breeze.*

Chris was sound asleep in half an hour, and Katie drifted off not long after.

The change of engine noise and pitch of the aircraft as it descended into Manaus woke them both. Katie pulled the curtain away from the window but was careful to block Chris's view. He still turned away. From the port side of the plane, she saw a wide brown river. *That must be the Amazon*, Katie thought. As they flew over, she also saw where another river, just as wide, joined it. This river wasn't muddy, but the water was dark. Both rivers met in a delta full of rivers and streams that twisted in sinuous lines.

Manaus was just across the dark river. The shore was covered with barges moored headfirst along the shore and stacked side by side. Not more than a hundred feet away, curved roofs of long warehouses mimicked the barges, stacked together in much the same way.

The plane descended over the city, and Katie saw a blue dome on a fancy building that shined like a jewel. A large semicircular staircase led down to a huge courtyard covered in the most amazing tile work, and a monument stood at the center.

The plane banked left and slowed as the landing gear came down. Chris gripped the armrests, and Katie patted the back of his hand. He clenched his eyes shut and tried to smile.

The cool air over the river mixed with the heat off the tarmac, and the landing was rough. Chris waited until all three wheels were on the ground before he opened his eyes, then sighed. The aircraft slowed and rolled up to the company hangar at the far end of the field.

"That wasn't so bad," Katie said as the aircraft stopped.

"This was the easy part," Chris replied. "We got one more flight to go, and trust me, it ain't fun."

Katie grinned, and Chris stood up with the rest of the passengers and pulled his bag out of the overhead.

"We need to go catch the cargo plane to camp," Chris said. "If you still want some company, you're welcome to stick with me."

"Sure!"

Everyone got off, and Chris grabbed her suitcase when the ground crew pulled it out of the tail. They walked through the hangar and into the office on the opposite side.

Another young woman greeted them from her desk.

"You must be Miss Winston," the woman said with a smile, and pushed her long dark hair behind her ears. "I'm Carolina. Did you have a good flight?"

"It was fine," Katie replied. "Thanks for asking. Chris kept me company the whole way."

"With his eyes shut no doubt," she replied. "Would you like some coffee?"

"No, thank you."

"What about me?" Chris asked.

"You know where it is."

Chris walked over to the coffee pot in the corner, poured a cup, and turned back to Carolina.

"I suppose South-Hem is late?" Chris asked.

"They always are. The truck from the warehouse

got here half an hour ago, but since the plane wasn't here, they went to lunch. Ameia just radioed to let me know they're on their way."

"Might as well get comfortable, Katie," Chris said. "We'll be here awhile."

"Carolina? May I leave my bags here?" Katie asked. "I think I'll go out and stretch my legs."

"No problem. Mind if I go with you?" Carolina replied, and walked around the desk. "Sorry, Chris, no boys allowed!"

Chris took a sip of coffee and shook his head. "Fine with me. I'll hold down the fort."

Carolina walked Katie over to the main terminal, pointed out the restroom, and bought them both a local fruit drink from her favorite vendor. They took their time getting back, and by the time they did the DC-47 had landed. It looked like the plane she'd been on for the past two days, except this one had two large doors on the port side near the tail.

A stake-side flatbed truck was backed up to the doors, and two men in coveralls wrestled boxes and crates into the plane.

Chris popped his head out of the cargo bay and yelled at the other two. "Come on, fellas! Can you pick up the pace a bit? We need to get going!"

The two men barked something back in Portuguese but didn't change their speed or enthusiasm.

"Would you like to wait inside?" Carolina asked.

"Thanks, but I think I better go help."

When Katie reached the plane, Chris had disappeared inside. She grabbed a wooden slat on the truck, put her foot on the bumper, and pulled herself into the bed.

The ground crew laughed as she picked up one of the boxes, but she smiled and carried it into the plane.

"I said we need to hurry, Goddamn it!" Chris yelled, then looked up from the crate strapped to the wall. "Sorry, Katie. I thought you were—"

"That's okay. It sounded like you could use a hand."

"Sure. Just let those other two get the heavy stuff." Katie grinned and returned to the truck.

The two men didn't want to be outdone by a woman, so they hurried to get the cargo loaded.

Once everything was lashed down, Katie looked at Chris, who was covered in sweat. "So what's the rush?" she asked.

"Change of plans. Weather's moving in, and we need to get going or we won't make it to Ameia. We're staying there tonight and flying into camp tomorrow, after the weather clears."

"Damn!" a voice yelled from behind, and Katie spun around. "If I had known the company hired a woman like you to work the ground crew, I'd have been on time." The man laughed through his yellow teeth, fished out the snuff from his lip, and threw it on the ground.

Katie looked down at him, and Chris stepped up to her side.

"Knock it off!" Chris yelled, and Ozzie Monroe smiled.

"Who are you?" Katie asked, and Chris rolled his eyes.

"Ozzie Monroe, sweetheart," he replied, and straightened the collar of his bomber jacket. "Owner and pilot of South-Hem Air. And who might you be?" Before Katie could answer, Ozzie leaned forward and looked up the leg of her shorts.

Katie took a step back, and Chris stepped in front of her.

"This is Katie. She'll be in camp a couple of days," he said. "So just stay the hell away from her."

A scrawny, greasy-haired man walked up next to Ozzie, looked up at Katie, and slicked back his hair with his hand.

"Ameia gettin' a new whore?" he asked.

Katie's brow dropped.

Ozzie laughed, then slapped the little man on the back. "Come on, Riley," he said. "Let's get this thing off the ground."

"Sorry, Katie," Chris said, and touched her on the shoulder. "Everyone not like—"

"Get that truck out of here and fire up the engines!" another voice yelled from a distance. "We need to go!"

It was Russel. He walked out of the hangar with a young Brazilian in a white suit and fedora.

Chris and Katie hopped down from the truck bed and walked to the nose of the plane.

"This is Joao Pedro Rocha," Russel said as they climbed up the stairs to the passenger door. "He's another tree counter, but this one's with the Brazilian Department of Fish and Game."

"Hello," Katie said as Joao Pedro walked by.

He touched the brim of his hat and looked at her chest but didn't say a word. Katie looked at Chris, and he shrugged.

Everyone took their seats, but unlike the DC-3, there were only three rows; the rest of the plane was cargo. Chris and Katie settled in the last row, and the ground crew shut the door.

Katie sighed and over at Chris's bag. "Shit!" she yelled, then stood back up.

Russel looked at her with a scowl.

"What is it?" Chris asked.

"My bags. They're still in the office."

Russel got up, unlatched the door, and dropped the steps.

"Sorry," Katie said. "I'll just be a minute."

Embarrassed, she ran in, grabbed her bags, and raced back to the plane. She stumbled up the steps and dropped her suitcase on Russel's feet, but instead of helping, he pushed it out of the way and shut the door.

"Can we go now?" he asked as he looked down at Katie, who was not quite back on her feet.

She stowed both bags behind the seat, sat down, and wiped the sweat from her forehead.

Chris looked at her and grinned. "You're gonna fit right in."

6
Ameia

Ameia was a little river town an hour and a half away by plane, but for a plane loaded with freight and flying into a headwind, it was a slow go. The pilot flew low and followed the river the whole way, which made for a bumpy ride but offered a great view.

The Rio Negro was one river, but it was streaked with long, thin islands that made it look like veins. The width of the river changed with the same irregularity, and Katie wondered what it would look like in a hundred years.

The shape of the window framed a painting that constantly changed. Colors in the sky, colors on the ground, and colorful birds that flew between them. Clouds reflected light and cast fingerlike shadows that stroked the trees.

The surface of the river was crisscrossed with wakes from the boats that slid across its surface. From the tiniest canoe to the longest barge, it was obvious to Katie the Rio Negro was actually a highway.

Half an hour from Ameia, the once-distant clouds now rolled overhead, and the sun disappeared in the shroud. The plane entered the front, and rain pounded the aircraft. Katie watched for lightning and listened for thunder, but it never came. She turned to check on Chris, whom she had neglected the whole flight. His eyes were shut and his hands were pressed to his ears, so she didn't bother him.

Turbulence shook the plane for ten minutes, and Katie was glad she hadn't eaten in Manaus. The rain slacked off just as they reached Ameia, and Katie could make out a narrow runway in the distance. It stretched all the way across the south end of town, with one end near the river.

The engines slowed, and she felt a thump on the bottom of her feet as the landing gear swung down. The plane banked left and descended over the river. She tried to look ahead but only saw water, and it kept getting closer. The engines slowed again, the nose pulled up, and just as Katie saw land below them, the wheels touched down.

Katie looked at Chris and watched him uncover his ears and open his eyes. She smiled and nudged him on the shoulder.

"I hate this shit," Chris said, and Russel looked back over his shoulder.

"Pussy."

The plane stopped between two similar planes near a small wood-clad office. Russel opened the door, and everyone filed out.

Two military jeeps were already there, and the soldiers gave them a ride to the hotel. The rain started again, so Katie didn't see much of the town.

When they arrived at the hotel, the rain turned into a downpour, and everyone got soaked wrestling their bags from the car to the porch.

Katie walked into the lobby and was struck by how pretty it was. The woodwork, vibrant colors, finished wood floors, and handmade rugs that mimicked the curves of the river. It wasn't gaudy or fancy but welcoming and clean. The woman behind the check-in counter seemed happy to see her, so Katie gave her a little wave from the front door.

"Miss Winston?" the woman asked, and ignored the men crowded around the counter. "I Pedrina. I own hotel. Happy you here."

"It's nice to meet you, Pedrina. Go ahead and take care of those gentlemen first. I'm in no hurry."

"No, I have room for you. They wait," Pedrina said,

then snatched a key from the board on the wall and left the counter.

"Speak for yourself," Russel said, and grabbed the key for room three.

"Yes, Mr. Russel. You room three. Always three."

Pedrina picked up Katie's bag and walked toward the stairs while the other men took a seat. Pedrina led Katie up to the second floor and opened her door.

The room was a small, oddly shaped corner room but nicely decorated. Pedrina set the suitcase at the foot of the bed, walked over to the tall curtain in the corner, and revealed a french door. She opened it and stepped out onto a small balcony.

Pedrina waved Katie over, so Katie set her rucksack on a chair and joined her on the balcony. Katie had a view of most of the town. Rain poured off the roof, but the wall blocked the wind, so the balcony was dry.

Pedrina pointed to the right, down the main street, and Katie could just make out the square in the center of town.

"Shop there," Pedrina said with a smile. "No eat. You eat here. My food best food. No sick." She pointed toward the river. "That Rio Negro." Next, she pointed at a long, white, single-story building to the left. "Market. When ready, we go."

"Thanks, Pedrina, but I think I'll stay in my room a little while and rest."

"Yes, yes, yes. You rest."

Pedrina hurried to the hallway door and looked back at Katie as she grabbed the doorknob.

"You rest. I back fifteen minute. We go."

Before Katie could reply, Pedrina shut the door, and Katie listened as she sang her way down the hall. Katie sat down on the bed and chuckled.

I'll only be here one night, Katie thought. *Half the reason I came to South America was to experience the culture.* She laid back on the bed for five minutes, then got ready for the next event.

Exactly fifteen minutes later Pedrina knocked twice and opened the door. "Miss Katie? We go now?"

Katie spun around, surprised Pedrina walked right in, but grinned as she finished buttoning her short-sleeved shirt.

"I'm ready," Katie replied, then noticed a little boy about seven years old peek around Pedrina's hips. "Well, hello. What's your name?"

"Rodrigo," the boy replied. "I carry the bags."

"That sounds like a fun job."

"It is," he said, then raced down the hall holding a canvas bag like a cape.

Katie and Pedrina caught up with him at the entrance, and he pulled two blue ponchos from the others hanging on the wall. He handed one to Pedrina, the other to Katie, and grabbed one for himself.

"Should we wait until it stops raining?" Katie asked, and Pedrina looked at her as if she'd just told a joke.

The trio donned their ponchos, pulled the hoods up, and walked onto the deck. Water poured off the steps like a waterwheel, but Pedrina and her son headed down like it was a sunny day. The market was only a block away, and Katie expected they would run for it, but they didn't. The three crossed the street and strolled casually along the sidewalk.

They passed a takeout restaurant, where the cashier stood behind a sliding window. A long tin awning covered a counter that ran the length of the restaurant, and locals were lined up, having a bite to eat. Pedrina made some comment about the place, but with the rain pounding off Katie's rubber hood, the only word she heard was "cat." Katie smiled and tried not to assume.

When they reached the intersection, they crossed the street. The entrance to the market was at the corner, and the awning on this building extended all the way to the road.

They walked in, and Katie saw that it wasn't one big supermarket; it was numerous small shops around the outside walls and an open courtyard in the middle. Vendor spaces were marked by thick blue lines on the wall, and each vendor had one long table in front from which to sell.

Most of the tables were covered in raw fish, fruit, and dry goods, but several vendors prepared hot food right at the table. Katie thought some of it looked good, but every time she pointed at something, Pedrina would say "Dirty!" and pull Katie away. Her little boy, however, got into everything. If he wasn't touching something, he was about to, but Pedrina had him trained to drop whatever it was just by giving him a look.

As they reached the back of the building, Katie saw a wide opening in the wall and a long ramp down to a dock. Fishermen in ragged shirts pushed wooden carts full of strange-looking fish into the market and unloaded them at their respective booths.

Men and women barked at shoppers for attention and bartered over the price. Every vendor knew Pedrina, and Katie enjoyed watching aggressive negotiators change when Pedrina stopped at their booth. The ones she didn't like worked twice as hard to make a sale, but the one's she did didn't haggle at all.

Katie became accustomed to the racket and commotion and focused more on specific goods. There were so many imported products.

"Pedrina? So many things not from here. Where do they come from?" Katie asked.

"Yes, many things from Manaus."

Pedrina bought several fish, including four piranhas to use in soup. She filled the bag with vegetables, bananas, and a pineapple, then headed for the door. Katie followed, and Rodrigo brought up the rear.

At the hotel, Katie insisted on taking a break, though Pedrina tried to get her to stay in the kitchen. Katie went to her room, kicked off her boots, and shut her eyes.

A few hours later, Pedrina's girls knocked on her door, and she woke to the sound of children giggling. Katie opened the door and found two little girls no older than five tugging at each other's bright dresses.

"You come," the elder of the two said, and grabbed Katie's hand.

"Wait a minute," Katie replied. "I have to get my shoes." She pointed at her bare feet.

The two girls squatted down and looked at her toes. The pink nail polish pulled them in, and the youngest one touched her big toe.

Katie was certain these were Pedrina's kids and smiled. "Tell your mother I'll be right down."

"Okay, we wait," the older one replied, then stood up and pushed her way into Katie's room. "You come now."

"Alright, girls. Give me a minute."

Katie disappeared into the bathroom and made sure to lock the door. When she stepped out a few minutes later, the girls were trying on her boots.

The girls let Katie put them on and escorted her downstairs to dinner. One long wooden table took up most of the dining room, and dinner had already been served. All of the men from the airplane were there, as well as several others Katie had never seen before. She scanned the table for a good seat, and the pilot, seated at the far end, waved his hand for her to come over, but she ignored him. The only other spot was across from Joao Pedro, the man from the Department of Fish and Game. Katie smiled and sat down just as Pedrina came out of the kitchen.

"Ah, you here! I make special just for you," she said, and brought over her dinner.

It was a beautiful piece of grilled fish on a bed of seasoned rice with a slice of pineapple on top.

"This looks great, Pedrina. Thanks so much."

The kitchen door swung open, and Pedrina's youngest daughter walked around Joao Pedro holding a tall beverage with both hands. She raised it, and Katie noticed her intense concentration. The bottom of the glass didn't clear the table, it tipped, and the fruit drink sloshed onto Joao Pedro's leg. He pushed back from the table and stood up, but the girl was undeterred. She looked at him as if it was his fault, then pushed the glass through the puddle toward Katie.

"Thank you very much, um . . ."

"Luiza," Pedrina replied. "Her name Luiza. She four year old. Other one Bruna. She three."

"Well, thank you, Luiza, and thank you too, Pedrina. I hope you didn't go to any trouble."

"No trouble. You eat."

"How about a little service down on this end of the table?" Ozzie shouted. He held up his empty glass.

Pedrina rolled her eyes and walked back toward the kitchen. "I get you drink, Mr. Ozzie. You wait."

Joao Pedro finished sopping up the juice from his pants and scooted back up to the table.

"So, Joao Pedro," Katie said, "you work with the Brazilian Fish and Game Department?"

"Yes."

"What's your specialty?"

"My what?"

"Your specialty . . . Your expertise?"

"Political affairs."

"No . . . sorry . . . I meant, your degree. What kind of biology did you study?"

"I didn't expect to have a job interview this evening. I'm not any kind of *ologist*. I have a degree in political science, but if you need to know more, I'll send you a résumé."

"Jesus . . . Sorry I asked. I was just trying to make conversation."

"This position is a stepping stone to bigger things," Joao Pedro said. He pushed his plate away and stood up. "And I won't let you or the INPA screw it up."

Joao Pedro left, and everyone stared at Katie. Without a word, she took a bite of fish and washed it down with a drink.

The others returned to their meals and conversations, and at a table full of people, Katie ate alone. When she was done, she excused herself and went back upstairs.

She wasn't tired enough to sleep, so she sat down on the balcony and watched the town through the rain. A steady amber glow came from the square, and streetlights led outward like dotted lines into the dark. Lights along the near shore defined the river, but beyond that the world was black: no moon, no clouds, no land, no sky.

She looked into the nothing and thought about all the people she'd met in the last two days. *I don't get the attitude. What the hell did Joao Pedro mean about screwing things up? They all hate me for some reason.* As someone most people liked, she found it strange being unwelcome and unwanted.

The rain stopped, and a gentle breeze blew across the balcony. Katie heard the door to the entrance of the hotel open below and footsteps on the porch.

"I'm going down there now, damn it! He's not leaving until dawn," Chris said.

Katie stood up and looked down.

"Everything okay?" she asked, and Chris stopped. He looked back at the porch, then up.

"Hi, Katie. Yeah, everything's fine. I just have to go help out at the dock. Wanna go?"

"Sure! I'll be right down."

They met in front of the hotel and walked along the main road to the center of town. Streetlights surrounded the square, but two bright lights illuminated the steeple of a small church at the far end. Most of the shops were closed for the night, but Chris pointed out the good places from the bad. They crossed the square and walked along the main street past tin-roofed houses, a couple of small grocery stores, and a bar. The buildings on the left side of the road, along the river, changed from homes to warehouses. A few people milled about the street, but for the most part it was dark and quiet.

As they walked by the last warehouse, Katie looked through the large window and saw a small light shining on a metal desk thirty feet away. A puff of smoke rose, and she noticed a man sitting in front of the desk, smoking a cigar. Just before she ran out of window, Katie saw another man inside a chain-link enclosure full of wires and electronics.

"What's this place?" Katie asked.

"Sid's," Chris replied. "Sid's Boat Sales & Salvage. Come on. I'll introduce you."

They turned left, alongside the building. The ground sloped down as they walked toward the river. Lights illuminated a large covered dock with a barge tied up close to shore. As they walked closer, Katie saw the barge was actually pulled up against a wall made of railroad ties. Two long steel plates extended onto the deck.

"So where's the ...?" Katie started to ask as they reached the end of the building, but a blast of yellow distracted her. A huge Caterpillar bulldozer was parked behind the building. "That's big."

"Yeah," Chris said. "That's the new D8H. Twice the size of the last model."

Katie nodded. He was excited, so she got excited too. "Looks like Grover's on the boat. Come on."

From the bank, Katie saw a man in the tiny wheel-house of the barge, but through the dim light and dirty glass he was a shadow. Chris walked Katie onto the dock, and as they passed under the first light, the figure stepped out of the wheelhouse. He walked to the edge of the barge, hopped onto the dock, and the whole thing tipped about a foot. Katie grabbed Chris's arm to keep from falling in.

"You okay?" Chris asked.

"I'm fine. Sorry. I nearly fell in."

As the man approached, his size became more apparent, and ten feet away, Katie had to look up to see his face. *That's the biggest man I've ever seen*, Katie thought, and tried to turn her fear into a smile. At six feet nine and over three hundred pounds of muscle, Grover dwarfed Katie, who barely stood chest high. He smiled and held out his hand.

"Evenin'," the man said in a deep baritone voice. "I'm Grover . . . You must be Katie."

"Yes, sir," Katie replied, and shook the three fingers she could get her hand around. "It's nice to meet you. Chris said you guys had some work to do, so I'll just watch from over here. I don't want to get in the way."

"You won't," Chris said. "Just stay on the dock until we get her loaded."

Chris jumped on the barge, while Grover walked up the bank to the bulldozer. Two men stepped out of the building and met him. Katie couldn't make out the conversation, but when Grover pointed her way, she smiled and waved. The men walked her way, while Grover climbed up into the seat of the dozer.

"Good evening, young lady," Sid said, and shook her hand. "I'm Sid, and this is Cage." The gas engine of the Cat sputtered, turned over, and settled into a steady drone. "I thought we better introduce ourselves now, before he starts that thing up."

Katie looked confused, since the engine was already running, and Sid just smiled.

"I understand you're headed for the construction site with me tomorrow," Cage said.

"I guess so. I'm looking forward to doing some real f— "

A loud, deep rumble stopped Katie midsentence as the diesel tried to turn over. Metallic thumps, a loud, deep pop, and the cylinders fired. Smoke rolled out of the exhaust stack as the engine roared to life.

The two men smiled. Lights along the top of the cab flooded the bank with light, and the giant machine crept down the hill on its tanklike treads. As it approached, Grover stopped, and Chris checked the position of the steel planks. Chris backed up to the middle of the barge, and Grover drove forward.

The metal tracks clattered, and the planks moaned under the weight as the dozer rolled across. The front of the barge dipped, but Grover kept moving.

The heavy lines attached to the dock tightened, and the pile guides slid down the pilings that held the dock in place.

Chris directed Grover to the center of the barge, and the keel settled back into the water.

Grover shut off the engine and looked at Katie. "There's some straps in the shed. You mind grabbing 'em?"

"I'll get it," Cage said, but Katie waved him off.

"No, no, I've got it," she replied, excited to be asked, and hurried out to the shed at the far end of the dock.

She opened the door and found ropes everywhere, some neatly coiled, but most just thrown. Katie stepped in for a closer look and saw a boat hook, rain gear, and things she didn't recognize, but no straps. Finally, she spotted a bag on the floor, looked inside, and found them. She slung the shoulder strap over her shoulder and hurried back down the dock.

Grover smiled and reached down over to the edge of the barge. "I'll take that."

Katie held the long strap up, and Grover swung it onto the deck. "Okay, you're next."

"Oh . . . I don't know," Katie replied, but before she could stop him, he had a hand under each armpit and lifted her onboard.

"Nothin' to it," the big man said with a smile. "Now hand me one of those straps, and we'll get this thing lashed down."

Katie pulled one of the wide woven straps from the bag, and Grover unrolled it. The heavy steel hook clattered on the rusty deck, and Katie grabbed it before it bounced over the edge. "Just hook it to the cleat."

Katie hooked her end, and Grover attached his above the tread. He tightened the ratchet just to take up the slack, and in no time the three of them had all the lines in place.

"Alright, Katie, I'm exhausted. You'll have to cinch 'em down."

"What?"

"There should be a bar in the bag that looks like a tire iron without the bend."

She reached in, felt around, and found it under some oily red rags. Katie held it up and Grover nodded.

"That's the one. Now, girl, all you have to do is stick it in a hole on the ratchet and pull."

Katie struggled at first to get the rusty bar into the hole, but she wouldn't let them help.

"Get in there, damn it!" Katie yelled, and both men smiled when it went in.

"Now pull," Chris said. "Flex those big muscles."

Katie laughed and almost lost her grip.

"You havin' fun yet?" Grover asked. "You want some help?"

"I can do it, but it might go faster if one of you holds the ratchet."

"Looks like she's got everything under control," Sid said. "If you don't need me or anything else from inside, I'm going to lock up."

"We got it from here. Thanks for staying. I'll see you in the morning."

It took all of Katie's weight, but she tightened every strap.

"You're a hard little worker," Grover said, and gave her a pat on the back.

Katie lurched forward. "Thanks. What's next?"

"Next?" Chris replied. "Next we head back to the hotel and get some sleep."

The three hopped off the barge and headed up to the main road. They talked the whole way, and Katie heard about Grover's college football career. She also heard about his wife and two little girls back in Alabama. By the time they reached the hotel, Katie was happy. She made some friends.

As they walked up the steps to the entrance, Ozzie and Riley were having a smoke on the porch.

"Well, look at this, Riley," Ozzie said with a sneer. "So, Katie, did you take care of them one at a time or both together?"

Chris and Grover stopped, and Katie opened the door. She went back for her two friends, took them by the arm, and ushered them inside.

Josue finished formula. "Thanks, Wita" a heavy ...

"Mose," Oliva replied. "Next we hang back 'til the ... aloud and ...I sense sleep.

They both hopped off the bunk and she waited on ... the full spread. They killed the whole day and came ... heard about Ozzie's College football ... as she also ... proud about his wife and two little girls back in ... Alabama. By the time they reached the hotel, Kane was happy she made some friends...

As they walked out the front to the entrance, Ozzie and they were, again, a smoke on the porch.

"Will y'all at this, Riley?" Ozzie said, "seems every ... time, Kane, the guy take care of them on an at door or ... both together?"

Oliva and she drew to speed and she opened the ... door. She went back for her two friends, took a hand in the arm and ushered them in ...

7

Unwelcome

The next morning started two hours before dawn when Katie's alarm went off. She switched on the lamp, shut off the alarm, and sat up in bed. Katie had half an hour to pull herself together but spent the first five minutes in thought. *Every day more people seem to hate me, but every day I also make a friend.* She smiled, cleaned up, and went downstairs.

Katie was the first one of the three to the front door, and she stood at the entry alone.

"You're up early," a man said from across the room, and Katie spun around. "Sorry. I didn't mean to startle you."

A bald man about thirty looked at her from behind the reception counter and set his coffee down.

"That's okay," Katie replied. "I am up early. I'm meeting a couple of friends at five thirty."

"Care for a cup of coffee while you wait?"

Katie looked at his sleeveless button-down shirt, tattoos, and ear ring, and almost said no.

"Sure," she said, then walked over to the counter.

The man disappeared into the kitchen and returned with a yellow-and-green ceramic mug of coffee and a basket of cream and sugar.

"Here you go."

"Thanks. Sorry, I didn't get your name. I'm Katie."

"Caio Pereira," he replied, and set the mug and basket on the counter. "You met my wife and kids yesterday."

"Oh! You're Pedrina's husband. She must keep you on your toes."

Caio smiled. "She does."

"So . . . I guess the two of you work here together."

"Sometimes. I'm a pilot and run my own little transportation and shipping business, and I'm gone a lot."

"Sounds exciting," Katie said. "Do you fly around here or farther away?" Caio didn't respond, and Katie could see he was searching for an acceptable response. "It's not important. I was just curious."

"Most runs are day trips."

Katie took a sip of coffee, and Caio pulled the guest register out from under the counter. As he set it down, he watched Katie study the tattoos on his arms. She looked up and realized she'd been staring.

"You've got quite a few tattoos," Katie said, and Caio smiled. "When did you start getting them?"

"I got my first one when I was ten, but most of these I got when I was in the service."

"So, you were in the army?"

"Air force. That's where I learned to fly."

"How did you end up here?"

"Pedrina. She and I met in Manaus. She knew the family who owned this hotel, and since I was gone most of the time, we bought it. It was pretty rough when we took over, but after I left the service and started flying freight, we were able to fix it up. Of course, a lot of trade goes through this little town, so the hotel is always busy."

Just then Chris and Grover walked in.

"Morning, Katie," Chris said, then noticed Caio. "Hey! Caio! I didn't expect to see you before we left."

"Chris, Grover, good morning. Want some coffee?"

"We'd like to," Grover said, "but we need to get going. I've got a long boat ride ahead of me today."

"I know," Caio replied. "I noticed your new dozer on my way in."

"I didn't think you could fly at night," Katie said.

"You can't."

"Alright, girls," Grover said as he opened the door. "We're burning daylight."

The sun wouldn't be up for another hour, but they got going.

As they walked through town, fishermen crossed the road on the way to the river.

At the barge, Katie stowed Grover's gear in the wheelhouse and watched twelve fifty-five-gallon drums being loaded on the deck with a small crane. Lastly, they slid the two steel planks onto the deck and secured them with a chain.

Light shimmered off the river and flashed in her eyes as the sun began to rise. Katie hopped off the barge onto the dock and walked out to the end. Trees emerged from darkness, and the first hint of the sun skipped across the surface of the river. Fishermen started their engines and, as if waiting for the sun to signal, pulled away from the shore. Paths crossed and wakes intersected, splitting long lines of bright light on the dark surface.

Katie watched the scene, and the image burned a place in her memory.

"Katie?" Grover said. "You okay?"

Katie turned, and Grover looked down at her from the keel of the boat.

"Perfect."

"Morning!" Cage shouted from the shore, and walked out onto the dock. He pitched his duffel next to the wheelhouse, slid an aluminum case onto the deck, and jumped onboard. "Sorry for the delay. I had to repack some equipment."

"Okay, Katie," Grover said. "Stand by the stern line while I'll start up the engines."

"Aye, aye, captain. Just say when."

Katie looked down the dock and waved at Chris, who released the spring line. The two engines started in turn and drummed a steady beat. Water, sucked in from the river to cool the engines, poured from a small hole in the transom and splashed back into the river. Grover stepped out of the wheelhouse, checked the flow, and waved at Katie.

"Alright! You first."

Katie loosened the locking loop from one end of the cleat and unraveled the figure eight.

"Leave one loop around the cleat so you can hold the boat," Chris yelled, then untied the bowline.

The current of the river held the barge against the dock while Katie and Chris pitched the lines onto the deck. Cage coiled and stowed them in a metal box behind the wheelhouse and waved at Katie.

"You did good," Grover said. "Thanks for the help."

"You're welcome."

"Chris, we'll meet you upstream." Grover stepped into the wheelhouse and backed away from the dock.

As the bow turned upriver, Chris walked up next to Katie. "We best get back to the hotel. I hope Caio has some coffee left."

Sid leaned against the frame of the door at the back of the shop and watched the barge head out into the river. Chris and Katie disappeared around the side of the building, and Sid walked over to the chain-link cage. He sat down at a small wooden desk, uncovered a radio, and flipped on the power. The tubes inside buzzed. He donned a headset, held down the button on the mic, and let the field lab know the barge was on its way.

By the time Chris and Katie got back to the hotel, all of the guests except Russel, Ozzie, and Riley were seated in the dining room having breakfast.

Caio stepped out of the kitchen with a pot of coffee and saw Katie. "Ah! Katie, you're back! Pedrina was afraid she wouldn't—"

"Katie!" Pedrina yelled, and pushed past her husband. "I think you leave no goodbye."

"I wouldn't do that," Katie replied with a big smile. "Chris and I were down at the dock helping Grover get underway."

"Yes, Caio tell me. You sit. I bring food."

Katie looked at the table, and there wasn't an open seat.

Pedrina noticed the same and walked over to the person with the cleanest plate. "You done—you go." She grabbed the man's plate.

Katie touched her on the arm. "If there's room in the kitchen, I'd rather eat with you."

Pedrina looked at Katie, smiled, and took the man's plate anyway. "He still done."

Chris and Katie both went in the kitchen, and Pedrina showed them to the family table under the window on the far wall. Caio poured them all some coffee, and Pedrina brought over a large plate of fruit as well as little cakes about three inches across.

The whole family had breakfast, but Katie received all the attention. At first, Katie talked about what she saw from the plane, but when she mentioned she worked at a zoo, everyone listened.

Thirty minutes later, Russel pushed open the kitchen door and stuck his head in.

"We're leaving in thirty minutes," he said, and left without waiting for a reply.

"We better get our stuff," Chris said, "or they'll leave us behind."

"Thanks for the breakfast, Pedrina," Katie said as she got up from the table. "I enjoyed meeting all of you."

Katie went up to her room, packed, and was back downstairs with ten minutes to spare.

Two military jeeps were parked out front, and the men were on the porch smoking. Pedrina came into the lobby and gave Katie a big hug.

When they parted, Pedrina grabbed her by both arms. "You careful," she said with a stern look. "Understand? Careful. You alone."

"I will," Katie said.

"I serious. Animal, good and bad. Man, good and bad. You alone. You careful." Just then Chris walked up and could see he'd interrupted an important conversation. "Chris good. You near him. Grover good too."

"Thanks, Pedrina," Chris said, and gave her a pat on the back. "I think you're good too. Katie, we better get out there."

Pedrina managed to squeeze in one more hug, and they left for the airstrip.

When they arrived, the drivers pulled up next to the

plane. Ozzie and Riley had just completed the preflight inspection of the outside, and Riley lit a cigarette. He walked over to Katie's Jeep and watched her step out of the car.

"Can I give you a hand . . . or two?" he asked with a sneer, and looked at her breasts.

"No, thanks," Katie replied, and pulled her bag out of the back seat.

"Just trying to be friendly."

He and Ozzie laughed as Katie walked to the tail of the plane, and Luiz, the one-man ground crew, pushed her suitcase in the cargo hold. Everyone got onboard, and Luiz pulled the chocks.

The plane taxied to the far end of the runway, turned back toward the river, and took off into the wind. It headed north across the Rio Negro and began a long, steady climb.

Katie looked out at the lines of puffy white clouds and the trees below. Yesterday she couldn't see anything through the rain, but now she could appreciate the immensity of the jungle that lay ahead. Not long after, she noticed a smaller river that twisted back and forth to such a degree that there must be five miles of river for every straight mile of land. The pilot adjusted course and followed it.

A flock of bright-green birds leapt from the canopy, and to Katie, it seemed like the leaves themselves had come alive.

Occasionally she noticed a tin roof or thatched hut, but as they flew farther upriver, the signs of man disappeared.

Half an hour into the flight, Katie noticed a wake on the river and, a moment later, a flash of yellow through the trees. It was the dozer.

Katie elbowed Chris. "I see Grover. Wanna look?"

"Are you kidding!" Chris replied, and Katie remembered he hated to fly.

"Sorry."

Grover stepped out of the wheelhouse and waved.

Eventually, the plane veered off to the right, and Katie saw where a high cliff separated the lowlands from the jungle plateau above. Time had clawed out the edge of the plateau, and she thought they must be getting close.

The plane banked left and began its descent. As it dropped, it banked around into the sun. They descended closer and closer to the canopy, and the jungle sped by. The trees suddenly dropped away at the edge of a steep cliff wall, and the jungle was far below. Another cliff rose a few seconds later, and without warning the wheels touched down.

The trees along the landing strip slowed as the plane rumbled along, and Katie thought she might be sick. She looked at Chris. He still had his eyes shut, and she wished she had done the same.

Chris opened his eyes as the plane turned around and had collected his nerves before the plane stopped. Everyone except for Chris and Katie gathered their things, and the engines shut down.

"I almost threw up," Katie whispered to Chris, and he gave her a sympathetic grin.

"Don't feel bad. The first time I flew in here I did."

Russel stopped at the door. "You girls coming, or are you going to sit here all day?"

He walked out, and Chris and Katie followed.

A well-built man of about forty met Russel at the bottom of the step.

"Russel," he said.

"Schroder."

Katie was right behind him, and Schroder welcomed her with a cold, sullen look.

"Katie Winston?"

"Yes, Hello. It's good to—"

"Schroder," he interrupted. "Chief of security. Grab your things and follow me. Mr. Brice wants a word before you settle in." Schroder looked at Chris, who stopped behind her. "You need something?"

"Nope."

"Then stow your gear and get down to the dock. Grover will be there in a couple of hours." Chris walked off, but Katie, a bit taken aback by the exchange, didn't move. "I don't tell people to do something twice."

Katie slung her rucksack over her shoulder, retrieved her suitcase from the tail, and tried to catch up with Schroder, who was already on his way to the office.

She didn't see much of the camp from the plane, but what she did see looked military. There were small and large military tents, a few tin shacks, and two wood-clad buildings with tin roofs. These two buildings were roughly fifteen feet wide and thirty feet long.

A sign next to the door of the second building said *TMV Global Field Office, James Brice, Project Manager*. Schroder walked up three wooden steps and went inside. Katie followed and shut the door. There was a large table to her left with blueprints on top, and a man sitting at a desk to her right. The walls were covered in more blueprints, a map, Gantt charts, rosters, and other construction documents.

Schroder stood in the far corner, leaned against the wall, and folded his arms. The man behind the desk tipped back in his chair and scratched his head.

"Miss Winston, I'm James Brice. I'm in charge of this project."

Katie guessed he was in his fifties, but his weather-beaten skin and gray hair made him look older.

"Thanks for having me," Katie said. "It's nice to—"

"I didn't invite you, young lady, and to be completely honest, I don't want you here."

"If you have a problem with the study, and the government requested it, you should take it up with Mr. Rocha."

"I don't have a problem with a study, and Mr. Rocha has already been taken care of. My problem is with you."

"How can I be a problem? I just got here."

"You're a woman. Dropping you in the middle of nowhere with a bunch of men is always trouble."

Katie stood there in disbelief.

"The thing is," Schroder added, "the sooner you leave, the better. In fact, as soon as the boys unload the plane, we'd like you to get back on it."

"I can't do that! I was asked to come here and look around, and that's what I'm going to do." The hair on the back of her neck stood up. "If you're worried about your men not being able to control themselves, that's their problem, not mine. As for me, I'm not leaving until I'm done!"

Schroder stood away from the wall and put his hands on his hips.

Brice leaned forward. "Figures," he said, then scoffed. "It's bad enough they send us a woman, but she's a damned feminist as well."

"No matter what I am, I'm here to do a job. I was also told everything I'd need would be provided. Just take me to my gear."

"Sure thing," Brice replied. "Everything you'll need is right here."

He reached into a small cabinet, took out a pair of binoculars, and set them on the desk. Katie shook her head.

"Like I said, your work's already been done. This project's moving forward, so you might as well get back on that plane and go back where you came from."

Katie slung her rucksack over her shoulder, picked up her suitcase, and opened the door.

"I don't suppose you have a place for me to sleep?"

"Sure! You're in the VIP shack with Mr. Rocha." The two men smiled. "Second shack on the left."

124

Katie started out the door.

"Wait! Miss Winston, you forgot your equipment!" Brice yelled, and Katie looked back over her shoulder.

"I brought my own binoculars. You can shove those up your ass."

Katie's face was on fire. She clenched her fists and felt every muscle as she marched toward the VIP shack. She flung open the rickety aluminum door without knocking and found Joao Pedro standing shirtless next to his open suitcase. Before he could say a word, she tossed her bags to one side, grabbed his suitcase, and threw it out the door.

"What the hell?" he shouted, and Katie grabbed his arm.

"You're moving!" Katie replied, and threw him out as well. She latched the door, sat down on the cot, and buried her face in her hands. She sat there for a while, kicked off her boots, and lay down. The voices and engines in the camp became static, and she thought, *Feminist? Jesus Christ.* A grin loosened the tenseness of her face.

The travel caught up with her as she rested her eyes, and a peaceful moment became a nap. When she woke, she sat up and looked around the room. *At least there is a floor*, she thought, and put her feet down.

The small bookcase at the foot of the cot was empty, and since there wasn't a closet, she assumed it was for clothes. She was surprised to see a wooden table and chair. It looked sturdy, but it also looked like it had been through a couple of wars.

One bare, incandescent bulb dangled from a rafter in the middle of the room, but daylight, diffused through a dirty burlap curtain, shone through a window in the western wall. The opposite wall had another.

Katie went to the east window, raised the curtain, and saw the office. She scoffed and let it fall back down. At the western window, however, she had a view toward the valley, and she rested her elbows on the sill. As she looked out, she thought, *Someone should really clean this glass.* Then she wondered, *Why am I looking through the glass at all?*

She put on her boots, dug the binoculars out of her rucksack, and put on her flop hat. Since the field from camp to the cliff was tall grass and weeds, Katie cut over to the airstrip and walked along it instead. When she reached the edge, she looked down just as a ray of sun slipped through a passing cloud and cast a spotlight on the canopy below. Birds of every color fluttered among the treetops, while more organized flocks sailed higher in the sky.

The valley was narrow, long, and deep. To the north, Katie saw the vapor drift away from a waterfall. To the south, the valley narrowed to a point like the tip of a spear. Also to the south, about a hundred yards away, was a steel platform that extended fifteen feet over the edge. She looked through her binoculars. The platform was clearly an observation deck, so she made her way over to it.

The structure was made of several I-beams, but the platform itself was a series of smaller beams with a metal grate on top for a deck. A tubular steel railing enclosed it, but the whole thing looked shaky to Katie.

A large gas-powered winch was bolted to a concrete slab where the steel beams began, and big a spool of cable lay on the ground nearby. A tall steel framework stuck out another three feet from the edge of the platform in line with the winch, and Katie took a look. *This must be where a lift would go*, she thought, and remembered her cold welcome. *The lift hasn't been installed for a reason*. She walked along the rail and looked at the cliff on the other side of the valley.

She'd never been afraid of heights, but her stomach tightened up; it was a long way down. Katie noticed the toes of her boots were an inch over the edge, and as her eyes fought to focus on the boots or the trees below, she felt queasy.

127

"Seven hundred twenty-three feet," a man said, and Katie spun around. It was Russel. He put one foot on the platform, took a pack of cigarettes from his shirt, and tapped one out. "I heard you had a pleasant conversation with the boss."

Katie turned back to the valley and watched the birds. Russel stepped up, lit his cigarette, and walked to the railing at the opposite end of the platform.

"I'm only here because I was asked to come," Katie said. "I want to help, but I never should have come."

"Hmm," Russel replied. "That's surprising. I didn't expect that kind of attitude from a woman who just told the boss to stick a pair of binoculars up his ass."

Katie looked at him, and Russel smiled.

"I didn't like you much," Russel said, "but don't feel bad. I don't like most people, but as of about two hours ago you changed my mind." Russel took another drag and flicked the ash into the valley below. "Don't let them make you change it back."

"What's wrong with them? Do you know what they said?"

"I can imagine. There's a lot of odd ducks down here, but most of us just want to make a few bucks and go home. You should stick around."

Russel ran his hand along the rail, took another drag, and walked away from the edge.

"Thanks," Katie said as Russel stepped off the platform. "Oh, I don't see a lift, so how am I supposed to get down there?"

"Brice would tell you to jump," Russel said with a smile. "But there's a narrow trail down the face of the cliff on the other side, but it's too dangerous to use. The only other way would be to follow the river in. I heard that end is completely blocked off, but you might find a way in."

"Thanks, Russel. It's too late to find out today, but I'll check it out tomorrow."

"You want to walk back to camp with me?"

"No. I'm going to stay out here awhile."

"Alright, but head back before it gets dark. Once the sun goes down, you can't see a damn thing unless the moon's out."

"I will."

8

High Ground

Katie walked south along the rocky edge of the cliff and stopped often to look at the jungle below. The sun was still high, but she kept what Russel told her in the back of her mind.

Half an hour later, Katie came to a large stone, climbed up, and took a break. She scanned the valley through her binoculars. Midway along the cliff on the opposite side, vegetation crept down the rocks at an angle. *That must be the trail Russel was talking about*, Katie thought. From her perspective, though, it looked like twisted vines and leaves.

Herons flew over the waterfall, floated into the middle of the valley, and settled atop the dense mat of trees. Katie adjusted the focus and watched them squabble. Squawking echoed off the cliff walls, and they fluttered and pecked to maintain their place.

One bird began to flutter more violently than the rest, and leaves shook all around it. As the rest of the flock flew away, Katie saw the bird jerked down into the canopy, and its squawking stopped.

The sound of a high-pitched motor, from the top of the cliff opposite her, pulled her attention away from the bird, and she focused on the tree line. She tried to pinpoint the noise but only saw trees and shadows. It came from farther down the valley to the south but got louder.

Light glinted off a piece of metal for only a second, then flashed once more. When the noise reached a small break in the trees, she saw a motorcycle speed past and disappear again.

Katie was familiar with motorcycles; they were all over São Paulo. In the city, however, people rode street bikes or scooters; this was neither.

Not long after, the engine stopped, and Katie turned her attention to the valley again.

Casmir Dubanowski—Doobie to his friends—sat on the back of his 1961 Husqvarna off-road motorcycle and waited for his ears to stop ringing. When he could hear the jungle again, he got off and rolled the Husky onto its stand.

Doobie took an orange from the small bag lashed to the seat, walked to the edge of the cliff, and sat down on the trunk of a fallen tree. As his thumbnail pressed into the rind, he remembered the roach in his pocket and stopped. He smoked it until it burned his fingers and dropped it in the dirt.

He went back to work on the orange and watched the birds rise and fall. The last wedge of orange had seeds, and as he spit them out, he heard the clatter of footsteps and rustling leaves. Doobie sat there and listened.

Leaves along the cliff shook, and something leapt up over the edge and scrambled past his motorcycle. It was a small deer. Three more followed, and Doobie walked over and looked down.

Everyone knew about the path, but no one had ever tried to go down. He waited to see if any more deer would pop up, then decided to see how far down he could get.

The first few steps were easy, as the path was about three feet wide. Tree roots and vines followed the ledge like a railing, so he kept going. Another bundle of roots reached down from above, crossed the ledge, and joined the other to form a tunnel. Doobie ducked down and moved inside.

When he emerged from the other end, the ledge was only a couple of feet wide. Doobie looked back in the direction he came and decided he'd gone far enough. Before he headed back up, he took a moment to enjoy the view.

It's like standing in thin air, he thought, and he was completely in the moment. Just then he heard footsteps again. *The damn deer must be heading back down*, he thought, but the noise wasn't coming from above, it was coming from below.

He leaned forward to peek over the edge but was struck from the side. He fell onto the ledge and almost went over, but the roots and vines held him back.

It was another deer. The impact had knocked the deer off its feet as well, and it struggled to get up. Must have broken its leg, Doobie thought; then he saw the long, bloody cut along its stomach.

The deer staggered forward but teetered over the edge. Doobie slung his arm over the bundle of vegetation and expected to see the animal plummet to the ground, but it was gone.

Then he heard it.

Leaves thrashed and the deer snorted. Doobie leaned out farther and saw the animal's legs sticking out of the leaf-covered vines below. *Damn*, Doobie thought. *That's one lucky deer*.

Then he saw the hand.

He only saw it for a second, but that was long enough to see it was covered in dark-gray hair and had the deer by its hind leg. Something tugged on the root under his arm, and he heard more footsteps moving up the path. These footsteps weren't clicks of hoofs on stone; they were softer.

The vine jerked, and Doobie got to his feet. He looked down the path but saw nothing. Leaves rustled and he looked down just as the same dark hand reached up and grabbed the root. Doobie took two steps up the path and wanted to run, but he also wanted to see what it was.

Movement drew his attention back down the path, and something was sitting on it. *That's one big monkey*, Doobie thought. Then it stood up. Its slim body was covered in hair. It had long muscular arms with strange hands.

Doobie froze, unsure whether to run or stand his ground. The creature leapt toward him. It had a large head and big eyes, but all Doobie saw were teeth. Doobie turned, took one long step, and expected to be hit, but he only heard a thud and hiss.

He looked back and saw the deer laying dead on the path, with the creature underneath. Another creature looked over the root, and Doobie scrambled up the path.

As he squeezed through the tunnel of roots, a long claw pushed through and cut his arm. The pain dropped him to one knee, but he got up and kept moving. The silhouette of the creature moved alongside him, and Doobie watched for the claw to come through again.

He didn't notice the one behind him until it grabbed his leg, and Doobie went down. He kicked free and raced out of the other end of the tunnel. The other creature leapt in front of him, and Doobie stiff-armed it in the chest

It clawed his arm as it went over the edge, but he heard the creature grab the roots on its way down. The creature behind him stopped to help the other, and Doobie made it to his bike.

One swift kick, and the engine turned over. He popped the clutch and twisted the throttle. The rear tire threw a blinding tail of debris toward the path just as the creatures reached the top. They ducked out of the way, and Doobie had a head start.

The motorcycle blasted through the jungle. The large tires absorbed the shock of smaller roots and rocks, and Doobie jumped the rest. Just when he thought he had gotten away, one of the creatures leapt onto the trunk of a tree beside him; then he saw the other.

Doobie changed course every time one got close, and the creatures barely seemed to keep up. He reached a patch of leafy saplings and couldn't see ahead but, with a creature now on both sides, sped through.

The limbs whipped him in the face, and he had to close his eyes. When he popped out the other side, he opened them, but it was too late. He crashed into the tall, wall-like roots of a kapok tree. The front fork broke, Doobie hit the tree, and the rest of the motorcycle crushed his spine.

Doobie lay draped over the wreck. The heat of the engine and exhaust pipe burned his skin, but he couldn't feel a thing.

The two creatures walked out of the dense foliage, stopped a few feet away, and sat down. Doobie couldn't move. He watched them.

They watched him as well and exchanged a few sounds. Then one of the creatures pushed its claw into Doobie's calf. Nothing. The creature lifted Doobie's leg and dropped it. The other creature did the same with his arm.

One creature pointed toward the camp and tapped its finger next to its eye. The other creature leaned in and took a closer look at Doobie's head.

Overcome with fear, Doobie screamed, but as soon as the first sound came out, the creature snapped his neck.

Katie walked far enough down the valley that through her binoculars she could almost see where it came to an end. It was just as Russel said. The cliff walls on either side had sheared off and blocked the entrance.

If the river gets out, Katie thought, *there must be a way in*. She considered walking farther but checked her watch and looked up at the sky. *Best not push my luck.*

She headed back to camp, and without stopping every five minutes to look around, she made good time. Katie was back in her shack an hour before sunset, kicked off her boots, and lay down on the cot with her journal.

She thumbed through the notes and sketches she'd made and wrote down a few questions.

Her stomach growled an hour later. She hadn't had anything since breakfast but hadn't felt hungry until then. Still, the cot felt good, and her feet were free from her boots, so she shut her eyes and dozed off.

Not long after, the sound of engines and shouting woke her. By the time she got her boots on and opened the door, the noise had stopped and it was quiet again.

Katie walked over to the first white building. It served as a mess hall and place for the men to relax after work. She climbed the steps and opened the door. To her surprise, Joao Pedro was the only one there. He was seated at a small table in the corner reading a book.

"Good afternoon," Katie said, then noticed the sunset out the window. "I mean evening."

"Hello," he replied over the top of his book, and went right back to reading.

The refrigerator was just to the left of the door, and Katie checked out what was inside. There was a lot of lunch meat and drinks, but also a large metal pan of spaghetti and meatballs on the bottom shelf.

She shut the door, scanned the kitchen counter, and found a basket of fruit. Katie grabbed two bananas and an apple, then sat down at the table in the corner, opposite Joao Pedro. She took a bite of apple and looked over at him.

"I'm going to see if I can find a way into the valley tomorrow," Katie said. "Would you like to come?"

"No."

"How do you plan on completing your assessment?"

"I already did."

"You've seen the valley?"

"Of course I did. I flew over it yesterday. It looks like the rest of the jungle, so it won't be missed."

"How can you say that without seeing what's down there?"

"Go down there if you want. I've seen all I need to see. Now, if you don't mind, I'd like to get back to my book."

Katie was dumbfounded. *How could the Brazilian government put someone like that in charge of something like this?* she thought, and finished her apple. She almost left but decided to stay. As she peeled the first banana, she calculated how long it would take her to reach the end of the valley and how far upstream she could go before she'd have to turn back. Then it hit her: even if she reached the far end of the valley, she didn't have a way down.

She thought about Chris and Grover and remembered Chris driving down to the river to meet him. *Someone could drive me down from the plateau the same way and follow it all the way to the entrance of the valley. If they drop me off in the morning, they could pick me up at sunset.*

Katie smiled and finished her banana. She had a plan.

Voices seeped through the door, and it opened. Ozzie and Riley walked in and went straight to the fridge. They took out two drinks and the pan of spaghetti and plopped down at the nearest table. They noticed Joao Pedro first, then saw Katie.

The two men got back up, grabbed their drinks and tray of pasta, and walked over. Ozzie set the tray down and slid it to the middle of the table. The tray pushed Katie's fruit onto her lap.

"You don't mind a little company, do you?" Ozzie asked. "You look kinda lonely sitting here by yourself." He gave her a toothy grin and slapped Riley on the back.

"I'd rather eat alone, if you don't mind," Katie replied as she put the banana peel and apple core back on the table.

"What else you got over there?" Riley asked, and noticed the banana. "Well, looky there. She's got a banana, and we got meatballs. How about we have a little party? Ozzie, what do you think?"

"I think she was saving that banana for later. The first time I saw her, I knew she needed a long, hard one."

Katie stood up, but Ozzie grabbed her shoulder and pushed her back into the chair. "No, no, girl. You're not going anywhere. This party's just getting started." He plucked two meatballs from the tray. "Come on, sugar, put my balls in your mouth."

Katie slapped his hand away, and the meatballs hit Riley's shirt. Ozzie laughed, but Riley jumped to his feet.

"Look what you did to my shirt, bitch!" he barked, then back-handed her across the face.

Katie fell out of the chair and landed on the floor. As soon as she began to push herself up, Ozzie knelt down on one knee beside her, reached around her, and grabbed both breasts.

"Let me give you a hand," he said, then wrestled her up and against the wall. Katie spun around and slapped him. "What did I tell you, Riley? She likes it rough." He knuckled up his fist and punched her in the face.

Katie fell into Joao Pedro's table and slid off onto the floor. Joao Pedro, already on his feet, looked down at Katie, who was barely conscious, then looked at Ozzie and Riley. Ozzie took a flask out of his pocket, took a swig, and handed it to Riley, who did the same.

"You want a piece of this?" Ozzie asked Joao Pedro, but he clutched his book against his chest and slid along the wall toward the door.

"No," he replied, and hurried out of the building.

"Pussy!" Ozzie yelled, then turned back to Katie, who tried to get up off the floor. Blood dripped from her mouth, and she coughed. "Speaking of pussy," Ozzie said, then grabbed Katie by the hair.

Katie screamed, and Ozzie covered her mouth with his hand.

"You do that again and you'll get another punch."

He moved his hand down and ripped open her shirt. Ozzie let go of her hair and wrapped his arm around her neck. Riley stepped in front of Katie, took out a knife, and slipped it under the fabric of her bra. He cut it, folded his knife, and grabbed her breasts. Katie tried to push him off but didn't have the strength.

"Don't fight it, girl," Riley said. "You're gonna get it whether you want it or not."

"You know what I want?" Ozzie asked, and bent her over the table.

Katie screamed, but Ozzie pushed her face harder into the wood.

"I wanna see that ass." He yanked her pants and panties down to just above the knee.

Ozzie unfastened and unzipped his pants, then smiled at Riley as he pulled out his penis. Before he could do anything with it, the mess-hall door flew open so violently that the hinges almost tore from the frame. Grover ducked down and stepped inside.

Ozzie went limp as he backed away, and Katie slid off the table onto the floor. She pulled herself into the corner and curled into a ball.

For a long, tense moment, Grover stood there and looked at the two men. He thought of his daughters, and the fire inside him swelled.

Chris stepped through the door, but Grover pushed him back outside, slammed the door, and locked it.

"Hey!" Ozzie shouted. "We were just having a little bit of fun. Besides, she started it!"

Chris tried to open the door again, and Grover shoved the refrigerator in front of it with one hand.

"Look," Riley said as he stepped forward. "We haven't fucked her yet, so it don't count!"

Grover looked at him, then saw the blood on the floor. He took a long, deep breath, walked over to the nearest table, and flipped it over. With one foot on the top, he wrapped his massive hand around the wooden leg and pulled until the screws broke.

"Now just a goddamned minute!" Ozzie shouted as he and Riley eased along the wall. "She ain't hurt that bad. I only hit her once!"

Riley made it to the fridge, but Grover hit him across the back. Riley stepped away, and Grover smashed him in the mouth with the wooden leg. There was a sharp crack of breaking bones and the clicking of teeth across the floor. Riley went down and didn't get up.

Ozzie threw a chair through the window and ran to jump out, but Grover flung the table leg and knocked him to the ground. Grover didn't hear the men outside shouting for him to stop; it was just noise.

He grabbed Ozzie by the throat and picked him up. With no more effort than it would take to throw a doll, Grover threw Ozzie against the wall. Ozzie staggered to his feet, and Grover hit him twice in the sternum. Both punches broke ribs, but it was the punch in the groin that dropped Ozzie to his knees.

Ozzie moaned, coughed up blood, and hugged himself, while Grover retrieved the table leg. Ozzie didn't see the swing, but his teeth joined Riley's on the floor, and he was out cold.

Grover dropped the leg, walked over to Katie, and threw the table out of the way. She was in a fetal position, pants down, and her whole body trembled. He unbuttoned his shirt, took it off, and draped it over her as he knelt down. He worked his huge arm under her and sat her up against the wall.

She looked at him with the eyes of a terrified child, and he wrapped her in a hug. A moment later, she released the grip she had on herself and hugged him back. She squeezed him with all her strength and cried.

"I've got you now, sweetheart," he whispered, and stroked the back of her head. "It's all over. They won't hurt you again."

While Grover consoled Katie, the men outside moved the steps over to the broken window, and Chris climbed inside. He rushed over to the corner, knelt down, and put his hand on Katie's shoulder.

"Jesus Christ," he said. "Are you okay?"

Katie couldn't look at him but took a long, ragged breath. "I am now."

"Keep the rest of them out," Grover said, and Chris went back to the window.

Brice and Schroder were anxious to get in and assess the damage, but Chris kept everyone at bay.

It was ten minutes before Katie released her grip on Grover, but he held on a little longer. Eventually, she stood up. Katie was oblivious to the state of her clothing, and Grover worked his thumbs between her shorts and skin and pulled them up.

"Thanks," Katie said, as she straightened the waist, then realized her shirt was open. "Sorry." She tried to button it, but the buttons were gone. She looked down. "I lost my buttons."

Grover picked his shirt up, wrapped it around her, and buttoned it up.

Chris couldn't hold off the others any longer, and two men crawled through the window. They pushed the refrigerator out of the way, and a flood of men came in.

Grover made sure Katie didn't see her two attackers sprawled out on the floor as he and Chris walked her to the door.

Brice grabbed Grover by the arm as he passed by, and Grover stopped. "Look what you've done, you goddamned animal! These two won't be able to fly for weeks!"

Grover looked down at Brice but didn't say a word.

"Don't you have any self-control?" Brice said.

"Of course I do," Grover replied. "When I walked in, I wanted to kill them."

Grover and Chris got Katie back to her shack, put her to bed, and stayed until she fell asleep.

9

Steel

Early the next morning Grover went by to check on Katie, and Chris was asleep in a chair outside her door. Grover touched him on the shoulder to wake him, and all four limbs sprang to life.

"Back off!"

Grover patted him on the back as Chris stood up.

"Better go get ready for work. I'll look after Katie."

Chris walked off to his tent, and Grover knocked on the door. Katie opened it, and he was surprised to see her already dressed.

"Good morning, Katie," Grover said, and Katie stepped aside to let him in. He tried not to stare at her black eye and swollen lip or let her see how much it bothered him.

Grover had always been a rock people could hold on to, but unlike stone, he absorbed their pain. But he couldn't let on.

"Good morning," Katie replied with a shameful look, then looked away. "Sorry about last night. I never thanked you."

Katie gave him a hug and pressed her head against his chest. She heard the beat of his heart, heard him breathe, and felt his hand on her head. She shut her eyes and felt safe.

"You don't owe anyone a thank-you or an apology. You didn't do anything wrong. I'm just sorry I didn't get back sooner."

"I'm glad you showed up when you did. I felt so helpless."

"Today's a new day," Grover said. "Caio's on his way to fly them out of here, and you'll never see them again." He noticed Katie's suitcase on the bed. "Why are you packing?"

"Brice came by about an hour ago, and we both agreed it was time for me to go."

Grover stood there and thought about it a moment. He thought about all the times he let one inconsequential person change the course of his life and sighed.

Katie looked up at him for his approval, and he looked down at her battered face. She teared up, and Grover lifted her chin. In her eyes he saw the eyes of his little girls, and he was terrified at the all-too-real possibility that one day they'd find themselves in the same place. *What will I do then?*

"Grover?"

"No," Grover said. "I've got a better idea."

He smiled and walked over to her cot.

"When I was a kid—I mean, before I started growing—I got picked on quite a bit." He opened her suitcase, turned it upside down, and dumped her belongings on the cot.

"What are you doing?"

"I'm no different than everyone else. I regret some of the decisions I've made in my life, but I always try to live by the one bit of advice my daddy gave me: 'Never let someone else make a decision for you when you can make it for yourself.'"

He tossed her empty suitcase into the corner. "If you want to do your job, do it. Those two got in your way, and I moved 'em. Next time it'll be up to you."

"I had every intention of doing my job," Katie replied. "But no one wants me h— "

"I don't care about them, Katie. I care about you, and I think what you really lost was confidence and control. When I was your age, I lifted weights to get mine back, but I've got something better in mind."

Grover pulled a set of keys out of his pocket and tossed them to Katie.

I've got twenty-five tons of steel with your name written all over it."

"Excuse me?"

"Chris is making a fuel run, and I'm a man short. You're working with me today."

Katie looked at the Esso Drop Boy key chain in her hand, and it looked up at her with a smile. It took her a second before she understood.

"No, no, no, no, no! I can't drive that thing! I don't even drive a car!"

"That's good. A Cat doesn't have a steering wheel, so you're already ahead of the game . . . No confusion."

"Oh come on," she replied. "I can't!"

"You can. You lost something yesterday, and today you're gonna get it back. Now, grab your hat and let's go."

Katie looked up at him, then down at the key. Her forearms tingled, followed by her neck and back, and an angry, determined expression washed over her face.

"You're right," Katie said, and snatched her hat off the table.

They walked outside and headed through camp. As they passed the construction office, Schroder and Brice came out.

"Your ride will be here in about an hour," Brice said, surprised to see her without her bags.

"I changed my mind," Katie replied without stopping. "I decided to stay and finish my job, but it'll have to start tomorrow. Grover needs my help today."

"Hey, goddamn it! I'm the boss here, and I want you on that plane!"

Neither Katie nor Grover replied or looked back. They walked right out of camp to the maintenance depot.

As they came around the front of the big metal shed, Katie saw the two dozer blades. The giant machines were parked side by side, and the newer one dwarfed the older.

"You already met the big boy," Grover said as he put his hand on the side of the blade. "This one's only a year old. The little guy's a bit older; it's a '55."

"I'll take the little one," Katie said, but Grover shook his head.

"Nope, the old one's kind of tricky and doesn't respond nearly as well as the new one."

"Yeah, but look at the size of this thing."

"Ah," Grover replied with a dismissive wave. "It looks big from down here. Wait till you get up there. It's huge."

Katie rolled her eyes, walked around to the side, and looked back at Grover. "Where's the ladder?"

Grover laughed, put his hand on her shoulder. "You don't need one. Just start climbing till you reach the seat."

"I don't want to fall," Katie said as she stepped up onto the heavy bar connected to the blade.

"If you do, I'll catch you," Grover replied.

Katie looked back and smiled, then worked her way onto the tread and up into the cushioned seat.

Grover followed, and as he stood on the guard above the tread, he got Katie's attention with a tap on the shoulder. He reached over, moved all of the levers into the right place.

"Use the key right here. That'll connect the battery. Then you can start the pony engine."

He showed her the switch, and she turned it on. The engine started, just like it had in Ameia, and it sounded like a car.

"The little engine turns over the big one," Grover said. "Now you can start the diesel. You have to heat up the plugs first, so turn that switch this way. Keep your eye on the gauge."

"I'm watching it."

"See how the needle's moving from red to green?"

"Yeah."

"When it gets into the green, the plugs are hot and you can turn it the other way."

A moment later, the engine was ready, and she turned the key. The giant diesel engine trembled, sputtered, then roared.

She remembered it being loud when she watched them load it, but sitting on top of it was a completely different experience. Her whole body shook, and she looked at Grover with wide eyes and smiled.

He spent the next two hours teaching her how to operate it, and by the third hour she was confident enough to run it on her own. Before he stepped down, however, he handed her the little, hundred-page factory *Operations and Maintenance Instructions Guide* just in case she forgot which lever did what.

Brice was going over schedules and logistics with Schroder when Caio and Cage landed. The security team and a couple of workmen unloaded the C-47 in less than an hour, and Caio and Cage walked into the office to talk to Brice.

"Mr. Brice, I'm Cage. I believe I'm supposed to report to Schroder."

"That's me," Schroder said, and shook his hand. "I understand you've been out of the country for a while recovering from an injury."

"Yes, sir, but I was down here prior to that, so I'm—"

"Yeah, I know all about it. Some kind of wild animal attack or something. As long as you're fit to work, I don't care about the whats and whys. Do your job the way I want it done and we'll get along fine."

"Yes, sir."

"Green meat pulls night shift, so go find your tent and get some sleep. Report to me at sundown."

"Yes, sir," Cage replied, and left.

"Caio," Brice said. "You unloaded?"

"Yep, unloaded and ready to head back. I heard you've got a couple of passengers going with me."

"Three. Two need a hospital, and the other you can dump at the morgue."

"Ameia doesn't have a morgue."

"Then stick him in a freezer at your hotel until you make another run to Manaus. I don't care what you do with him, but he can't stay here."

"What happened to him?"

"Schroder will take you to the doc. Just get them on the plane."

Katie pushed another swath of dirt from the center of the trench up the bank but stopped when she saw a Jeep pull up at the top. Chris stood up behind the wheel and laughed.

Katie smiled, waved, and watched him shake his head with a grin. She motioned for him to back out of the way and finished her run.

At the top, she drove over the mound and stopped the dozer in front of the Jeep. Chris came over, climbed up to the cab, and leaned in.

"You trying to put me out of a job?" Chris asked, then smiled.

"Not at all. This isn't work, it's therapy!"

"Is it working?"

"You better believe it."

"Looks like you and Grover got a hell of a lot done today."

"Yeah, but I'm sure if Grover was driving this we'd have done a lot more. He insisted I drive the big one."

"I would have too. That little one's tricky. So how'd you like it?"

"Other than it being so damn loud, I love it! I think I could push a whole mountain down with this thing."

"People do. It's getting kinda late. You guys about ready to call it a day?"

"You'll have to ask the boss. Squeeze in, and I'll take you over." Katie threw the Cat into reverse, backed down into the ravine, and made her way to Grover, who was bulldozing the tree line.

Grover saw Katie, then noticed Chris. He backed out of the fallen trees, navigated around the uprooted stumps, and pulled up alongside.

"You ready to call it a day?" Chris yelled.

Grover couldn't hear over the roar and pointed to his ears. Chris raised his arm and pointed at his watch. Grover looked down at his own and nodded his head.

Katie dropped Chris off at the Jeep, and the three of them headed back to camp. Chris arrived at the maintenance shed first and watched Grover park next to the building. Katie brought up the rear and pulled in beside him. She stopped, put it in neutral, and dropped the blade.

She sat there a minute, then looked over at Grover, who had already powered his dozer down. He looked back and started to laugh. *I taught her everything she needed to know*, Grover thought, *except how to turn it off.* She raised both hands and shrugged.

Chris climbed up, walked her through it, and the engine clattered to a stop. For the first time all day it was quiet.

"Well, how do you feel?" Grover asked as he got up out of his seat.

"Other than some lost hearing and a sore butt, I feel great!"

Grover and Chris laughed, and all three met in front of the blades. Katie looked up at Grover and tugged his sleeve.

"Thanks, Grover, I really do appreciate it."

Grover put his arm around her and pulled her in for a fatherly one-handed hug.

"You did good. You're a lot tougher than you think."

They stopped at the mess hall to get something to eat and found the cook had prepared a casserole of sorts. It looked a little like chicken potpie, but the meat was off. Katie took a closer look where someone had dug some out and sniffed.

"Hmm . . . fish."

Hunger overpowered the presentation, so they shoveled out a bowl and took a seat.

Some of the other men in camp were already eating, and while they offered a pleasant hello, none of them made eye contact with Katie.

Katie attacked her dinner, and Chris stopped eating to watch.

"Jesus, Katie, slow down. It's not gonna run away."

Katie looked at him with a mouth full of food and almost laughed it through her nose.

"So, Grover," Chris said, "what's on for tomorrow? Is Katie dozing or me?"

Katie raised her hand shoulder high, and the two men waited for her to swallow.

"Sorry," she said. "As much as I'd like to help, I've got my own work to do, so you boys are on your own."

"That's good to know," Chris replied. "I'd hate to lose my job."

"Glad to hear it, Katie," Grover said. "But before you ditch us and go back to your real job, I've got a graduation present for you."

Grover leaned back, straightened his leg, and shoved his hand in his pocket. "The day I left Alabama to come down here, I stopped to fill up with gas." He pulled the little Esso key chain out. "And the attendant gave me this little guy." He removed the dozer key and held it up. "Today you showed me how much you could overcome, but more importantly, you showed yourself. I want you to have this as a reminder."

Katie took the key chain and gave him a hug. "Thanks, Grover. You mean a lot to me, and now this little guy does too." Katie looked at the Oil Drop Man and smiled.

"So, what's your plan for tomorrow?" Grover asked, but Brice and Schroder walked in before she could answer.

"Well, there they are," Brice said. "Because of you I've got two men in the hospital and one in the morgue."

"Someone died?" Katie replied.

"I was going to tell you—" Grover started to say, but Brice cut him off.

"Yeah, dead."

"That wasn't her fault!" Chris barked. "Doobie ran into a tree!"

"He wouldn't have been out there if it hadn't been for her!"

"What?" Chris replied.

"I knew she wanted to go down there; that's why I never installed the lift. That trail's the only other way in, and Doobie was there to make sure she couldn't use it."

"If that's true," Katie said, "he's dead because of you!"

"How about Ozzie and Riley?" Schroder yelled. "That's all your fault. The last thing we needed in this

161

camp is a damn woman, and you should have been smart enough not to come."

"It's my fault they tried to rape me?"

"You should have known something like that was going to happen, but you came anyway."

Grover watched Katie's anger grow and saw her hands curl into fists. He was ready to break up a fight, and just when he thought she'd come over the table, her hand opened and her expression changed. Katie took a deep breath and looked down at the key chain. She loaded her fork and took another bite. She took her time and chewed. After she swallowed, she turned to Grover.

"To answer your question, plan wise," Katie said, "since Mr. Brice won't install the lift and I can't use the trail, I'm going to drive back toward the river and see if I can find a way in from the southern end of the valley."

"Caio's coming back tomorrow morning," Brice said, "and you're getting out of here. I've put up with enough of your bullshit, and I'm done! That's it!"

Brice and Schroder turned to leave and expected someone to make a snide remark, but none did. They all went back to eating, and Brice and Schroder walked out.

"You're not really going down there alone, are you?" Chris asked. "That can't be safe."

"Let's see," Katie replied, then looked around the room. The man she was looking for was in the corner, as expected. "Mr. Rocha, you're here to survey the valley. Wanna come with me?"

Rocha looked up from the book he was pretending to read, turned the page, and didn't say a word.

"Looks like I'm on my own."

"Katie?" Grover said. "I like your new confidence, but Chris is right. Going down there alone is dangerous."

"Grover, I know animals like you know dozers. I'll be fine. Besides, it's not like I can get lost."

"You don't need my permission, but you need to take a radio and a gun."

"A gun?"

"There's snakes and predators and all kinds of creepy shit out there, and you need to be prepared."

Katie looked back over her shoulder at Joao Pedro and smiled. "Hey, Joao Pedro! You sure you don't want to come? It sounds like it's going to be a lot of fun!"

10

A Way In

Grover knocked on Katie's door just after dawn.

"Morning, Grover. Did you come to see me off?"

"Of course, and I brought you a couple of things."

Katie sat on the cot. "What did you bring me?" she asked as she pulled on one boot.

"First off, this is a tent. I know you don't plan on being out there overnight, but if you have a problem and can't get back, you'll need one. The last thing you want to do is sleep on the ground. This is a covered hammock, so all you need to set it up are a couple of sturdy trees."

"Thanks, Grover," Katie said, and he handed it to her. "Wow, that's light."

"Yep, easy to carry." He reached into his pocket and took out a walkie-talkie. "Keep this on. If you need me, I'm on channel four."

"Okay."

"One more thing," Grover said, and took a revolver in a leather holster out of his pocket. "This is for emergencies: snakes, animals, and whatever or whoever you might run into. Just please be careful with it. I don't want you to shoot yourself by accident."

Katie unbuckled her belt, slipped it out from under the loops, and Grover handed her the gun. She fished the belt through the slots in the holster and put it back on.

Grover looked her over with a smile.

"With those boots, a gun, and a black eye, you look like a real explorer."

Katie laughed, and Grover pulled the gun from its holster. "Have you ever fired a gun?"

"No, but I'll figure it out."

"The main thing to remember," Grover said as he showed Katie the side, "is to keep the safety on until you need to shoot." He pointed out the tiny lever. "Flip it this way to lock it and that way to fire."

"Got it," Katie replied, and he handed her the gun. She looked at it for a minute, stuck it in the holster, and snapped down the strap.

Katie tied the rolled-up hammock to the bottom of her rucksack, and Grover opened the door. She slung the bag over one shoulder, and they walked over to the maintenance depot. Katie dropped her bag in the Jeep and felt Grover's hand on the back of her neck.

"You know I don't like this, right?"

"Yeah, but it's got to be done, and I'm the only one willing to do it."

"That's what scares me."

"I'll be fine. If I run into any trouble, I'll call."

Katie smiled and got behind the wheel.

"Just be careful."

Katie started the engine, pressed the clutch, and put the transmission in gear. She gave him a confident wave and drove away.

The supply road was well kept. Grover graded it when he drove the dozer from the barge to camp, so it was an easy drive. The jungle around the road, however, was dense, though she passed through several tiny clearings.

The road took her away from the valley before a gentle slope turned back toward the river. She descended down from the plateau, and the terrain leveled out at the base of the cliff. The road continued straight toward the main river, but Katie turned right and followed a cliff.

The face was much higher than the jungle, and the top disappeared in the canopy. The jungle wasn't quite as dense, and to her surprise there was a path to follow.

The path meandered around large trees and boulders but never strayed out of sight of the cliff. All things considered, she made good time.

After a couple of miles, she came to a giant monolithic stone that had sheared off the face of the cliff and fallen like the trunk of a tree into the jungle. She stood up behind the wheel for a better look but couldn't see a way around it. *I have to be getting close,* Katie thought, and sat back down. She pulled the jeep forward until the bumper touched the stone, shut off the engine, and listened to the jungle.

She reached into the back seat, grabbed her rucksack, and stood up. Katie climbed over the windshield onto the hood and tossed her rucksack onto the stone. She pulled herself up, donned her pack, and looked ahead. To her right, the top of the cliff was visible through a break in the trees. She lowered herself down the other side, tightened the shoulder straps, and set off on foot.

The trail she had followed in the Jeep continued, so the hike along the base of the cliff was easy. She imagined for a moment it was the same trail used by Portuguese explorers in search of gold or Jesuit priests in search of souls.

After twenty minutes, the trail narrowed and the elevation rose. The ground turned from dirt to stone, and walking was difficult. A short time later, she heard water and saw the river she'd been looking for through the trees.

This must be the river flowing out of the valley, Katie thought, and was excited to see it. She followed it upstream and in no time reached the stones that blocked the entrance.

She sighed, put her hands on her hips, and looked up. It was massive. She tried to think of how she might describe it, and she had it. *Stones as big as skyscrapers that fell into and on top of each other*, then she remembered Dr. Ribeiro's camera.

Katie wriggled out of her pack, fished out the camera, and slung the strap around her neck. She took several pictures, then realized there was nothing in the shot to give it scale, so she stopped.

She put her pack back on and followed the river. The source was a gap at the bottom of two gigantic slabs that leaned back against each other. It would take a mountaineer to climb over the rubble, and the river was moving way too fast to swim, so she stood there in disgust. *I made it all this way and can't get in*.

Unwilling to accept defeat, she took a closer look around. She followed the base of the obstruction to the right, climbed over small roots and under bigger ones, and a clicking sound made her stop. *That's not footsteps*, Katie thought. *It sounds like fingernails clicking on a table or kitchen counter.*

The noise moved closer and she was certain it was on the other side of the tree in front of her. Katie crept up to the trunk and took a peek. A big black pig walked away from the cliff into the jungle, but two more smaller pigs appeared to walk right out of the stone. She watched them trot off, then went over for a closer look.

There was a crack in the stone that went all the way through, no doubt caused by the tremendous load it had to bear. Katie cupped her hands to shade her eyes and stared into the darkness. There was light at the other end.

She pulled a flashlight out of her rucksack, flicked it on, and moved into the darkness. When she emerged on the other side, she was surprised to see the ground so level. She thought about the geology, and it kind of made sense.

The tree next to the opening was enormous, as were many other trees in her field of view. Since most of the sediment and organic decay couldn't wash out of the valley, all of the plants were well fed. Still, the size of the trees stood out most. The biggest trees were two hundred feet tall or more, and there wasn't a limb on some of them for the first hundred.

Vines the diameter of trees themselves rose from the earth and rooted themselves in the bark. Katie examined the nearest one and watched a long line of ants carry bits of leaves. She looked along the procession but stopped at a dead branch. *Kind of strange that one little branch would have grown so close to the ground while the rest are so far above.*

Katie looked closer and realized the branch wasn't part of the tree at all; it had been jammed between the vine and trunk. She also noticed an odd tuft of long, dark-gray hair tied to the end. She touched it and it felt coarse. She thought about it and decided the Yanomami must have put it there as a warning.

Shade kept the ground from being overgrown, but it was still full of palms and ferns. A game trail led back toward the river, so she stowed her flashlight, took out a notebook and pencil, and headed off into the jungle.

She followed the trail along the rubble to the river and discovered a pond. The river couldn't escape fast enough, and the choke point caused the river to back up as the water waited its turn to pass.

She left the game trail and walked to the edge. The damp ground was full of tracks, but most were made by deer. The other prints were a mishmash of different animals, including one that was as big as Katie's fist. It was the print of a large cat. She didn't expect to see every kind of animal in the valley, so she took a picture of the prints, hoping someone could identify them later.

She made a few notes, returned to the game trail, and followed it upriver. Every few steps, however, she'd stop to take a closer look at something.

Insects were everywhere. Birds darted from limb to limb or soared among the trunks.

She took so many pictures and notes that she barely made any progress upstream, but there was so much she wanted to document around her.

She hadn't looked at her watch all day and didn't realize it was getting late until the shadow of the cliff crossed the river. Katie stopped, took off her pack, and unhooked her canteen. As she took a drink, something ran through the undergrowth in the distance. She froze and listened. There was a short, muted cry of an animal nearby, and the birds scattered.

It sounded close, so Katie slung her rucksack over one shoulder and hurried up the trail. A faint popping and cracking brought her to a standstill, and she listened. She couldn't tell what the noise was over all the other sounds, but she continued on.

The noise stopped, and something raced off into the jungle ahead. Ten steps later the noises made sense. A dead animal was draped over a log next to the trail with its midsection torn out. It was long and covered with hair, and from a distance it looked like some kind of sloth.

When she reached it and knelt down for a closer look, however, it was obvious she was wrong. It had hands, similar to a monkey, but the digits were separated, like a koala. Also like a koala, it had talon-like claws that would have made it a fantastic climber. Strangely, it seemed to be missing its middle fingers. Its arms and legs were both long, like a monkey, but when she touched its bicep, the muscle felt hard. *This little guy must have been incredibly strong*, Katie thought, then looked at its head. It was unique. It had apelike features, but the eyes were large. Katie looked at each one and imagined the creature had the vision of an owl. Still, there was something familiar about the face, something almost human.

Katie was so focused on the creature she didn't write a note or take a picture. She also didn't realize she was being watched.

The female had been searching for the elder of her two children for the last hour and looked down from the tree above. It watched Katie and dug its claws into the bark.

Katie lifted the dead creature's arm and saw it wasn't missing its middle finger after all. The digit was neatly folded into a perfect indentation in its palm, but unlike the other fingers, the claw on this finger was thick and long. It stretched the length of its forearm but was concealed by long, wispy hair.

The female watched and unfolded its claw. Just as it was about to leap, however, Katie lifted the creature off the log. Its mother stopped.

Katie laid the animal on the ground, straightened its legs, and folded its arms across its chest. Katie knew a predator killed it and would be back to finish its meal, but there was something about it. She couldn't leave it in such a horrible state.

She closed its eyes, stroked its head, and touched the side of its face. "I wish I had met you when you were alive."

A low growl rumbled behind her, and she turned. It was a jaguar. Katie watched it, and it watched her from the shadow of a fern. They didn't take their eyes off each other.

Katie reached over, grabbed the strap of her rucksack, and stood up. The cat crept out from under the fern and growled. Katie clutched the bag against her stomach and backed up along the trail.

The cat stayed behind, and when it was out of sight, Katie heard the cat collect its meal and race off into the jungle. Katie put the rucksack on, walked about ten feet, and felt the camera on her chest.

"Shit! I forgot to take a picture."

The image of the creature was burned into her memory, but without a picture or the animal itself, her recollection would be easy to dismiss.

With that failure in mind, she made a conscious effort to document everything, and once again lost track of the time. This time, it was Grover's voice that snapped her out of her trance.

"Katie?" Grover said over the walkie-talkie. "I hope you're on your way back, over."

Katie looked at her watch, took the radio out of the bag, and shook her head. *He's not going to be happy.*

"Grover," Katie replied. "Sorry, I lost track of time. It'll be dark before I can get out of the valley, over."

There was a long pause, and Katie imagined him cursing.

"I'll come get you, over."

"You'll never be able to find me. Besides, I'm fine. I see a good spot to camp and wood for a fire, so I'll be okay, over."

"I'd feel better if you weren't alone. You sure you don't want me to come down, over?"

"Don't worry, Grover. I'll be fine. I have the hammock, I'll build a fire, and I have your gun, so I'll be safe, over."

"Okay," Grover replied, knowing he didn't have a choice at this point. "Just keep a fire burning all night and check in with me in the morning, over."

"I will, over."

"Over and out."

Cage sat on the edge of his cot and stared at the radio next to its metal case. The frequency returned to static, and he watched the little bulb flicker as the radio scanned channels. He only just met the woman but clawed the fabric of the cot in thought. *She's been down there all day, and she's still alive? She can't be. How could she be? What's different? She's a woman? Maybe they don't see her as a threat. Maybe it's because she's alone. They let Jackson go. Hell, they let me go, but that was just so we could tell everyone else to keep out.*

Still, she's been down there all day, and she hasn't even seen one.

Maybe they left. No, Sid said they were down there. Jesus, she doesn't even know what she's walked into. I should go get her. I can rappel down after dark, and no one would know I'm even gone. She'd be easy to find in the dark with a fire going. Be easy for them to find her too.

Those things—whatever they are—they're down there, and ... I can't do it. Jesus Christ, I didn't even want to come back here.

Cage rubbed the back of his head. "She'll never survive the night."

Cage couldn't stand his own company any longer, so he got ready for work and walked over to the mess hall for something to eat. Several workers were already there, but there were five soldiers at one table that looked out of place. They looked like they just rolled in from a mission.

Cage picked up a plate, loaded it with meat loaf, mashed potatoes, and green beans, and sat down at the empty table next to the group of men.

"You fellas look like you've had a rough day," Cage said with a smile. He forked a chunk of meatloaf and shoved it in his mouth.

177

"Rough year, son," the oldest of the men replied. "I'm Skinner. This is Perez, Smith, Uri, and Gonzalez."

"Cage. How long have you guys been down here?"

"Too long. You?"

"Just got back in country. I was here about a year ago."

"Injured or rotated out?"

Cage unbuttoned the top two buttons of his shirt and exposed part of his scars.

"That's a good one," Smith said. "Looks like the one on Uri's back."

"Did you say your name's Cage?" Skinner asked.

"Yeah."

"Well, damn, boy, I know you, or at least I know about you. Grab your slop and sit over here." The men made room, and Cage moved to their table. "Cage here was first contact. He's the fella that survived."

"Yeah, that's me, but since we don't have the room, probably best not to talk about it."

"You're right . . . you're absolutely right. No sense scaring the sheep, but we could tell you some stories. I read your report when they brought us in on this, and given what we've been through, you're damn lucky to be alive. At least we came prepared."

"What kind of team?"

178

"Until all of this started, we worked recovery, but given what we've been doing here, we're more like dog catchers and exterminators. The lab rats call us the bag team. Can you believe that shit?"

"Mad dog catchers maybe," Perez said, and the rest of the team laughed.

"I was just lucky," Cage said.

Skinner looked around the room, smiled, and pointed his fork at Cage, while a piece of meat loaf dangled from his fork.

"Amen, brother. We'll catch up later. But tell me: What do they got you doing?"

"Site security. I had to finish out my contract, and since I already knew the area, this is where I landed. They got me on nights, but come find me when you have time."

"Will do."

Katie walked into the small break in the undergrowth and looked around. *This is the perfect place to camp*, she thought. *It's not on the river, so the bugs shouldn't be bad. I've got a dead tree for firewood and two live ones for the hammock.*

"Okay," Katie said. "First things first."

She took off her rucksack and dug out her hatchet. She gathered up enough twigs for kindling and chopped a couple of limbs into two-foot lengths. Next she tore a page out of her journal, twisted it, and laid it on the ground. She put the kindling on top and made a teepee of larger sticks.

Katie pulled the flint from its small leather case and smiled. She remembered debating with the salesman over which was more practical, a lighter or flint. He sold her on the flint, but this was the first time she tried to use it.

She took out her knife and raked the back side of it along the flint. It barely made a spark. She changed the angle, raked it again, and like magic a barrage of sparks flew out and a few landed on the paper. She blew on the embers just enough to keep them red, and the paper caught fire. The kindling followed, and slowly the larger sticks began to burn.

"Damn! That worked great," Katie said, then cut firewood.

When she had enough wood for the night, she released the straps holding the hammock to the bottom of her rucksack and unfurled it between the two trees. There were two lines on each end, one for the hammock itself, and another to form the peak of the roof. Katie tied everything up and gave it a try. The rope slipped a little bit, but it worked.

"Okay, I've got fire, shelter, water in my canteen, and food in my bag. I think that covers it."

A monkey howled in the distance and sharpened her awareness of her surroundings. *The jaguar*, she thought. *Somehow I need to secure the campsite. The gun would scare anything off, but if I'm asleep, I'll need some way to hear it coming.*

She walked around the small clearing and assessed her resources but didn't find anything that would work. Katie ventured off a little further and found several palms that were covered in long thorns. She cut a few fronds and used a bit of rope to drag them back to camp. She laid them on the ground around her tiny camp so that anything that walked in would step on them.

Katie got in her floating tent, took some fruit out of her rucksack, and set the bag at the other end of the hammock by her feet. She ate dinner and wrote in her journal until she fell asleep.

11
Stone

The next day began well before dawn when a flash of light and cannon shot of thunder jarred Katie from sleep. A steady rain extinguished the fire and became a downpour. Water tested the strength of the fabric above her, and the tent roof drooped against her arms.

Katie lay, eyes wide open, but without a fire or moon she was blind. She thought of wide-open spaces and sunshine, but always returned to thinking she was in a coffin, being buried on a rainy day. She raised her hand to her face, saw nothing, and remembered what Russel told her about how dark the dark could get. She never imagined this.

Grover's tent hammock kept her dry, but it swayed. Without any visual reference, her senses misread a few inches as feet, and she tried harder to imagine herself anywhere else. The regular flash of lightning helped, and it was the first time she ever hoped for more lightning to come.

The rain and thunder chased away any chance of sleep, but at dawn the storm passed. Water dripped from the leaves above and for a while longer mimicked the rain. A short time later it became a mere patter. The storm rumbled in the distance, and as the sound of thunder softened, Katie drifted off to sleep.

A noise woke her an hour later, and she listened for it to come again. There was just enough light to make out shapes and shadows, but with the roof draped over each side of the hammock, she was still blind to everything outside.

Sightless, she heard everything: distant birds, drops of water, and rustling leaves. Among the noise there was a low, guttural vibration that sounded out of place. As Katie tried to place it, she heard footsteps and didn't move.

She heard it breathe. It was an animal. Then something nudged the hammock.

It sniffed the fabric and lapped at the pool of water resting atop her arm. She felt its tongue. It purred, and Katie felt its body move under the small of her back—the head, shoulders, and spine—as the creature pushed up against her. Katie fought the urge to scream but managed to stay still and quiet. As the creature moved out from under the hammock, the roof along the edge moved with it, and Katie saw the jaguar's back. Just as the fabric slipped off the tail, the jaguar stepped on a thorny frond. It growled, hissed, and ran off into the jungle.

Katie didn't move again until the urge to pee insisted she do something about it. She peeked out and was grateful there was enough light to see. Katie swung her feet down and took the pistol out of its holster. She stood up, took a careful look around, and yawned. When she convinced herself it was safe, she chose a spot with a tree at her back and enough of the clearing in front of her to see and took care of business.

Katie thought of what she was doing and almost laughed. *Pants down in the middle of the jungle with a pistol in my hand, afraid any minute I might be attacked. Of course, I've been in a few public toilets where I felt the same.*

Katie broke camp, packed her rucksack, and checked her watch. *No sense turning back now and wasting a day*, Katie thought, then remembered Grover. She fished her walkie-talkie out of her pocket and pressed "Talk."

"Grover, come in, over."

Grover picked up the radio that had been on his chest all night and answered. "Katie? Are you alright, over?"

"I'm fine. Your tent hammock was a real lifesaver, over."

"I'll bet. That was a hell of a storm. Are you on your way back, over?"

"No, it's early, and I should have time to hike to the waterfall and still make it back by late afternoon, over."

Silence.

"You're giving me an ulcer. You know that, right? Over."

"I know. I'm sorry. It's just that I'm already down here, so I might as well make the most of it, over."

"Have you come across anything dangerous, over?"

This time it was Katie who was silent as she considered what to say.

"Nope," Katie replied. "I haven't seen a thing, over."

"You're keeping an eye out for snakes aren't you, over?"

"Yeah, but the weird thing is, I haven't seen any, over."

"Good. Just keep your eyes peeled for 'em, and I'll see you this afternoon, over."

"Sure, but it'll be *late* afternoon, over."

"Be careful, and call if you need me, over."

"Will do, over and out."

Unlike yesterday, Katie forced herself not to stop and make a note of every little thing. She set a reasonable pace and was determined to make it to the waterfall before noon.

An hour in, the trail split. One path went off to the right, and the other turned toward the river. *I know the river will take me to the falls*, Katie thought, and made a left.

The game trail was muddy, but not as muddy as she expected, given all the rain. The tracks in it were fresh, and she'd stop to look when one looked particularly interesting. Most of the prints were from birds, deer, and small mammals, so she didn't stop often.

At the river, the trail split again. One path led downstream and the other up. Katie continued upstream until the river itself split. She hiked a bit farther and could see where the river joined back together. The split was actually a long, narrow island, and the river around her side was rocky and shallow.

A single enormous vine stretched across the river from the island to a tree, which supported it from the other side. Two birds flew out of the jungle behind her and perched on the moss-covered vine. A thin sheet of mist drifted over the rippled water, and Katie raised her camera to take a picture.

She set the shutter speed and aperture to get as much depth of field as possible and pressed the button. The camera clicked, the birds flew away, and Katie advanced the film with her thumb.

"I sure hope that one comes out," she said, and lowered her camera.

A growl startled her from behind. Katie turned and saw the jaguar standing in the trail. She took a step toward the water, and the big cat moved with her. Katie took two more and stepped into the shallow water. The boots gripped the stones, but it was difficult to balance.

The cat moved forward, crouched, and Katie took another step. The cat charged. The rock shifted under her boot, and Katie fell back in the river. The jaguar missed its target, and Katie saw it pass over her. It scrambled to its feet and turned. Katie tried to stand, but it leapt again. Katie threw herself to one side, and the cat landed near the bank.

As Katie lay on her side, she felt the gun press against her hip. She grabbed the grip and pulled, but it wouldn't come out. *The strap!* she thought, and unsnapped it.

Just as the barrel cleared the holster, the jaguar leapt again. Katie reached out and grabbed the animal by the neck with both hands and pushed. Inertia carried the cat over her, but without thinking she held on.

The cat landed on its back, and Katie rolled on top of it. She held its head under the water. The cat kicked and clawed but couldn't get out from under her weight. The kicking slowed, and Katie loosened her grip. The jaguar's hind paw met Katie's arm, and she screamed as the claws tore through her skin. She pulled away, and the cat wriggled free.

Dazed and half-drowned, the cat collapsed in the river, while Katie crawled upstream and slung her arm over the vine for support. Her left arm was throbbing, and as she sat in the water she watched a thin stream of blood wash down the river.

Her heart was racing, and she tried to catch her breath. She looked at the cuts on her arm and winced, then looked back at the dying cat.

It stood up.

The creature shook off the water, sniffed the air, then sniffed the surface of the river. It smelled the trail of blood as it drifted by and looked upstream.

"Son of a bitch," Katie said, then reached for her gun.

It was gone.

The cat crept toward her, and she put her right hand on the river bottom to push herself up. She felt a large, round rock under her hand and wrapped her fingers around it. The jaguar leapt, and Katie struck it in the head.

The big cat went down but tried to get to its feet. Katie struck it again, and it fell. Katie hit it again and it stopped moving. She straddled the creature, grabbed its head with both hands, and pounded it on the bottom.

A torrent of water and blood splashed in her face, and she yelled, "Why? Why?"

Whatever had come over her subsided. She looked down at the dead animal, stared into its eyes, and felt its fur in her hands. *A few days ago I helped save one of you*, Katie thought. *Now look what I've done.*

She stood up, walked back across the river, and lay her rucksack on the bank.

She sat there in silence and watched the water roll by, the stones that changed its movement, and the distorted reflections on the surface. She didn't think. She didn't consider what to do next or even feel the pain burning down her arm. She just watched the water.

Her mind had taken her away, but the pain of her body brought her back, and she snapped out of it. Katie's hand brushed the empty holster on her hip.

Damn gun, she thought. Then she thought of the old adage "Better to have it and not need it than need it and not have it." She thought of Grover. *I can't wait to see his face when I tell him that I had the gun* and *needed it but lost it when I tried to use it. I'm such an idiot.*

Katie stood up, looked at the spot on the bank where she fell in, and scanned the river bottom for the gun. The river wasn't deep, and the water was clear, so it didn't take long. She held it up, let the water drip out of the barrel, and pushed it into the holster.

She took one last look at the dead jaguar and stepped out of the water. She slung her rucksack over her shoulders, and the strap brushed the wound on her arm. *I need to clean that up.* There was a log not far up the trail, so she walked over and took a seat.

She opened her pack and was amazed that everything was still dry. The adrenaline that masked the pain had worn off, and her left arm was on fire. Other parts of her body complained as well, but the cut on her arm was the loudest.

She took out her medical kit and pulled out a roll of gauze, iodine, and peroxide. She lined them up next to her on the log and unbuttoned her shirt. As she took it off, she looked around to make sure no one was watching, then chuckled at the thought and shook her head. She peeled off her wet shirt and draped it over the log.

Katie used the peroxide first. As soon as it hit the cut, the sting brought tears to her eyes and the pain shot down her arm. With the blood washed away, the cut didn't look so bad, and she felt better. A few drops of iodine, however, brought her to tears again but disinfected the wound. She wrapped it up in gauze and put her shirt back on.

Patched up, rested, and ready to go, Katie stood up. A warm, squishy sensation surrounded her feet, and her boots gurgled.

She sighed. "Shit."

Katie sat back down, took off her boots, and poured out the water. Her feet were the only part of her that didn't hurt, so she hadn't noticed they were soaked.

She wrung the water out of her socks and hung them on her rucksack to dry, then got a fresh pair. She shook all the water she could from her boots and put them back on.

Uncomfortable and in pain, she swung her rucksack onto her back and moved on.

Half an hour later, something moved in the bushes along the river on the opposite bank. Katie stopped next to a tree and watched. It was a tiny deer. It drank from the river, then scampered off toward a clearing not far away.

Even from a distance, Katie could see the clearing was full of shrubs covered in berries. The little deer disappeared among them, but as Katie watched, she saw several larger deer as well. She raised her camera to take a picture and felt a trickle of water spill in her palm. She looked at the camera, shook it, and heard the river slosh around inside.

With her thumb on the bayonet release, she gave the lens a twist, and water poured out of the body. The pictures were gone, but the camera might be salvageable, so she put the lens back on and stuffed it into her rucksack.

Katie kept going and not long after caught a glimpse of the waterfall through the canopy. Fifteen minutes later she found another trailside log and took a break. Like the last one, this one offered a nice view of the river, so Katie took off her rucksack and had a drink. Her stomach reminded her she hadn't eaten, so she dug out an orange as well.

As she peeled it, her canteen fell off the back of the log. Katie retrieved it and returned to her orange. The canteen fell off again, and Katie looked down at it. She stared into the shadows under the foliage behind her, sighed, and returned the canteen to the log.

Katie went back to her orange but raised her elbows high enough to watch the canteen. A dark, harry little hand reached out, grabbed the strap of the canteen, and pulled it off the log. Katie picked it up one last time but set it in front of the log instead. A faint huff of disappointment came from behind her, and she smiled.

Katie finished peeling the orange and pulled off a wedge. She placed it on the log beside her and watched it out of the corner of her eye. It reached out its little hand again, and she saw both its hand and forearm. It looked just like the arm of the carcass she found the previous day. Katie set down another wedge toward the front of the log, and the creature retrieved it the same way. She almost saw its head.

"Okay, you little booger," Katie said, and slid off the front of the log. She twisted around Indian-style and faced the log, then placed another orange wedge on top. "How about you come out and say hello?"

The creature peeked over the log, looked at Katie for a moment, then jumped up, sat on top of it, and snatched up the orange wedge. It looked like the other creature, but this one was darker and appeared to be younger. It popped the orange wedge in its mouth and smiled, then reached out to Katie for another. She obliged and watched the creature's long, furry fingers close around the piece of orange.

Katie ate a piece of orange herself, and the two were content to simply look at each other. When the orange was gone, Katie showed the creature her empty hands. It looked at her, then reached over and grabbed the top of her rucksack with its foot. It lifted the flap and sniffed the air. Its expression changed from curiosity to excitement, as if it had just solved a puzzle, and it hopped off the log.

The creature held the flap open and stuck its face inside. It sniffed then and made a soft, guttural sound. It pulled its head out, looked at Katie, then stuck its hand in the rucksack and pulled out a small white paper sack.

It sniffed the sack, and Katie reached out to open it, but the creature pulled it away. It jumped on to the log, sat down, and tore a small hole in the sack. Katie remembered to take pictures this time and raised her camera.

As she framed the shot, saw the water droplets, and removed the strap from around her neck, Katie shook her head and stuffed the camera into her rucksack.

Sugar sprinkled out of the hole in the sack onto the creature's hand, and it tasted the tiny granules. It laughed. The creature looked at her, and Katie reached out once more, and this time the creature gave it to her. Katie opened the sack and pulled a cookie out. The creature took the sack and the cookie and sniffed both. It licked the cookie, and Katie made a biting gesture. The creature took a bite. Its eyes grew wide and it smiled as it chewed. It swallowed, took another bite, and rocked back and forth.

"It's good, isn't it?" Katie said, and the creature just looked at her. "Mrs. Baker made those cookies, and I carried them all the way here from São Paulo."

The creature listened and ate, and when the sugar kicked in, it swung its long legs. Katie looked at the claws on its toes. They were the same as the talon-shaped claws on its fingers, but Katie needed a better look.

"Can I look at your feet?" Katie asked, then slowly reached out for its foot.

The creature stopped eating and watched her hand but let Katie touch it. She rested his heel in the palm of her hand and leaned in. The bottom of its foot was black, and the orientation of its toes was as strange as its hands.

"You're not a monkey or an ape," Katie said. "But whatever you are, you've adapted perfectly to life in the trees."

Katie ran her thumb across the sole of its foot, and the creature laughed and pulled its foot away. Katie looked at the creature and took out her notebook. She turned to the first blank page and started to sketch. When the creature finished its cookie, it reached out and pushed the top of the book down so it could see what she was doing.

"You want to see?" Katie asked, then turned the book around.

It tapped the picture with the back of its hand and patted itself on the chest. Katie nearly dropped the book. She sat there speechless for a moment, amazed at what the creature had just done.

"Oh my God . . . You recognize yourself. That can't be."

The creature turned the book around and pushed it toward her. It tapped the book, then tapped itself under the chin with the back of its hand.

"You want me to finish?"

Katie smiled and finished the drawing while the creature watched. When she was done, the creature was anxious to see it but also wanted to see the stick she used to draw it. The creature took the pencil from her hand, looked at it, then started to put it in its mouth.

Katie reached out and grabbed it. The creature jerked back, but Katie held on long enough to get the pencil.

"No eating the pencil," Katie said, pointing at her mouth and waving her finger.

The creature's eyes widened, and then it squinted in thought. A moment later it touched itself on the mouth and shook its head side to side. Katie's mouth fell agape.

The creature patted itself on the chest, pointed to its eye, and made a scribbling gesture on the back of its left hand with its index finger. It pointed at the pencil, and excitement shot down Katie's spine.

"This is impossible. We can't be having a conversation."

The creature pointed at the pencil again. Katie held it out, and the creature took it.

"I wonder," Katie said, and slowly stood up. She straddled the log, sat down, and lay the book down in front of her.

The creature turned around on the log as well and watched Katie turn to a blank page. Katie took the creature's hand, and it gave her an apprehensive look but let her place its hand flat on the page. She took his other hand, turned the pencil around so the lead was down, and helped the creature trace its hand in her book. The creature smiled, and after tracing two fingers, he stopped and moved her hand away. It traced the rest of its hand by itself. To her astonishment, the creature switched the pencil to its other hand and traced that hand as well.

"You're very smart," Katie said, and the creature touched her mouth. It looked at her a moment, turned the page, and took her hand. This time it lay her hand on the book and traced hers. Katie felt its rough palm and couldn't believe what she had found.

As the creature traced each digit, Katie looked at its face. Its brow was furrowed in intense concentration and its tongue peeked out of its mouth. Katie almost laughed but held it in.

When it was done, Katie moved her hand away, but the creature returned to the page. It looked over at Katie's hand, then its own, and added long claws to the tracing on the page. It smiled at Katie and she laughed.

A terrifying howl cried out in the distance, and the little creature looked scared to death. It jumped up and tried to push Katie off the log. It waved its arm underhanded like it was throwing something away, then leapt over her head. It landed behind her and pulled at the collar of her shirt.

Its little claws scratched her neck, and Katie got to her feet. She looked down at the creature, and it pointed up into the jungle behind her. Katie turned, looked up, and saw branch after branch shake, each time closer than the last.

She caught a glimpse of a shadow first; then she saw it. It was another creature, but it wasn't a child.

Katie reached for her bag, but the creature pushed the back of her legs. The adult dropped below the canopy and crouched on a high limb. It howled again, and Katie just ran.

She raced up the game trail along the river and didn't look back. The creature gained on her fast as it leapt from tree to tree and scrambled along the limbs. Leaves fell, and the creature howled. The roar of the waterfall grew, and the creature dropped down from the trees to her right, and she sprinted with all the strength she had.

A pool at the base of the waterfall came into view, and she ran for it. Just as she reached the edge, the creature leapt, but another creature tackled it. She threw herself off the bank, dove into the pool, and struck her head on the bottom.

Everything went black.

12

Out of Reach

Two hours before sunset, Chris and Grover returned to the maintenance shed, parked their dozers, and shut off the engines.

Grover took out his walkie-talkie. "Katie, just checking to make sure you made it back to camp, over." He waited a moment, then pressed "Talk" again. "Katie, talk to me, over."

"She probably turned off her radio when she got back," Chris said as he climbed down from the dozer. "I'll bet she hit the sack."

"Probably. Still, I'll feel better when I know for sure."

The two men stopped by the auto depot on their way into camp, but the Jeep Katie took was still gone.

"Someone else took it out, that's all," Chris said.

"You sure are a glass-half-full kind of guy," Grover replied, and picked up the pace to Katie's shack.

When they got there, Chris knocked, but Grover didn't wait for a reply. He opened the door, and Katie wasn't there.

"Let's check the mess hall," Grover said.

They walked in the mess hall and saw several men eating dinner, including Russel.

"Russel?" Chris asked. "Have you seen Katie? She should be back by now."

"No, sorry. Did she take a radio?"

"Yeah, but she's not answering."

"There's still a couple of hours of daylight left. I'm sure she'll be back."

"I'm not," Grover replied. "She camped out down there last night but swore she'd be back this afternoon. At least last night she radioed to let me know she was okay."

Russel sat there a moment, checked his watch, and looked out the crack in the plywood covering the broken window.

"It's too damn late to go after her. If she doesn't make a fire, we'd never find her in the dark."

"I can't just sit around and do nothing."

"Me either," Chris added.

"I'm with you," Russel said. "But there's a dozen reasons you can't get her on the radio, and not all of them mean something bad happened. It might be a dead battery or she just lost it. If she doesn't show up by dark, then we'll go after her at dawn."

Brice and Schroder walked in just as Russel finished his sentence.

"Who are you going after?" Brice asked, certain he knew the answer.

"Katie hasn't made it back," Chris replied.

"She wasn't supposed to go down there in the first place. If something happened to her or she can't find her way back, I say good riddance."

"You've got to be kidding," Russel said.

"Hey, that bitch made her bed and she can lay in it."

"We've got to do something!" Chris shouted.

"No, we don't. She's not our responsibility. None of you are going to do anything other than the jobs I hired you to do," Brice added. 'You hear me, Grover?"

Grover looked down at Brice. "I hear you. I just don't give a shit. If she doesn't show up tonight, I'm going down there to get her tomorrow."

Brice stepped forward and pushed his finger in Grover's chest. "You work for me, asshole, not the other way around. On my job you do what I say."

Grover grabbed Brice's hand and squeezed. Schroder reached in to pull Brice free but couldn't.

"Stop me," Grover replied, and tightened his grip just shy of breaking bones.

Brice tried to hide the pain but couldn't, and after a few seconds Grover let him go.

Brice cradled his hand. "You're fired! How about that?"

"Suits me fine," Grover replied, "but I'm not leaving without Katie."

Grover walked to the door and looked back at Brice. "Don't let me forget to punch you in the face before I leave."

Grover walked out and slammed the door.

"Anybody else losing their jobs today?" Brice asked, and Chris made his way to the door. "You have anything smart to say?"

"Nope," Chris replied, and caught up with Grover, who was headed toward the cliff.

"You quit too?" Grover asked.

"Hell yeah. That guy has lost his mind. So what's the plan?"

"The quickest way down would be to rappel, but that's a long way down. Also, I don't know how," Grover said, and looked at Chris. "You?"

"Nope. We could drive down to the end of the valley and figure out how she got in."

"I was thinking about that, too, or we could try the trail down the cliff on the other side."

"Rappelling sounds safer than that," Chris said. "What about the lift? It would take some time to put it together, but all the parts are still in the crate."

"That would take all morning," Grover replied.

"Or half the night?" Chris said, and Grover stopped.

"Now that sounds like a plan. Still, I'd like to see if I can spot any smoke. If her radio is on the fritz and she's set up camp, she'll have a fire going by now."

Chris and Grover stood on the top of the cliff for half an hour and looked for smoke.

"Alright, Chris," Grover said. "Best head for the maintenance shed and get started."

Cage stood outside his tent and watched Grover and Chris walk back to camp. He heard Grover's radio call go unanswered and knew she was gone.

Skinner walked up to Cage with the rest of his team.

"Alright, boys," Skinner said. "I want two of you on the river, and three at the top of the trail."

They all had on heavy vests with high, thick collars as well as arm and leg protection. Cage fought the urge to smile, but Skinner knew what Cage was thinking and smiled for him.

"First lesson: protect yourself."

"What's the second?"

"That's easy: when in doubt, kill it."

Cage grinned. "I can certainly understand that. So, tell me, Skinner, what's really going on here?"

"If you were assigned here, you know there's more of them down there."

"Yeah, Sid read me in on it."

"Then you know this is the last tribe."

"Tribe?"

"Tribe, troop, family, whatever you want to call 'em. We call 'em tribes. Anyway, this is the last one. You found the first one. We started with them after you left and spent a year getting here."

"How many tribes did you find?"

"Including this one, four. The first one was the worst. When we were brought in, they sent us in pretty much blind, like your team. Only difference was that we had better tools."

"The lab wanted my team to catch an adult."

Skinner laughed and slapped his thigh. "Those lab rats. That's what they told us too. Course, they stayed in camp, so giving the order was easy for them to do."

"Did you get one?"

"Eventually, but we attacked that troop for weeks."

"Weeks?"

"Yeah, weeks. They're a tight-knit bunch and smart. They figured out what we were up to, and every time we managed to dart one, the others jumped down and carried it off. I lost three men before we made it back with one. After that, I laid down the law with the lab rats: we weren't catching any more adults. That first one was a male, and they shipped it Stateside as quick as they could. They didn't want the Brazilians finding out about 'em, I guess.

"After one of those damn things killed another one of my team, a good friend of mine, I made the lab rats tell me what we were doing. They said they wanted to breed the goddamned things. Can you believe that? They want to train 'em like dogs to do recon and package retrieval and any other sneaky Agency shit they can think of. They needed adults for breeding, but get this: they wanted all of the infants and really young creatures they could get. I suppose the thought is, if you're going to train a lion, you don't start with an adult, you start with a cub.

"Turns out that simplified things for my team. Once we had two adult females for the male to breed with, all we focused on were the babies. And get this: they insisted we kill the rest. We snatched all the little ones we could, and they're already Stateside. They didn't want the Russians or Cubans getting their hands on these things, so I guess extermination made sense. We mopped up the third tribe a week ago, and now we're here."

"You're collecting the creatures here?"

"That was the plan, but the casualties have started to attract attention, and the lab rats have a gaggle of babies, so they've got something else planned for this bunch. As it turns out, a defense contractor wants to field-test some kind of mass defoliant or some damn thing. Obviously, they can't test it on humans, and since these things are similar to us, like chimps, they'll make good test subjects. They're just going to leave those things down there, bomb the shit out of 'em, and see what happens. This valley's nicely contained, and we don't think they can get out, but they left us here to make sure. If any of 'em survive and try to crawl out, we'll just pick 'em off from up here. Fish in a barrel, that sort of thing."

Cage stared at the sunset and tried to process everything he heard.

"Hey," Skinner said, and nudged Cage's arm. "You still with me?"

"Yeah, yeah, fish in a barrel. I got it. It was good talking to you, but I need to grab some chow before I go on duty."

"Course, I'll be around. Good talking to you."

When they got to the shed, they pushed a broken-down jeep out so they'd have room to work. The elevator part of the lift was still in the wooden crate it arrived in a month ago and had to be dug out from behind a bunch of spare parts and sheet metal in the corner.

It was a large rectangular wooden crate about eight feet long and six feet tall and three feet deep, so they knew assembling it would be a chore.

Chris pried open the narrow end, and they pulled out all the pieces. They propped the big pieces against the wall and separated the smaller pieces into piles on the dirt floor. No instructions. It was a simple cage, like a portable jail cell or shark cage.

Grover cut open a heavy cardboard box filled with bolts, washers, and nuts and looked over at Chris.

"This might take longer than half the night."

Chris agreed with a shake of his head, but Russel answered, "Maybe not."

"Hey, Russel," Grover said. "You sure you want to help?"

"Six hands are better than four," Russel replied. "Besides, I never liked working for those two assholes anyway."

After half an hour the three men found their rhythm, and two hours later they tightened the last of the bolts and stepped back to admire their work.

"What's next?" Chris asked. "Besides a cold drink?"

"The winch still needs to be wound with cable," Grover replied.

"I'll get the oil and gasoline," Russel said. "You guys get a Jeep and a long length of chain."

They loaded up the Jeep, and not knowing what tools they'd need, Grover threw a big steel toolbox in the back as well.

As they drove through camp, Chris stopped at the mess hall, jumped out, and ran inside. He came out with three cold Cokes and passed out the drinks

"Thanks," Grover replied, and popped off the cap on the dash with a firm slap. "Let's go."

When they reached the platform, Chris parked with the headlights facing the winch. They unloaded the Jeep and went to work.

The winch was brand-new, so it didn't take much to get it started. Russel shut it off, and the three looked at the huge spool of cable.

"Any ideas?" Grover asked.

"Actually," Russel said, "I was thinking we could run the chain through the spool, connect the chain to the bumper of the Jeep, and let the winch pull it off from there."

"That spool looks pretty damn heavy, and I don't think it'll spin sitting in the dirt," Grover said. "We're going to need something bigger."

Grover looked at Chris.

"I'll go get it," Chris said. "But we might as well get the cage while we're at it and save a trip."

The three jumped in the Jeep and headed back to camp.

At the maintenance shed, Chris fired up the big dozer, while Grover and Russel pulled the elevator out of the bay. Chris stopped the dozer next to it, and Grover and Russel attached the chain. Chris raised the blade, and it lifted the elevator off the ground.

"Meet you there!" Chris yelled, and the three men headed back to the cliff.

Russel got in the Jeep, but Grover went back into the shop for a can of bearing grease and a piece of sheet metal.

211

As the goliath rolled past the office, Chris saw Brice and Schroder standing in the door. He waved and smiled, to which Brice shouted something and gave him the finger.

At the platform, Chris set the cage down and waited for Grover and Russel to free the chain. Afterward, he pulled up to the spool and used the blade to stand it upright. He repositioned and pulled up to the spool again.

Grover and Russel held the sheet metal against the blade, and Chris pulled forward. They ran the chain through the hole, fastened the chain to each side of the blade, and smeared some grease on the edge of the spool.

Grover gave Chris the signal, and Chris raised the spool about six inches off the ground. Russel cut the strap holding the cable in place, and Grover pulled off enough cable to fasten it to the winch.

Once it was secure, Russel fired up the engine and began to wind the cable. Their jerry-rigging worked perfectly, and the steel cable unraveled from the spool onto the winch. They took turns greasing the spool, but it was a long cable and took a while to load.

With the last of the cable on the winch, the three men turned their attention to the cage. They wrestled it onto the platform, released enough cable to string through the pulley above the hole, and attached the cable to a fitting on top of the cage.

They stood the cage up, and with Chris on the winch, Grover and Russel slid the lift in place. The vertical beams on each corner held it in position, and Grover pulled a lever that pushed the locking pins in place.

Russel looked down at his watch. "Well, we managed to get it done before midnight."

"Sunrise is in six hours," Grover replied. "Chris, meet me back here at six. I'll need you to look after the winch."

"I'm going with you."

"No, I need you up here to make sure Katie and I can get back."

"But the lift is radio controlled."

"I understand, but if both of us go, there's nothing keeping someone from pulling the elevator back up while we're down there."

"You're not going alone," Russel added. "You need someone down there to watch your back."

"Alright, we meet back here at six."

Half an hour later, Grover was sacked out on his cot but couldn't sleep. Most nights he fell asleep right off, but worry kept him up.

Best case, Grover thought, the battery in her radio was dead; worst case, Katie was. He refused to think about the latter. She was following the river to the waterfall. *The lift is about halfway, so we'll make straight for the river and turn upstream. What if she's hurt and laying on the ground? She could be ten feet away and I might not see her through the leaves and scrub. Regardless, I have to try. I have to do something.*

Exhaustion finally caught up with him, and Grover fell asleep.

At five forty-five Russel pulled up outside Grover's tent, and Grover was ready to go.

"Get any sleep?" Russel asked.

"Not much. You?"

"No. I stopped at the office and picked up rifles, pistols, and a couple of radios."

"Run into anyone?"

"Yep."

"They give you any trouble?"

"Yep, but once I explained that my uncle is on the Senate Appropriations Committee, they let me take them anyway."

"Wow," Grover replied. "I had no idea you had family in Congress."

"Yeah, I don't."

Grover smiled and shook his head.

"I'm telling you, Grover, there's something else going on here. I've worked on a lot of construction projects, but none like this."

"Agreed. So, let's go get Katie and get the hell out of here."

Chris stepped out of his tent, stretched, and looked across the dirt road at Grover and Russel. The three men piled into the Jeep and headed for the lift.

A new day chased the darkness from the horizon, and they stopped at the lift. The three unloaded the Jeep, fired up the winch, and tested the lift. They ran the lift all the way down and back up, and it worked perfectly.

The clouds turned orange, and Grover slung a rifle over his shoulder.

"Chris, you sure you're okay watching the lift?" Grover asked. "Not to sound paranoid, but there's no telling what Brice and Schroder might do once Russel and I get down there."

"I'll be fine," Chris replied as he pushed a clip in his rifle. "There's too many witnesses around for them to do anything. Besides, you'll probably find her and be back in an hour, so I'll be fine."

"Just watch your ass. That's all I'm saying."

"Understood. I'll be fine. Now, get in, and let's get this show on the road."

Grover and Russel stepped into the lift. Chris released the locking mechanism, and Russel pressed the down button on the controls. The elevator slipped through the platform and slowly descended into the valley.

The sun cleared the earth, and a warm light struck the trees along the top of the cliff. The noise of the winch engine drowned out every other sound, and Chris leaned over the rail. When the lift was halfway down, Chris leaned back and took a quick look around. In camp, shadowy figures made their way to the mess hall, but as he turned back to the lift, two other figures caught his eye. They stood along the edge of the cliff at the end of the runway, and one of them checked his watch.

The sound changed. Chris walked toward the winch, but the noise was something else. The noise grew louder, and he realized it was coming from the south. He looked down the valley and watched three dark objects fly out of the pink clouds.

Something white blew into Chris's periphery, and he looked back toward the runway. A smoke grenade sent a long white plume into the sky and carried it south on the wind.

"What the . . .?" Chris said, then hurried back to the edge of the platform.

He looked down at the elevator and took out his walkie-talkie. Before he could press the button to talk, Russel called him.

"Chris, what's going on up there, over?"

"Look down the valley! Three planes are headed this way, over."

Closer now, it was easy to see that these aircraft were much bigger than the cargo planes the company used.

"They can't land something that big here," Russel said to Grover.

"Get back up here!" Chris shouted into the radio.

"Too late," Russel replied, and stopped the lift.

The three planes descended in a straight line, then separated into formation. The roar of engines reverberated off the cliff walls and filled the valley with noise. As they reached the southern tip of the valley, thin lines of mist spewed from the wings and settled on the jungle below.

Russel and Grover covered their noses and mouths with their shirts and closed their eyes. When they opened them, they watched the aircraft pass over the north end of the valley, and the dusting stopped. The three planes turned east, and Grover looked at his arm.

"Doesn't burn or smell. Any idea what that was?" Grover asked.

"If I had to guess, I'd say nothing good. Let's get Katie and get back up so we can wash this off."

Russel started the lift, and they continued down.

Chris watched them for a moment, then looked back toward the end of the runway. The two shadowy figures were walking his way. Dawn gave them detail, and Chris could see it was Brice and Schroder.

Their distance and casual stroll gave Chris time to consider the position he'd volunteered for, and his stomach twisted into a knot. *My only job is to keep anyone from tampering with the lift*, Chris thought. *I have a rifle, but what if pointing it isn't enough?*

Time to decide grew short, then ran out. Chris raised the rifle and pointed it at the two men. "That's far enough!"

Brice nudged Schroder's arm, and both men stopped.

"Chris," Brice said. "Looks like you pulled guard duty. What say you put that rifle down? We're not here to interfere with your little rescue mission."

Chris didn't say a word or lower the rifle.

Schroder whispered something to Brice, but Brice shook his head.

"Fair enough, Chris," Brice continued. "If I were you, I wouldn't trust me either. I just came over to let you know that I've delayed the return flight to Ameia, so once you boys get Katie, the four of you can load up and get out of here; no muss, no fuss."

"What the hell did they just spray down there?" Chris yelled. "There's people down there!"

"Don't blame me, boy. I warned all of you not to go down there."

"What was it?"

"To tell you the truth, I don't know. I heard it's something special, but you fellas won't be here to find out, so it doesn't matter."

Brice turned and took a few steps toward camp, then looked back over his shoulder.

"Good luck," Brice said. "Schroder, we better let him get back to his post."

Chris lowered the rifle, looked down at his trembling hand, and sighed.

13
Sunup

Hammering was the first sound Katie heard when she regained consciousness, and she opened her eyes. A misty dappled light squeezed through a thick wall of leaves, but among the shadows there was a shape. Someone was seated on the ground a few feet away.

Katie pushed herself up to a seated position as well, and her head throbbed.

"Chris?" Katie asked, but he didn't answer.

The shadow moved, and Katie rubbed her eyes. It was the juvenile.

It stood up and walked toward her with an almost-human gait and touched her on the head. Katie's memory came back, and she smiled through the pain.

The creature made a sharp whoop and a combination of whistles, then looked at the cut on Katie's head. It touched her face, and she felt the coarse texture of its finger and its claw on her skin, but she stayed still.

The creature inspected her wound, and Katie noticed her surroundings. She was inside a dome-shaped shelter of woven limbs and leaves. Sunlight flickered through the walls but also the floor.

She turned her head and realized she was leaning against the trunk of a tree. She looked back at the little creature.

The floor of the shelter trembled, and she heard something moving on the other side of the trunk. Two adults stepped into view. Her memory of being chased through the jungle came to mind, and she pushed herself away. She tried to stand, but one of the creatures grabbed her by the shoulders, forced her back down, and held her there. It knelt on one knee and leaned in, inches from her face.

The creature looked at her, and Katie saw her reflection in the creature's eyes. She was terrified. The creature put its hand under Katie's jaw, opened her mouth, and looked at her teeth. It made a curious huff and turned its attention to the wound on Katie's forehead.

The creature brushed Katie's hair aside and held it there while she took a closer look. Its mouth, now eye level to Katie, opened just enough for her to see the creature's teeth, and she imagined being torn to pieces.

The creature released Katie's shoulder, and the other adult handed it a thick green leaf the size of a human hand. It popped the leaf into its mouth, chewed it for a few seconds, then took it out and pressed it against Katie's head. The creature leaned back, took Katie's hand, and pushed it against the leaf. It grunted, then patted the back of Katie's hand. Katie held the leaf in place, and the creature smiled.

Her terror slipped away, as did the pain in her head. Katie smiled back, and both adult creatures sat down.

The juvenile climbed onto the adult's back, draped its arm over its shoulder, and looked at Katie. That was when Katie noticed the breasts under its hair. *She must be the little creature's mother*, Katie thought.

They looked at each other for a long, quiet moment, then the mother made a guttural noise and touched herself on the mouth. The child hopped off her back and returned to its spot along the wall.

The hammering started again, and when it stopped, the little creature stood up with a handful of nuts in one hand and the camera in the other. The creature smiled and demonstrated how well the camera cracked open nuts.

The child handed Katie the shelled nuts and sat down next to her. It rested its arm on Katie's lap and played with the camera a little more. The door on the back of the camera was gone, along with the film, and she heard other parts rattle inside. It was ruined, so there wasn't any point in asking for it back.

The little creature was fascinated by the lens and tapped on the glass with its claws. Content to study its new toy, the creature stretched out and rested its head against Katie's arm. A moment later, it lifted her arm, settled its head against Katie's side, and pulled her arm around its head onto its chest. Katie looked down at the creature with a smile and watched him inspect the camera.

The creature's mother reached out with its long arm and straightened the hair on her child's foot. Katie looked up at her, and the creature smiled.

The mother turned toward the other adult, made a few strange sounds, and the other creature replied in kind.

That's not random noises, Katie thought. *They were too similar and structured for that.* The creatures exchanged noises again, and the other adult disappeared behind the tree.

They're talking! But not in some undiscernible way, like dolphins, whales, or chimpanzees. That was a conversation. I have to write this down.

As soon as she thought it, she remembered losing her notebook and sighed. Katie looked at the female and opened her mouth to ask, then thought of the child, who had seen the bag. Katie tapped on the little creature's shoulder.

When it turned and looked at her, Katie made a gesture with both hands in front of her. The leaf fell off her forehead, and the female tried to get Katie to put it back.

"No, no, no," Katie said. "My bag." Both creatures just stared. "Okay, how about this?" Katie held both fists up to her shoulders, then pointed over her shoulder to her back.

The juvenile slapped Katie on the leg and hopped to his feet. It said something to its mother, then hurried around the trunk of the tree. A moment later, it returned with her rucksack, and Katie smiled. It repeated the same sounds to its mother and handed Katie the bag.

Katie tried to repeat the sounds, and both creatures laughed. The mother said it again, slower this time, but the extreme jump in pitch and tone made it impossible for Katie to pronounce. The female gestured toward her child, then pointed at the base of the curved wall.

The creature scurried over to a small pile of sticks, but when he picked it up, Katie saw that it was a basket.

The child brought it over and set it next to Katie's rucksack.

Katie picked it up. The basket was shaped like an eggplant, with a small opening at the top and a round bottom. The vertical branches were bent into a U-shape, and thinner, horizontal branches held the structure together. Long vines were woven over the surface to fill in the gaps, and it was sturdy.

The basket also had a braided strap that extended from one end to the other. Katie couldn't believe it. She held the basket close and ran her fingers over all the woven ridges, then took a closer look at the strap. It wasn't just braided, though that would be miraculous in and of itself. Two of the vines were a different color, and the braiding created a pattern. Maybe they simply found the basket or took it from one of the Yanomami tribes, Katie thought, and it made sense.

The child touched Katie's shoulder to get her attention, then hurried back over to the wall. When it returned, it held out a smaller, half-finished basket and patted itself on its chest. The child sat down and demonstrated its skill. It fished the thin vine over, under, over, and under again, then used the claw on its index finger to tap the vine down against the row beneath it.

Katie grinned and pointed to the two shoulder straps on her own rucksack. Both creatures watched as Katie wiggled the strap on the finished basket.

The female made a short guttural sound and gave a quick nod to the child. The child stood up, took the basket from Katie, and slung it on its back, with the strap running diagonally across its chest. The child hopped up and down and showed off how well the basket remained in place, then leapt onto the trunk of the tree like a squirrel.

Katie was amazed at how little effort it took the creature to hold itself in place. It crawled around the trunk and emerged from the other side. It hopped down, removed the basket, and sat down next to Katie again. Katie pulled her rucksack onto her lap and checked to see what was left inside. A few minor things were missing, including her notebook, but what concerned her most was the gun. It wasn't in the holster.

The male returned, but he wasn't alone; a larger creature stepped out from around the trunk as well and stood beside him. The larger male scowled, gestured at Katie, and made several agitated sounds. The smaller male pushed the larger one aside and pointed southeast toward the camp.

The larger male shook his head, stepped toward Katie, and she noticed a long scar across his chest. He said something to the smaller male, and the smaller male stepped in front of him. He slapped himself three times on the chest, growled, and shoved the larger male against the tree.

Katie sat still and tried not to look up at them. The smaller creature repeated himself and pointed toward the camp again. The larger creature sighed, and Katie looked up.

The larger creature looked at the other male and grabbed Katie's forearm. The creature lifted Katie to her feet, and the contents of her rucksack spilled onto the floor.

The creature huffed as Katie knelt back down to collect her things and shook his head. The female and child helped pick everything up, and Katie packed it away.

The larger male grunted twice.

"Alright," Katie said. "I'm hurrying. Just give me a minute . . . Jeez." She slung the rucksack onto her back and looked at the smaller male for instructions.

The child wrapped its arms around Katie's leg and held it tight. It said something to its mother, and the mother smiled. Katie touched the child on the top of its head, and the little creature gave her one last squeeze before letting go.

The larger male gave Katie a light push on her chest with the back of his hand, then stepped around the trunk of the tree. Katie followed, and as she reached the opposite side, she saw a semicircular hole in the floor next to the trunk.

Katie stepped close enough to look down but couldn't see the ground through the limbs and leaves. The creature knelt down, took Katie by the wrist, and turned his back while pulling her arm over his shoulder. He reached back with his other hand, pulled Katie's arm under his, and pushed her hands together. She locked them and felt the scar under her forearm. The creature climbed onto the tree.

"Oh shit. Oh shit. *Oh shit*. Don't look down."

The creature looked back over his shoulder and huffed.

"I'm okay," Katie said with a tremble in her voice. "Just don't drop me."

Katie held tight as they moved through the hole, and she felt the creature's strength. They descended through the canopy, and when they had traveled far enough down to see the ground, Katie couldn't help but look.

As soon as she opened her eyes, she felt dizzy, and the perspective of the trunk retreating to the ground didn't help. Katie thought of where she was and became acutely aware that a firm grip was all that kept her from plummeting to her death. She tightened her grip and pressed her cheek against the creature's neck. The creature's torso twitched, and it made short repeating noises. Katie didn't know what it was at first; then it hit her.

"Stop laughing," Katie said, and tried to smile.

The creature stopped laughing, looked at her over his shoulder, and touched the back of her arm. The creature resumed their descent but stopped a moment later on an enormous limb. He knelt down and tapped her hands, still clenched in the middle of his chest.

Katie released him, and the creature turned around. He inspected her hands. They were white. The creature held out his own and, with his palms up, made fists several times. He reached over and tapped her on the breast with the back of his hand, and Katie made fists as well.

"I'm okay," Katie said, and color returned to her fingers. The creature grunted, and Katie pointed to the ground. "We're almost there."

The creature looked down, then off to the side and pointed along the limb.

"Oh no! Wait a minute," Katie said, and held her hands up in front of her.

The creature turned, knelt once more, and pulled her onto his back. When her feet came off the ground this time, however, he touched her knees and had her wrap her legs around his waist. As soon as she did, he leaned over and grabbed the branch with his hands and feet.

"I'm happy to walk back if you just take me to the ground."

The creature checked to see her hands were together, then set off across the limb.

Katie wanted to keep her eyes open, if only to be able to document it later, but two steps in she gave up.

After they crossed the river, the creature stopped. He looked south and listened. A voice called out. It was faint and masked by the chirping of birds; then she heard it twice more. Someone was yelling her name.

The creature descended down the trunk of the nearest tree. On the ground, Katie let go, and the creature faced her. It pointed toward the camp, took Katie by the wrist, and pushed her hand against her chest. It let go, made a sweeping gesture around them, and touched himself on the chest.

231

Katie smiled, nodded, and touched the creature on the upper arm. The creature turned, climbed up onto the lowest limb, and looked back. Katie heard her name again, and the creature disappeared into the canopy. She stood there, lost in thought.

"Katie!"

"Katie!"

"Over here!" she yelled, and Grover and Russel raced down the path in her direction.

Grover gave Katie an off-the-ground hug, and for a few seconds he wouldn't put her down. He never told Chris or Russel, but he was certain they'd find her dead.

When Grover put her down, he noticed her head and leaned down for a better look. "Jesus, Katie, what happened?"

"I jumped in the river and hit my head."

"When I couldn't raise you on the radio, I thought . . . Did the battery go dead, or did you lose it?"

"It's a long story," Katie replied. "I'll tell you on the way back. I left the Jeep at the far end of the valley."

"The company can pick it up later," Russel said. "Grover, Chris, and I got the lift running last night, so that's our ride back up."

"What about Brice?" she said.

232

"Don't worry about him. He got the ass about it, but it's nothing you need to worry about. Once we get back to camp, we're out of here."

"We can't leave!"

"What?" Grover asked.

"There's something down here, and they have to stop construction."

"That won't happen, Katie," Russel said. "They sprayed the whole valley with something this morning. I don't know what it was, but I think it's going to kill all the trees."

"No. No. No. No. No! We have to stop it!"

"We can't."

"I have to ... I have to get to Ameia and make a phone call. My boss at the São Paulo Zoo knows people. He'll help."

"What did you find?" Grover asked.

"I'll tell you on the way. We have to get going."

By the time Katie, Grover, and Russel reached the top of the cliff, the two men knew everything. Grover didn't know what to say. *After everything she's been through, she's still alive,* Grover thought, and though it terrified him to hear it, he was proud of her. The young woman he met a few days ago now had such a determined, confident look, he was sure nothing would stop her.

Chris heard the highlights as he drove them back to camp, and when they reached the management office, Katie hopped out before the Jeep stopped.

Cage stepped out of his tent, yawned, and rubbed his eyes. "I'll be damned," he said, then smiled and went back inside. He flipped on the radio, turned to Sid's frequency, and passed along the news.

She raced up the steps and pushed open the door. Schroder had watched them drive up and stepped between Katie and Brice's desk.

"I'm surprised to see you," Brice said, and stood up from his chair.

Schroder grabbed Katie by the shoulders, and Katie kneed him in the groin. Schroder went down, groaned, and tried to stand up. He took a hunched-over step toward Katie, but Grover grabbed him by the back of the neck before he reached her. Grover put him in a chair, and Brice sat back down with a smug grin.

"Better let her say what she has to say," a man said, and Katie turned toward the door.

Skinner and a lab tech were seated at the back of the room, and he gave Katie an approving nod.

"This has to stop!" Katie shouted. "I was sent here to make sure there wasn't anything important down there, and there is. It's something incredible. You'll have to build your dam somewhere else."

"Sure," Brice replied. "We'll just pack everything up and move where? Huh? You got another place that won't disrupt the lives of an undiscovered frog or bird? I told you whatever you found wouldn't make any difference, and it doesn't."

"I'm not talking about a frog, goddamn it. I'm talking about something that's almost human! If you kill everything down there, it's murder!"

"Jesus Christ," Schroder said. "Just listen to this nut!"

"Excuse me, ma'am," Skinner said. "I don't know what you saw, but you did say *nearly* human."

"I'm sorry. Who are you?"

"You can call me—"

"There's more humanity down there than there is up here, and no one—you hear me?—no one is going to touch that valley! What's down there is more important than any of this bullshit and may be the most important discovery in human evolution. Now I need to get to Ameia and make a call. I saw Caio's plane out there, and I need to go."

Brice raised his brow and stood up. "Funny you should say that. Caio's been waiting for all of you to get back, and all your belongings are already onboard."

235

"This isn't over."

"Yeah, it is," Brice replied. "This is bigger than a dam, and the clock started ticking this morning. In three days that valley will be as barren as—"

"I think that's enough," Skinner said as he stood up. "I appreciate your enthusiasm, young lady, but you're done here."

"I don't work for you, and you haven't seen what I've seen."

"That may be," the lab rat said, "but we're all just guests in Brazil, and this is what they want. They accept the price of progress, as we have in the US. And progress always comes at the expense of something else. The choice is up to those already there. They can leave or get crushed under the weight."

Katie walked over to the door and stopped. "You have no idea what you're doing."

Katie left the office, followed by her three friends, and as they passed the mess hall, the door opened.

Caio waved and hurried down the stairs after them. "Ready to go?" he asked. "Brice told me to wait."

"We're ready," Grover replied. "Let's get the hell out of here."

In fifteen minutes, the DC-3 lifted off the runway, and Katie looked down at the valley below. She sighed and shook her head. Grover patted her on the knee, and she laid her hand on his.

"It'll be okay," Grover said.

Katie looked up at him, then down at her hand. She still felt the creature's fingers on her skin, saw its eyes look up at her, and heard the sounds they made.

"We have to save them."

14

Plan B

When they landed at Ameia, Katie was the first one off the plane and made straight for the airstrip office.

Luiz met her halfway. "Can I help with your bags?" he said as he approached with a smile.

"Do you have a phone?"

"Yes."

Katie grabbed his arm, turned him back toward the office, and escorted him inside. "I need to put a call through to São Paulo."

"Sorry, local calls only."

"I'll take care of the long-distance charges," Katie replied. "Just hand me the phone."

"The manager will be back in an hour or so and—"

Katie reached over the counter, picked up the phone, and set it down in front of her. "What's your name?"

239

"Luiz."

"I know you're just trying to do your job, but I need to do mine. So, I'm making this call. I'll take it up with your boss later."

"Okay, but he can get kind of mean."

Katie looked at him and smiled. "So can I."

"I'll go help with the bags."

Luiz walked out, and Katie dialed Murilo Ribeiro's number. After a couple of rings, his secretary, Rosalice, answered.

"*Olá*, Parque Zoológico de São Paulo."

"Rosalice? This is Katie. I need to speak to Dr. Ribeiro. It's urgent."

"*Olá*, Katie! Are you having exciting time in Amazon?"

"More than I expected, but I really need to talk to Dr. Ribeiro. It's important."

"Okay, I'll put you through."

A moment later, Katie heard two clicks, and her boss answered the phone.

"Hello, Katie. It's good to hear from you. Are you on your way back?"

"No. I found something, and I need your help."

"I received a call yesterday that the survey deadline had passed and the construction project was cleared to move forward. Box up whatever samples you collected and bring them back with you."

"You don't understand. There's a group of amazing creatures down there, and we have to save them."

"What does the man from Fish and Game think?"

"Joao Pedro wasn't interested in hearing about it. He wouldn't even go down in the valley with me. Honestly, I don't think he works for the Department of Fish and Game at all. He's more of a politician."

"Katie, I don't know what I can do. You going up there was really just a formality. It sounded like the project was moving forward with or without your results. I think your professor only sent you so you could get some field experience."

"I understand, but there's a species of ape living here that has never been seen before. We can't let them be exterminated!"

"So, they're like an orangutan?"

"No. They're more evolved. They make things and have a language."

"Animals make tools all the time, like chimps using sticks to fish termites out of a mound."

"True, but have you ever seen a chimp weave a basket?"

There was a long pause on the other end of the line as Katie awaited his reply.

"That's unprecedented. Are you sure they actually crafted the basket and didn't steal it from a village nearby?"

"Dr. Ribeiro, I watched one of the juveniles do it. I'm telling you, we have to stop this!"

"I agree, but tell me, Katie, what do they look like?"

"They're kind of a cross between an ape and a man. No, that's not right. They're different from both in a lot of ways but similar. I've given it a lot of thought, though, and maybe the best way to describe them is this: imagine the point in evolution when apes adapted to life on the ground. They walked upright, their skeletal structure changed, but they were still very much apelike. Now imagine what would happen if some of them returned to life in the trees. Over a few million years they'd adapt to become superior climbers, but unlike their biped cousins, these creatures would need the use of all four limbs, so they didn't develop hand tools. One of their fingers adapted to become their principal tool, and . . . Well, they're just amazing!"

"I wish I were there to see them for myself, but I'm sure you took lots of pictures."

"I tried."

"If you're right, Katie, this changes everything, and I don't mean just stopping the construction project. If they can communicate, science may have to redefine the definition of human and reconsider where we came from. Maybe mankind didn't evolve solely in Africa but in South America as well. Don't worry, Katie, I'll do everything I can. I have friends in the capital that can shut this down immediately. Where can I reach you?"

"I'm in Ameia at the Hotel Pereira Amazonia. We just landed, but you can call me there."

"Congratulations! This is incredible."

"Thanks, Dr. Ribeiro. I'll be waiting for your call."

He hung up the phone, sat back in his chair, and rapped his knuckles on the desk. He became more aware of the importance of the moment. *If she found what she says,* Ribeiro thought, *this is the most important moment of my career.* He smiled. He reminisced for a few minutes, thought of all the adventures hanging on the wall, and knew the next one would be the one everyone remembered. He stood up and walked to the office door.

"Rosalice, I'll be making some important phone calls, and I can't be disturbed. I'm sure some of them will have to return my call, so when they do, be sure to put them right through."

Dr. Ribeiro grabbed the edge of the door to shut it, but Rosalice pointed across the room. "Sorry, sir, but there's a courier with a package that needs your signature."

"Sure," Dr. Ribeiro replied, and the man handed him a clipboard.

"Just sign here."

Dr. Ribeiro signed and took the small package, then noticed blue ink on his fingers.

"Goodness, I think your pen sprung a leak."

"Sorry about that, sir," the courier replied. "Those cheap pens do that all the time. That's why I wear gloves."

Dr. Ribeiro smiled. "I'm sure it'll wash right off." He shut the door, returned to his desk, and tore off the brown paper wrapping. He opened the box and found a wooden giraffe, just like the ones in the zoo's gift shop.

He looked for a note, thinking it must be from their supplier, but there wasn't one. He put the giraffe on his desk, dropped the empty package in the trash, and reached for the phone.

Katie walked out of the office and over to a shady spot where Grover, Chris, and Russel watched Luiz refuel the plane.

"So?" Grover asked. "Did you get through?"

"Yep. Once I told him what I found, he said he'd take care of it, so by the end of the day that project will be over."

An aircraft approached from the east. It was a much smaller plane than the DC-3, and as it swung out over the river to line up its approach, the gray paint and military markings became visible.

It looked strange. The aircraft had a long nose but the belly of a boat and an oversized prop engine on each wing. The wings themselves were attached to the top of the fuselage instead of the bottom, and the whole thing looked like an engineering experiment gone awry.

The roar of the engines reduced to a grumble, and the tires barked when it landed. The aircraft only needed half the length of the runway to land and turned toward the office.

When the pilot reached the mark on the tarmac, he slowed one engine to an idle, hit the starboard brake, and the aircraft pivoted around. He brought the second engine to an idle, then killed them both.

Caio hopped down from the DC-3 just as the door of the smaller plane opened, and Sid stepped out. Everyone met between the planes.

"That's quite an airplane," Chris said, and Sid looked back at it.

"Yeah, but it's a real ballbuster," Sid said, then turned back around. "Oh sorry, Katie."

Katie smiled and shook her head. "Water off a duck's back."

"Funny you should say that. They call this thing a Mallard."

"How about that?"

"Can I take a look?" Chris asked.

"You can do more than that. You're all going back to Manaus on it, so you'll have lot of time to look around."

"I thought I was taking them," Caio said. "I only stopped to refuel, and then we were headed out."

"Since I had to come up here for a couple of days, and the pilot's flying straight back, I guess they thought it made more sense for everyone to go with him."

"Okay by me," Caio replied. "I was getting worried I might not make it back before dark."

A military Jeep pulled around the side of the office and stopped.

"This must be my ride," Sid said. "Luiz, you mind grabbing my bag off the plane?"

Luiz hurried off, climbed on board, and popped back out with three bags. On his way back to the car, Sid stopped him.

"Just the one! The duffel bag and suitcase belong to the pilot and stay onboard."

Luiz set down Sid's bag and returned the others where he found them. When Sid's bag made it to the Jeep, Sid sat down, and the driver started the engine.

"You all have a safe trip home and eat a big American cheeseburger for me."

They all waved, and the Jeep drove off.

"Better go get our stuff," Grover said, and Russel and Chris walked off toward the plane. Grover touched Katie on the shoulder. "Won't be long until you're back to city livin'."

"I can't leave," Katie replied.

Chris and Russel stopped.

"Come on, Katie," Russel said. "You've done all you can do. It sounds like your boss is taking care of it, so let's go."

"Sorry, but I can't. Those creatures know me, and if I know Dr. Ribeiro, by this time tomorrow there will be a small army of scientists here, eager to say hello. I need to be here when they arrive."

Chris turned and started toward the plane.

"Where you going?" Grover asked.

"To get her bags."

"We're not done discussing this."

"Yeah, we are. You don't seriously think you can change her mind?"

Katie smiled and looked up at Grover. Chris kept walking, and Grover shook his head.

"If you're staying," Grover said. "I should stay with you."

Katie gave him a one-armed hug. "You should go home and see your family. I really am sorry I cost all of you your jobs. If there's anything I can ever do for you, just let me know."

The men moved their bags to the Mallard, and Grover gave Katie one last wave before the pilot closed the door. She watched her friends fly away, then called for a ride.

The car dropped her off in front of the hotel, and Katie climbed the stairs to the porch. Before she reached the door, however, Pedrina pulled it open and greeted her with a hug.

"Katie. Good see you," Pedrina said, and released Katie from her grip, then stepped back and saw the wound on her head. "Katie! What this? Some man?"

"No, I fell and hit my head."

"Ooh, that look bad," Pedrina replied, and brushed Katie's hair away from her forehead to look at the wound.

Pedrina touched Katie's black eye. They looked at each other a moment, but Pedrina didn't ask about it.

"You okay. You here now. That good."

Pedrina led Katie inside and signed her in.

"You in old room," Pedrina said, and as Katie stepped away from the counter, Pedrina noticed the entirety of her condition. Her eyes widened, and Katie looked down at herself. She was a wreck.

"How many times you fall?"

Katie grinned. "It's been a long few days."

"You want hospital?"

"No, no, I'll be fine. I would like to go get cleaned up if that's okay."

"Yes, yes, you go. I get you for dinner."

Rodrigo grabbed Katie's bags and wrestled them toward the stairs.

"Oh, one more thing. I'm expecting a call from my boss in São Paulo, and it's really important I take it. So, please get me when he calls."

"Okay. No problem. You go. I let you know."

"Thanks, Pedrina . . . It's good to see you."

Katie helped the boy get her bags upstairs, washed off the jungle, then filled up the tub for a soak. She felt like she'd been in the wild for weeks, and as if it had been equally as long since she could catch her breath. Submerged in hot water, she sighed and drifted off in thought. She imagined Dr. Ribeiro at his desk calling everyone he could think of to tell them what she'd found. His foot would drum a quick beat on the floor, and he'd be anxious to get on a plane. Katie could almost see the next picture he'd add to his wall. *Something this important will take precedence over any construction project,* she thought. *The government will have to intercede; besides, they haven't even started construction.*

In darker places of her mind, apprehension lingered, and no matter how hard she tried to convince herself everything would be fine, she didn't know for sure.

Katie folded her hands on her chest and looked at her thumbs, the wrinkles above each joint, and rough nails. She rubbed her thumb across her fingers and felt the tiny ridges.

My hands are so smooth, Katie thought, *compared to the creature.* She clenched her fist. *How different would my hand have to be to cling to the side of a tree or race across a limb? It's so effortless for them.*

She thought a lot about the creatures and thought about their home. As she tried to recall detail, she realized how much she missed. *How many creatures are there? How long have they been there? What do they eat besides nuts? Do they live as family units, like giant otters, or is it a whole community? Are there more of these creatures in other areas of the Amazon?*

She thought about, their language, but their reasoning fascinated her most. *They problem solve, make things, learn, and teach.*

She tried to recall the sounds they made and their context. *Lots of human tribes have language without writing. The biology of these creatures allows for a wider range of vocalizations, and they use the full range, but if they are capable of such highs and lows, could they learn English?*

The more she thought, the more doors opened, and she was just beginning to imagine the impact these creatures could have on the world. She smiled.

Overwhelmed but content, she dipped her washcloth into the water, rolled up a towel for a pillow, and covered her face. When the water became tepid and Katie's fingers were pruned, she got out, dried off, and dressed.

She grabbed her rucksack, put it in the chair, and opened the pocket to get her journal. The pocket was empty, and she remembered the journal and the gun had disappeared.

There were unused journals in her bag, but she hated that she'd lost the sketch of the creature and the tracing she made of its hand. Still, she had to get as much as she could down on paper and pulled a fresh journal and pencil out.

She went out on the balcony, tipped back in a chair, and put her feet up on the rail. For a while, she didn't open the journal. She couldn't decide where to start, so she watched the locals walk by.

The valley was the most important part, so she focused on everything after she crossed through the rubble. She started with the stick with hair tied to the end of it. *That must be how they mark their territory,* Katie thought. *Okay, the next thing was the juvenile the jaguar killed . . . The jaguar.* Katie sighed and bit down on her pencil. *That's going to be hard to explain. Come on, it was him or me! The imagery of that doesn't quite scream animal lover . . . Alright, I'll just move on.*

Katie wrote down every detail she wanted to remember, then went back and added the ones she didn't. Once she started, time passed without notice, and when she was done, she closed the journal and noticed where the pressure of the pencil left its mark on her finger.

She stood up, stretched, and looked down the road toward the center of town. The sun set, and the lights in the square came on. Katie was ready to get out of her room, so she freshened up and headed downstairs.

She followed the sound of rattling pans and children to the kitchen and found Pedrina preparing fish. The children fussed over the vegetables and argued with Rodrigo, who was the only one old enough to use a knife. The two girls and made sure he did it right.

Katie walked in, touched the youngest daughter, Bruna, on the head, and continued over to see Padrina. "Can I help?"

"No, no. You guest. Sit down."

"That looks great," Katie said, and smelled the fish.

"Caught today."

"Do you have many guests tonight?"

"Two and you. Government people. One US. He look like Brazil. He cute."

Katie rolled her eyes and grinned. "I met someone like that this afternoon. What's his name?"

"Sam."

"Sam, hmm. You sure it wasn't Sid?"

"No, Sam. I remember."

"Well, maybe it's someone else."

"He back for dinner. You see then."

"What about the phone call?" Katie asked. "Did anyone call for me?"

"No, no call. You need make call, call."

Katie looked at the clock and stood up. "I think I will. Should I use the phone at the front desk?"

"Yes, yes, that phone good."

"It's long distance. Is that all right? I'll pay for it."

"No problem for you."

"Thanks, Pedrina. I'll keep it short."

Katie went into the lobby, walked around the counter, and picked up the phone. It was getting late, but she expected Dr. Ribeiro would still be in his office, so she rang. Rosalice answered, but she sounded a bit off.

"*Olá*, Parque Zoológico de São Paulo."

"Rosalice? It's me, Katie. Is Dr. Ribeiro there?"

"Dr. Ribeiro? Dr. Ribeiro had a heart attack this afternoon right after you called."

"Oh my God! Is he okay?"

"He died. He died right at his desk, right here. No one even knew he had a heart problem. Even Mrs. Ribeiro didn't know."

"Is she okay?"

"No, she found him. He said he didn't want to be disturbed, so I didn't bother him, but when Lia showed up for lunch, she went right in. They said he had probably been dead for two or three hours, and I was sitting right here the whole time."

"I'm so sorry. I wish there was something I could do. It's getting late there. Maybe you should go home."

"I was just about to."

"Good, you take care."

"Bye, Katie."

Katie hung up the phone and stared across the room. She thought about the man, and the thought of him being gone made her sick. She looked at the cushioned high-back chair in the corner, went over, and sat down.

Grief filled her head with memories of conversations they'd had and his wife and little girl. Her thoughts returned to the reason she called, and she realized he probably died before he contacted anyone.

Pedrina walked into the lobby, and Katie went back to the phone.

"You okay, Katie?"

"No, I need to make one more call."

"Yes," Pedrina replied, and put the phone on the counter.

Katie picked up the receiver and called Dr. Powel. He answered on the third ring.

"Hello . . . Dr. Powel."

"Dr. Powel, it's Katie."

"Katie, Jesus Christ! It's good to hear your voice. Are you back in São Paulo?"

"No, I'm still in the Amazon, and I need to tell you—"

"Stay out of that valley!"

"That's why I'm calling. I found something down there, and they have to stop."

"They won't. It's bigger than whatever you found, so whatever it is, just leave it."

"You don't understand."

"Have they sprayed yet?"

"What? Yes, at least that is what I was told but—"

"When?"

"This morning, but whatever it was didn't do anything. Dr. Powel, I have to tell you some— "

"Two days, Katie. It's over. Get out of there as soon as you can."

"That's what Brice said. What the hell's going on?"

"It doesn't matter. In two days there won't be anything left. Trust me. I've seen it, and you need to get—"

The line crackled and suddenly went dead.

"Hello?" Katie said, and tapped on the cradle. Nothing.

"Okay?" Pedrina asked, and Katie hung up the phone.

"The line went dead."

"Happens. Maybe out for days. You eat. Feel better."

Katie followed Pedrina to the dining room and took a seat. *That's it,* Katie thought. *No help is coming, and there's nothing I can do.* Still, she couldn't let it go.

She had several ideas to save the valley, but once she thought them through, she decided they were all impossible. Without the phone, she was cut off from the world, but even if she had a phone, there wasn't anyone left to call.

Pedrina walked back in with a plate of fruit, and Katie looked at all the colors, then thought about the variety. A small glass bowl of pistachios sat in the middle of the tray, and as soon as Katie saw it, she had another idea and smiled.

"Pedrina?"

"Yes?"

"These pistachios . . . Where do you get them?"

"Oh, those special. Caio bring from Medellín."

"Is he home?"

"He in kitchen."

Katie got up, followed Pedrina, and found Caio leaning against the counter watching his children eat dinner.

"Caio," Katie said. "You fly cargo all over the place. Right?"

"Yes, I fly all over."

"How far can you go?"

"I can go as far as I want, as long as I can stop for fuel. Why? Do you need to go somewhere?"

The door to the dining room opened, and Sid peeked around the jamb.

"Sorry to interrupt. Did I miss dinner?"

"No, Sam," Pedrina replied. "I bring now. You sit."

Sid noticed Katie and stopped. "Katie, right?"

"Yes."

"I thought you left."

"Not yet. There's something I still have to do."

"Hmm. Well, it's nice to see you again."

"You too."

Sid ducked back into the dining room and shut the door. Pedrina took the broiled fish and vegetables out of the oven, plated four meals, and Katie helped her take them to the table.

Dinner conversation was modest, as everyone seemed to have a lot on their minds. The last of the hotel guests, a soldier, showed up just in time for dessert and sat down with a tired, troubled look.

"Long day, Colonel?" Sid asked, then popped a cube of fruit in his mouth.

"Yes, very. I've been working the plane crash. I was helping with the recovery."

"What plane?" Katie asked.

"A small plane on its way to Manaus. The pilot managed to survive, but the three passengers were lost."

Katie dropped her fork. "What do you mean, lost? Are you saying you can't find them?"

"No, ma'am. A fisherman said the plane just exploded. It's a miracle the pilot wasn't killed, but all the passengers are dead."

Katie's hands turned cold. She pushed herself away from the table and threw up.

15
Current

After a long night of crying and occasional sleep, morning arrived. A new clarity arrived as well, and Katie had a plan before she rolled out of bed. By the time she dressed, she felt a determination she'd never felt before in her life.

She made her bed, put her journal on the pillow, and wrote a note to Pedrina. In it, she explained she was going to hire a boat to take her to the valley, and if she didn't make it back, for Pedrina to mail the journal to Katie's professor in the States.

It was early, and Katie snuck out the front door without waking anyone up. She slung her rucksack on her back and walked to the market.

Vendors laid out yesterday's catch and tried to get Katie's attention, but she passed right by. She walked out the back side of the building and down the long ramp to the dock along the shore. Katie stopped, looked left and right at the jumble of boats, and put her hands on her hips.

A fisherman with a two-wheeled cart full of fishing gear and bloody bait pushed his way around her, and she touched his shoulder.

"English?" Katie asked.

"No English," he replied without looking back.

One after another walked by, and none answered her call.

As men passed, so did time, and a steady flow of boats cast off and motored away. Several boats remained, but only one looked big enough to travel any distance.

Katie took off her rucksack, set it on the dock, and leaned it against the rail. Another fisherman passed, and Katie tried again.

"English?"

"No, No . . . no English."

"Shit."

"I speak English," a man said, and she turned around.

It was Sid. He dangled a set of keys in in front of him and smiled. "I assume you're looking for a ride upriver."

"How did you—?"

"I'm a light sleeper."

Katie smiled, picked up her rucksack, and slung it over her shoulder.

"So which one's yours?"

"*Uiara*," he replied, and pointed at the big wooden boat she'd been watching at the end of the dock. "We best get going."

The faded hull was less than a foot above the water-line at midship but rose sharply to four feet at the bow. A white stripe along the top of the freeboard high-lighted the curve of the hull, and the name "Uiara" was hand-painted in red on the bow near the anchor.

The rest of the boat resembled a houseboat: it had a flat roof and vertical boards that made up the walls. It was enclosed from midship to stern, but from midship to the helm there were no walls at all.

A curved wall with three panes of glass protected the helm from the weather, but it was extremely far forward so the captain could see over the bow.

"The owner won't mind."

"Where's the captain?"

"Please . . . I wouldn't be much of a boat salesman if I couldn't pilot a boat. Besides, all we need to do is cross the Rio Negro, head upstream a bit, and take the first right. That crooked little river takes us right where you need to go."

They walked out on the finger pier next to the boat, and Sid opened the door in the gunnel. He hopped on, and the boat tipped. He grabbed an upright for balance and looked back at Katie.

"If you'll get the lines, I'll start her up."

Katie looked at the ropes attached to the cleats on the dock and tried to remember the order she and Chris used to untie the barge.

"Spring, stern, then bow," he said. "Kind of like you did with the barge. The current will keep the boat against the dock, so don't worry about me floating away."

"Okay," Katie replied, and untied the spring line.

She freed the stern and pitched the rope on the deck. The engine started, and Katie moved toward the bow. The diesel settled into a deep, steady rhythm, but it was soft compared to the dozer. Still, it had the same tone. Smoke and a stream of water poured out of the exhaust port in the transom.

"Sounds like a diesel," Katie said, and Sid looked over at her with a smile. A gust of wind pushed the exhaust over Katie. "Smells like one too."

Katie fanned the fumes away and untied the bowline. Once it was free, she looped it into a neat bundle, and threw it on the deck. She got onboard, shut the door along the gunnel, and locked it in place.

"You ready?" Sid asked.

"Yep."

Sid put it in reverse, and the boat slid along the dock until the current pushed the stern downstream. As soon as the midship cleared the end, Sid cut the wheel, shifted the transmission into forward, revved the throttle. The bow came around, and they headed out into the river.

The Rio Negro was over two miles wide at Ameia, but all the little islands made it feel like a maze. Katie sat down on a barstool by his side and they headed east. Sid focused on steering, but Katie quickly turned her attention from the river to the boat. There was a shelf under the dash crammed with clothing, a small radio, hat, and metal box, but underneath it she saw a piece of paper with tiny numbers and curved lines on it. She pushed everything on top out of the way and pulled it out.

"Nautical chart," Sid said, and Katie shook off the dirt.

"You going to navigate?"

Katie unfolded the chart, spread it across the console, and looked for Ameia. Once she found it, she folded it down to just the section she needed and looked out the window for landmarks.

Sunlight sparkled off the black river. Silhouettes of boats gained color, and birds left roost for sky. Water lapped against the hull, and the sound of the engine echoed across the surface. Katie stared out the window, and neither she nor Sid spoke until they reached the other side.

A hundred feet from shore, he turned upstream. "Know where we are?"

Katie looked at him, then down at the chart. "Right here. This bit of land is actually an island, so don't take the first right you come to. It's the one after."

"Got it."

Sid looked at Katie, who tried to hide her anxiety behind a smile, but it wasn't enough. He reached over and gave her a reassuring pat on the back.

"It'll be okay. You're doing everything you can."

"I know," Katie replied, and turned back toward the window.

They reached the river and passed several fishermen anchored at the mouth. Sid and Katie waved, the fishermen waved back, and the *Uiara* continued up the river.

The number of fishermen slowly dwindled from several to a few, then none, and an hour later they were deep in the Amazon and hadn't seen anyone for a while.

Katie made tiny pencil marks on the map as they reached each turn, which kept her busy, as they often made turns.

"So what's the plan?" Sid asked, and Katie looked up from the map.

"When I get to the valley, I'm sure the creatures will find me, and I'll convince them to leave."

"Do you think they'll understand?"

"Oh, I'm sure they'll understand. They're smart. My concern is they won't leave no matter what I say."

"Have you heard what's going to happen in the valley? I mean, do you know what this test is all about?"

"Not exactly, but it sounds like they plan to blow it all up."

"Blow it up?" Sid replied. "How the hell do you blow up a jungle?"

"I don't know. All Brice said was it would reduce the valley to ashes."

"Did he say when?"

"Sometime tomorrow. That's why I need to get them out today. Surely they can find another place to live, far away from all of this."

"What if there isn't?"

"There has to be."

"Why?"

"I didn't see a large group of creatures. My guess is they stay in small family groups, and when the young are old enough to reproduce, they leave their family to find a mate in another. There's got to be other troops out there and other places this group can move."

"Makes sense, but in my experience it's always a good idea to have a backup plan. What's your plan if this one falls through?"

"It can't," Katie said. "It just can't."

"Sorry, I didn't mean it that way. I'm just saying you need to consider all the what-ifs."

"What if I can't get them to leave and they all die? I can't think about it."

"No, no, no. For instance, what if they don't leave, and the jungle is destroyed but the creatures are still alive? What then?" Katie looked away from Sid and rubbed the back of her neck in thought. "Then they'd have to leave, right?"

"Right."

"So where do you think they'd go?"

"I don't know."

"They wouldn't go east," Sid said. "If there are other troops, they'd be away from civilization, not toward it. My guess is they'd head west toward the Andes."

"That makes sense."

"Then regardless what happens to the valley, they should be fine, as long as they don't get blown up first . . . Sorry, but you know what I mean."

"Still," Katie replied, "eventually people will find something in the Amazon they want, like oil or gold. They'll rip everything up to get it, and at best they'll leave a few parks. As much as I hate to admit it, you can't stop progress. What these creatures really need is a place where none of that can happen."

"Like a national park?"

"No. Parks are protected, but people visit, and these creatures would be captured and sold or even killed if neighbors saw them as a threat, like wolves."

"So, getting them to move to another part of the Amazon isn't a long-term solution. You think they need to be somewhere else altogether. Have you got any ideas?"

"Actually, I thought of the perfect place, but I'd have to get them back to the States," Katie replied.

"Okay. For argument sake, let's say you could. Where would you take them?"

"My family owns a huge piece of land at the foot of the Rockies. It's a lot like the valley, except for the climate, of course. There's a cliff along one side, and two rivers fall over it and meet at the far end of the property. The family owns a lot more land around it, but that part is like a huge island. There's plenty of deer and other things to eat, and it's far enough away from people no one would ever know they were there."

"Sounds perfect."

"Yeah."

"Hopefully you'll be able to get them to leave, but at least you've got a backup plan."

"Thanks, Sid."

Sid looked over at the chart. "We probably have two or three hours to go. How about you take the wheel for a while and give me a break?"

Katie hopped off the barstool and nudged Sid out of the way. "Absolutely."

Sid grinned, stepped back, and pointed at the chrome lever next to the wheel.

"That's the throttle."

"Got it," Katie replied. "Where's the brake?"

Sid looked at her, and she grinned.

"Just kidding. I've got the wheel."

"Would you like a Coke?"

"A Coke?"

"I stowed a few in the live well when I brought the boat up from Manaus, and I'm sure there's a couple left. You want one?"

"Sure."

Katie eased the boat around the next turn, and Sid walked aft. She heard him walk off, then back, and turned her head. A white blur passed downward in front of her face, and she felt the rope tighten around her neck.

Cage lay in his cot with a pillowcase folded over his eyes to block out the light in the tent but still couldn't sleep. Since the day he was attacked, the creatures lingered in his thoughts, like a tune he couldn't get out of his head.

Even when he forced himself to think of other things, he'd catch himself running his fingers over the scars on his chest. The stress was tough Stateside, but laying in a cot with more of them just outside the door didn't encourage sleep.

He thought about what Skinner said, what they'd done, and what the lab rats were doing Stateside. Mostly, he thought about Katie, Grover, and Russel. Those creatures were down there, and he couldn't figure out how all three walked out.

It shouldn't bother me, Cage thought, *but something's wrong.* A memory of his youth shook out of his bag of thoughts, and he remembered a little boy.

Jamie. Jamie something. What the hell was that kid's last name? He was a runt. I remember that. A real mama's boy from somewhere in Arizona. He never had a dog, never was around them, and that's weird. Real people are either dog people or cat people, though I'd argue the latter. Jamie was neither when they moved next door. Mom. Why do mothers always force their kids to be part of the welcome wagon when new people move it? She volunteered me to walk Jamie to school. It was a Wednesday; quiz day in Mrs. Budkey's class. I never studied.

Cage smiled.

What was that kid's last name? Good old Mr. Brock and his dog. Standard poodle ... No, it was bigger and scruffier than that. Big, like a Great Dane, but hairy. Otter hound! That's it. Big as a horse to a couple of third graders. I walked past that house every day on the way to school, and it just went apeshit. The old man knew I was terrified of it the first time I saw it, but he made me go inside the fence and say hello. The dog wasn't mean at all; it just wanted to play.

That's just dogs, Mr. Brock explained. They jump and bark and snap and race around like lunatics, but that's just how they play. Little kids must seem like a squeaky to a dog, and that's why dogs go after little kids first; at least that's the way the old man explained it. It still looked scary, but that dog turned out to be the nicest dog in the world.

But Jamie, Cage thought. *That poor kid. It wasn't my fault, but Mom whipped my ass anyway. She even dragged me next door to apologize. I tried to tell her I didn't do it on purpose. Me and Jamie were just walking down the sidewalk on the way to school, and I was trying to get him to trade his Ding Dongs for my single Hershey's Kiss. What kind of mother gives their kid one damn Kiss? After some strong debate, he decided to give up one of his Ding-Dongs and was rummaging around in his sack lunch to get it out.*

I was street-side on the sidewalk, and Jamie was next to the fence when that dog's head came over. I'm sure all Jamie saw was hair and teeth ... Shit his pants right on the spot. I'll never forget it. He'd never been around dogs before, especially one that big, and after that one experience he hated dogs the whole time I knew him. I guess someone can see a thing for the first time and get it in their head that that's the way those things are all the time.

McPherson! That was Jamie's last name.

That Skinner's a piece of work. I wonder if that's his actual name or a nickname. Nice enough guy. A little screwy, but who isn't?

Cage sat up, put on just enough to be presentable, and walked over to the mess hall for a snack.

"Just relax," Sid said as he leaned back and lifted Katie's feet off the ground.

Katie kicked and tried to work her fingers between the rope and her neck but couldn't. She grabbed his head, but Sid shook loose. Her right foot hit the wheel, and she pushed back. Sid leaned into her, and instead of pushing him backwards, only managed to push herself toward the ceiling.

Katie's lungs burned, and she felt the pressure behind her eyes and face. Her vision began to blur, but she saw a gaff hanging from two rusty hooks above her.

She reached for it and missed, then reached again. Her fingers knocked one end loose, and the gaff slipped free. The steel hook clattered against the dash. The handle swung down, it hit her chest, and she grabbed it.

Katie felt dizzy and weak, but she looked at the hook on the far end of the handle, swung it over her shoulder and pulled forward. Sid screamed, and the rope went slack.

Katie let go of the handle and Sid staggered backward. The hook was set so deep in his shoulder that she saw the tip just under the front of his shirt. Katie fell to her knees and gasped for breath but watched Sid.

He staggered to the back of the boat, held the handle of the gaff with both hands, and put the end of the gaff against the wall. With one quick motion, he lurched forward and forced the hook out of his body. He screamed again and fell to the floor.

Sid pushed himself up into a crouched position and glared at Katie as she staggered to her feet. The bloody gaff lay next to Sid, and he grabbed it. He used it as a crutch to get up, then turned to hook toward Katie and raced forward.

Katie grabbed the barstool and blocked the hook, but momentum carried Sid into the wheel. He hit his head and ended up on his knees. Sid looked up just as Katie brought the stool down, and he was out cold.

It was a long time before Sid regained consciousness, and when he did, he wished he hadn't; his head was throbbing and his left arm felt like it was on fire. He tried to reach up to rub his head but couldn't. His hands were tied behind his back.

He rolled over onto his good shoulder and saw Katie at the helm. He coughed up blood, and Katie turned around. She looked down at him and took a sip of Coke. Sid looked at the bottle and couldn't help but smile.

"Did you save one for me?" he asked.

Katie set her drink down on the console and watched Sid squirm. He tested the strength of the knots and how tightly his limbs were bound together. It wasn't just his hands; his ankles were tied together as well.

"*Why?*"

Sid didn't answer, and Katie turned back to the wheel.

"You're one of *them*, aren't you?"

"Them who?"

"Those bastards working for the construction company."

Sid laughed, and Katie returned a hateful glare. She reached up and grabbed the handle of the gaff she'd returned to its hooks.

"Untie me, Katie. This is ridiculous. I need a doctor."

Katie turned back to the wheel and steered the boat.

"This is so much bigger than building a dam," Sid said. "You have no idea what you walked into."

"What? Tell me. I'd really like to know what could be so important that you'd exterminate an entire species."

"You're so naive. Do you really think they started this project without knowing exactly what was down there? We've known about these things for over a year, and you were right: there were other groups in the Amazon."

"Were?" Katie replied.

"Yeah, were. This is the last of them. We dealt with the others, and by this time tomorrow they'll all be gone."

"Why? Why can't they be relocated? They need to be protected. They need to be saved!"

"You might be right, but there's no time. This isn't about a dam. The Russians are in bed with Castro, and we know what they're planning. We need chess pieces they can't see, and we need them now."

"Chess! Listen to yourself. You can't do this. These creatures have a right to live."

"Come on, Katie," Sid replied, and squirmed a bit more. "It's over. Untie me, and let's go back to Ameia. I'll put you on a plane today, and you'll be in a comfortable hotel room in Manaus by tonight. Leave, and put all of this behind you. What d'you say?"

Katie stared quietly out the window and navigated around the next bend in the river. She thought about everything and everyone, the friends she'd made and the ones she'd lost.

"No one knows these things even exist," Sid said. "So they won't be missed when they're gone. Besides, if you don't turn back now, I can't protect you. You don't want to end up like the others."

Katie snapped her head around and looked down at Sid, who freed his hands.

"What did you say?"

"Come on. Give me a hand."

"What did you just say?"

"You think that plane crash was an accident?"

Katie tightened her grip on the wheel and remembered the day Sid got off the weird little plane. *The bag*, she thought. *He made Luiz put those two bags back onboard.*

"You!"

Sid hurried to untie the rope around his ankles but didn't answer. Katie looked down at him, throttled the engine back to idle, and disengaged the prop. She grabbed the loose end of the rope attached to his ankles, opened the little door along the gunnel, and walked the rope around to the bow. Katie tied the rope around the anchor and threw the release.

Sid heard the splash and screamed as the rope pulled him across the deck. He reached for everything he could and managed to grab Katie's rucksack just as the rope pulled him through the door. The screaming stopped with a gurgle, and Katie watched Sid slip deeper into the murky water.

Katie went back inside, found a knife, and cut the anchor line. She looked down at the water and waited to feel remorse or guilt over killing him, but it never came.

16
Presence

Katie continued upriver past the company dock and assumed the next river she came to would be the one that ran out of the valley. When she reached it, she tied the boat to a couple of trees and followed the smaller river into the jungle.

An hour later she reached the end of the valley, passed under the collapsed stones, and stopped on the other side. She knew the creatures would find her, but she needed to make some noise.

Katie cupped her hands around her mouth and yelled, "Hello!"

She scanned the trees but only saw birds. Katie made her way up the trail and stopped every hundred yards to yell.

At the fork where the sentry released her, the creature leapt down. Katie turned and in that instant realized she hadn't thought about what she'd say.

Katie looked at the ground. "What do I say? What do I say?"

She looked at him and smiled, then patted him on the chest while she thought it over.

I know what I want to say, but how? she thought. *But how do I say it?* A long, uncomfortable moment passed for both of them as Katie's hand was still on his chest.

"Think, goddamn it."

The creature stepped closer.

"No, not you."

She reached out with both hands and grabbed his upper arms to focus his attention. The creature pulled away.

"Sorry," Katie said, and released him, then looked at him with excitement.

He stepped back, and Katie patted herself on the chest. The creature watched her as she turned, pointed toward the waterfall, then up into the trees. She repeated the gestures one more time and waited for the creature's reaction.

He turned his back, knelt down, and reached over his shoulder.

"Thank God," Katie said, and reached around him as she'd done before. She locked her hands, closed her eyes, and the creature leapt onto the trunk of the tree.

A moment later they were high in the canopy and raced across the limbs.

This time Katie forced herself to open her eyes. Her vision was filled with a blur of greens, grays, and browns. The creature's hair rose and fell in the wind, and soon Katie's eyes adjusted to the pace.

Like riding double on a motorcycle, she held on and tried not to throw off his balance. Katie expected to end up at the nest, but the creature carried her to the edge of the small clearing.

The troop was gathered around a dead deer. The sentry descended, and Katie let go. The youngest creatures raced over to greet her, but the alpha's son leapt into her arms and hugged her neck. The sentry joined the others, and the children led Katie through the field to the kill.

Katie was amazed at the efficiency with which the creatures skinned and butchered the animal. The long claw was the perfect tool to separate the hide and cut meat from the bone. The children were given the lower legs to play with, but it was in fact their opportunity to practice butchering for themselves.

As Katie watched, she almost forgot why she was there, but eventually her smile went away. She walked around and sat down next to the alpha and his mate.

Their child abandoned its deer leg and sat down beside her.

The alpha was busy cutting the hindquarter from the pelvis and merely acknowledged Katie with a nod. She reached over and put her hand on his knee. The alpha stopped cutting and looked at her, as did his mate.

I have their attention. Now what? she thought. Katie held up a finger while she thought.

"Okay, those people," Katie said, and pointed up toward the camp. "They are coming here"—she walked her fingers along her forearm—"to kill." She pointed at the dead deer. "You." She pointed at the alpha.

The alpha looked at his mate, gestured, then looked back at Katie. The creature pointed toward the camp, patted himself on the chest, extended his claw, and held it up to his neck.

Katie nodded, repeated his motions, then made a sweeping gesture at all the creatures around the carcass. She made a running gesture with her fingers along her arm and pointed at the top of the opposite cliff.

The alpha took her hand and put it back in her lap. He pointed at the camp once more, made a walking gesture with his long fingers, and patted the ground in front of him. Katie nodded, and the alpha reached out and cut the deer's throat.

"Shit, I explained it wrong."

Alright, Katie thought. *If people were coming down here to shoot them, they'd be able to defend themselves, but this is different. How do you explain a bomb to someone who doesn't know what a bomb is?*

A rock had been digging into her butt cheek since she sat down, and as she removed it, she had an idea. Katie tapped the alpha's child on the arm and pointed at the other children. The creature looked at them, then back at her, and cocked its head to the side. She pointed again and swung both arms in horizontal circles toward her chest.

The little creature smiled, hopped on top of the carcass, and leapt off the other side. It chattered and whistled, and the children ran over.

Katie stood up and assembled her little group of actors in a circle about ten feet across. All the adults stopped to watch, and a couple even stood up. Katie took her place in the circle, pointed at her eye, and patted herself on the chest. The children looked confused, then chattered and smiled.

Katie held the rock out in front of her and looked at the alpha. She showed it to him, just to make sure he understood to watch it, then tossed it into the air. As soon as it hit the ground in the middle of the circle,

Katie fell back and played dead. The children laughed and did the same.

The alpha stood up and looked at the bodies. A moment later, Katie and the children sat up. The children all laughed, and several practiced different falling techniques and poses of death. Other children gestured for Katie to do it again, but Katie's eyes were fixed on the alpha. Katie moved from sitting to kneeling and raised her hands in front of her face as if in prayer.

The alpha stepped into the circle, reached down, and picked up the rock. He looked at it, then slowly rolled his eyes toward Katie. He held the rock out and pointed at the camp.

"Yes!" Katie shouted, and stood up.

She gestured around her at the rest of the troop.

"All of you need to run away." She made the same running gesture with her fingers.

The alpha looked at the rock and let it roll out of his hand. When it hit the ground, all the children standing fell back down and laughed. The alpha looked back at his mate and walked up to the tree line. A moment later he ascended the trunk of the nearest tree and disappeared into the canopy.

Caio left Ameia at dawn and arrived in Manaus ninety minutes later. The ground crew loaded several large crates, a half-dozen metal cases, fifteen folding chairs, and a podium.

Three passengers in BDUs walked out of the hangar, but it was obvious to Caio they weren't soldiers. Two were spindly, and the other was too fat, and none of them could pass a physical.

A fourth man followed and looked completely out of place. *Don't see many brown tweed suits down here*, Caio thought, and met them all beside the plane. Caio reached out to shake the fat soldier's hand, but the suit pushed through and took his hand instead.

"Frank Baldridge," the man said. "I hope this plane has air-conditioning. I'm sweating my nuts off."

"I'm Caio, and sorry, no air-conditioning, but once we get moving you should be fine."

"Sure," Frank said, then clapped his hands. "Alright, fellas, load up and let's get going. Time's a wastin'."

As soon as everyone and everything was onboard, they were in the air. The flight to the construction site was rough, and the passengers complained, but bags were handy, so at least they didn't make a mess. The sky cleared before they reached the valley, and as soon as the tires hit the ground, Caio's pasty-faced passengers clapped.

He parked, stood up, and looked back into the plane. "I hope everyone enjoyed their flight today," Caio said. "On behalf of all of us at Caio Air, we'd like to thank you for choosing us and look forward to serving you again soon. Please take your vomit bags with you."

Since none of his passengers could tell if Caio was being sarcastic or serious, they gathered their little bags and walked out of the plane.

Cage watched the plane from his tent. The passengers unloaded, and security met them at the bottom step.

"You the film crew?" Raeburn, one of the security team, asked.

"That's us," the fat man replied. "I'm Holloway, the director, and these other two are my crew. This gentleman is Dr. Baldridge. He's the—"

"Yeah, yeah," Frank said. "I wasn't expecting first-class accommodations, but that was—"

"Just get your bags and settle in," Raeburn said. "You boys are in the shack over there." He noticed the little paper sacks. "What the hell's that? Did your mothers fix you a sack lunch?"

"We got them on the plane," Gary, the taller of the thin men, said.

Raeburn shook his head in disgust and walked off as the ground crew unloaded the plane.

"Welcome to Brazil. Nice to meet you. Glad you're here," Gary said.

"Yeah, and thanks for coming," Vickers, the shorter of the thin men, added. "What an asshole."

Caio went into the mess, stole a soda from the fridge, and took a sip just as a horn blared outside. Caio opened the door, and the horn blared again.

All the workers in the camp assembled in front of the management office, and Brice and Schroder stepped out. Schroder called roll, and when everyone on his list was accounted for, they made their way to Caio's plane.

"What are you waiting for?" Brice yelled at Caio. "Get these boys back to Ameia and keep them there until I tell you to bring them back."

Caio tipped his Coke bottle with a forced grin and headed back to the airstrip.

All the workers got onboard, and the stink of body odor and mud filled the plane. Caio pushed the cockpit door closed and cracked the side window. Five minutes later they were wheels up, and Caio banked left toward the river.

Caio loved flying. He loved the speed you really only feel near the ground, so he was rarely in a hurry to climb. He looked out the window and watched the trees race by.

The plane reached the far end of the valley; he buzzed the giant pile of stones. At the river, he dipped the wing and banked left. A flash of color along the river caught his eye, and in an instant he recognized the old boat. It was the *Uiara*. He and the owner were good friends, and Caio had been on it many times, usually after dark.

Caio straightened out and began a slow climb to five thousand feet and wondered why his friend would be there. When he leveled off, he settled into the monotony of flying and forgot about the boat.

When he reached the Rio Negro, he began his descent into Ameia, but halfway across the river he noticed another DC-47 parked at the airstrip.

It was a Brazilian Air Force plane.

Caio usually dropped straight in, but this time he leveled off at fifteen hundred feet and circled the field for a look. Four olive-drab rectangles were laid out on the ground near the office, and a group of soldiers were spreading out another.

Tents, Caio thought, then smiled. *At least they won't be stinking up the hotel.* He brought the plane around again and headed back toward the river. As soon as he leveled out, he looked right and saw the front of a big green helicopter the size of a bus.

Caio veered out of the helicopter's unusual flight path, then made another turn toward the river. When he landed, Caio parked next to the other DC-47. The helicopter was on the ground, but the two huge rotors were still spinning.

Aviation news in the Amazon was pretty sparse, but Caio recognized the helicopter as soon as he saw it from the side; it was a Chinook.

I'll bet Boeing brought it down here to sell a few to the navy, Caio thought, then held his breath and let his passengers off the plane. While they exited, Caio leaned against the tail and watched a line of people in suits and uniforms file out of the helicopter. They loaded up into military Jeeps and headed off to town.

Four men stayed behind. Three walked over to check on the tent raising, but the fourth, Joao Pedro, put his hands on his hips and watched the Jeeps drive away. *Must have run out of seats*, Caio thought, and laughed when Joao Pedro took off his hat and slapped his leg.

Luiz chocked the tires, then came over to greet Caio.

"You want me to top off the tanks now or wait until morning?" Luiz asked.

"Fill it up," Caio said. "I want to have a look at that flying bus."

As Caio walked up to the aircraft, he saw the crew inside, and one man looked up and waved.

"That's quite a machine," Caio said, and the man stepped down. He was pushing forty, clean shaven, with a light-yellow button-down shirt and green plaid pants.

"Yes, sir," he replied. "This is the farthest south this monster's been, but the government was dying to take it for a spin. Brett Aldridge, Boeing Corporation, USA," he added, and stuck out his hand.

"Caio."

"Who are you with?"

"With? Oh, with. No one. This is my gooney," Caio said, and pointed a thumb over his shoulder at his plane.

"You down here for the big test too?"

"No, I live here. I fly freight, but my wife owns the best hotel in five hundred miles."

"The best and only hotel in five hundred miles. Am I right?" Brett said, and slapped Caio on the arm with a smile.

"Just about. You're probably staying there tonight, unless they've got you bunked in one of these tents."

"The hotel's reserved for the bigwigs. Me and the crew are bunked right here in tent city, but hey, it's not that bad."

"Sorry."

"Don't be. I've slept in a hell of a lot worse, my friend. Come to think of it, if we had a few more tents and a bunch of people shooting at us, I'd swear I was back in Korea."

"So, have you got time to give me the nickel tour?"

"You bet! This is my baby. The first one of these took off the end of last year, and I jumped at the chance to show it off."

Brett spent nearly an hour showing Caio around the Chinook, and along with sharing everything there was to know about the aircraft, he told Caio about the test.

When the tour was over, Caio walked toward the airfield office to call a car. Before he reached the door, however, a car pulled up and Joao Pedro got out. The driver popped the trunk, and Joao Pedro yanked his suitcase out. The driver waved at Caio to hop in, and Joao Pedro walked past him without saying a word. Caio turned and watched him march toward the tents and heard him curse the whole way.

Caio arrived at the hotel, and there was a small group of men talking on the porch. There were two more groups in the lobby, and he could hear others in the dining room. He looked at Pedrina, who was behind the registration counter, and she returned a concerned look.

She left the counter, grabbed Caio by the arm, and pulled him down the hall to the back door. Two men were talking in the yard, so they went into the kitchen, and Caio pulled his arm away.

"Pedrina? What's wrong with you?"

"Katie's gone."

"I know. She went back to São Paulo?"

"No," Pedrina replied in Portuguese. "I sent the girls up to get her for breakfast, and she was gone, but her things are still here. I looked all over town, but she's gone."

"*Mãe*," Luiza, their four-year-old, said from her seat at the kitchen table. "*Papai.*"

"Her clothes are put away, her toothbrush is in the bathroom, and her suitcase was in the closet. I think something happened to her."

"Okay," Caio said.

"*Mãe!*"

"She'll be okay. I'll find her. She couldn't have gone far."

"*Papai!*"

"Luiza, please. We're trying to have a—"

"But I know where she is."

"Me too," Bruna added as she looked up from a sketch in Katie's notebook.

"Have you seen her?" Pedrina asked.

"No," Luiza said. "But she left a letter and her drawing book. I didn't know all the words, but Rodrigo read it. She went to save the monkey people."

"The what?" Padrina replied, and Caio remembered the boat he saw when he took off from camp. He knew exactly where Katie was, then thought of tomorrow's test.

"Oh shit," Caio said.

"Caio!"

"I know where she went. I saw the *Uiara* near the valley on my way back today."

"Who are the monkey people?" Pedrina asked, and looked to any of them for an answer.

Bruna flipped back a few pages and held up Katie's notebook. Her choice of colors was more fit for a parrot, but Pedrina clearly saw the creature.

"What's that?"

"That's the monkey people," Bruna said.

Caio grabbed a box of crackers out of the cabinet and moved Pedrina out of earshot of the children. "I just talked to a guy who said they're about to blow up the whole valley," he said, "and I'm certain Katie's in it. I have to go back up there and get her."

"Yes, yes," Pedrina said. "Go. Go quick."

Caio picked up two sodas, threw them into his small flight bag, along with the crackers, and headed back.

It was late in the day when he arrived at the airstrip, and the sun was on its way down. Caio hurried over to his plane, even though he knew he'd never reach the camp before dark.

"Where do you think you're going?" Joao Pedro asked as he cut Caio off. "The airspace is closed until further notice."

"I forgot my logbook," Caio replied without slowing down. "I'll just be a minute."

Luiz walked toward the plane as well and saw Caio look at him, then the chocks.

"Make it quick."

Caio opened the door, climbed the stairs, and shut it.

"Hey!" Joao Pedro shouted, and hurried over to the fuselage.

While he pounded on the door, Luiz pulled the chocks from the tires.

Caio slid open the cockpit window and yelled, "Clear!"

The first engine started, and the wind blew off Joao Pedro's hat. He ran after it, but when he reached the tail of the plane, he realized it was no use. Caio started the second engine, pressed down on the left brake, and increased the throttle.

The plane spun around, and the tip of the wing barely missed the long, drooping blades of the Chinook. Once the plane was clear, he bumped up the speed on the port engine and made for the far end of the runway.

Caio spun the plane round one more time, adjusted the flaps, and gave both engines full throttle. When the plane started rolling, he noticed a Jeep barreling across the tarmac to cut him off. It was Joao Pedro.

The tail wheel lifted off the ground, and Caio pulled back on the stick. The Jeep skidded to a stop in the middle of the runway, but the plane was off the ground. Joao Pedro dove out from behind the wheel onto the tarmac just as the left tire cleared the Jeep.

He sat up and watched Caio's plane head out over the river. When the noise of the engines faded, Joao heard men laughing and looked back toward the tents.

Caio turned northwest, and every mile he traveled the sun dipped closer to the ground. It wasn't long, however, before the clouds snuffed it out. He could barely make out the canopy, much less the river he usually followed. All Caio knew for sure was his bearing, altitude, airspeed, and how long it usually took to get there.

When the light died, the gray shadows turned black, and he was blind. Caio studied the instruments, corrected every time the compass moved too far one way or the other, but the longer he flew, the more he thought how easy it would be for the wind to blow him off course.

The only real landmark was the river, but the new moon was no help. *I can't see a damn thing from up here*, Caio thought. *I have to find the river.* He shut his eyes, took a deep breath, and let it out.

"Alright, Lord. Let's do it your way."

Caio throttled back, flipped on the landing lights, and let the plane descend. He turned his attention repeatedly from the window to the altimeter, and each time his breathing became more and more shallow. The lights on the wings were useless, but the one under the nose cast a bright beam of light into the abyss.

At a thousand feet his gut tightened, as did his sphincter. A hundred feet later, the lights revealed the canopy, and it was surreal. Caio leveled out and stared at the blur of treetops below.

"Come on, river. Where are you?"

The river cut a wide serpentine path through the jungle, and at best he'd only see a flash of reflected light off the water, but at least he'd have something to follow.

A moment later the leaves disappeared for an instant, he saw his light on the surface of the river, and the canopy came right back. When the next break came, he knew he was on track.

He focused on the here-and-gone-again rhythm and began to take normal breaths. Calmness allowed for other thoughts, and he considered the landing, the approach across the valley, and the cliff walls.

"Oh shit," Caio said, and his anxiety returned. *The river will take me right where I need to go, but the cliff walls of the plateau are right there. I can bank hard left and climb, but by the time I see the cliff it'll be too late. I need altitude, but I can't lose sight of the river.* He looked at his watch. *I have to be getting close.*

Caio noted the compass needle and decided he couldn't risk it. He applied a little pressure on the stick, increased his speed, and began to climb. The trees drifted off into the darkness, and Caio sighed. He glanced down at the compass just as the landing light struck the cliff.

"Shit!"

Caio gave the engines full throttle, jerked back on the stick, and banked left. The cliff raced toward him, and the blur of stone came into sharp focus.

"Go! Go! Go! Go! Go! Climb you son of a b— "

The cliff suddenly disappeared but was instantly replaced by limbs and leaves.

"Goddamn it!" Caio shouted, and the plane struck the very top of the trees. The props mowed through the thin branches, and the tough old bird took care of the rest.

Caio continued to climb and turn, and at two thousand feet he came full circle. He flew along the western wall of the valley by keeping half the beam in the trees and the other half in darkness. A moment later he saw a light in the distance. It was the construction site.

He turned toward it and buzzed the field. As he circled back around to the left, he looked down at the ground and saw two headlights move down the runway toward the cliff.

Caio continued out over the valley, counted to twenty, and came around again. The headlights of the Jeep lit up just enough of the runway for Caio to line up, and he dropped the flaps two clicks. He pulled the nose up to compensate, and just before he reached the Jeep he throttled back. The plane dropped, bounced twice, and sped to the end of the runway, then rocked to a stop.

Caio released the stick and grinned when he realized the tightness of his grip. He turned the plane around and parked in his usual spot.

The Jeep was already there, and a long shadow passed through the headlights. Caio cut the engines, powered down, and leaned back in his seat. His quiet moment of relief, however, ended when Schroder pounded on the fuselage and yelled. Caio unlatched the door, swung it open, and dropped the stairs. Brice and Schroder were right there, but Cage leaned back against the fender of the Jeep and watched

"What the hell are you doing back here?" Brice shouted. "You're lucky to be alive, you idiot. You know you can't fly at night."

Caio grabbed his bag and stepped off the plane. "Have you seen Katie?" Caio asked.

"Katie? What the hell are you talking about? You flew her out of here yesterday!"

"She came back."

"What?"

"She took a boat and came back up here. She left a note. The guy from Boeing told me what's about to happen, and if Katie's down there, we have to get her out."

Schroder ended Caio's rant with the butt of his gun, and Caio fell unconscious in the dirt.

"Cage!" Schroder yelled. "Lock this asshole in the office storeroom until I decide what to do with him."

Cage stood up from the fender and looked at Brice.

"You got a problem with that?" Brice asked.

"No, sir."

"Then get to it."

"I'll give you a hand," Skinner said from the darkness as he walked up from camp. "Evenin', fellas. What did I miss?"

"Just a little personnel problem. It's sorted out," Brice answered.

"I can see that," he replied, and looked at Cage. "Which end do you want? Hands or feet?"

17

Drop

Katie barely slept, and neither had the creatures, except for the young ones. The adults talked most of the night, and she had watched their gestures and heard the tone of their voice. They hadn't come to a unanimous decision.

The airplane landing after dark had them all on edge, and some reconsidered leaving, but not all. At dawn, the alpha's family, the sentry, and those who decided to leave packed their baskets and gathered in the branches around the alpha's nest. They left just as the Chinook rumbled into the valley and made a low pass over the trees. The troop's retreat was slow, given the children and baskets they carried, but they made their way toward the western cliff wall.

Katie held tight to the sentry, and whenever he looked in her direction, she could see the anger on his face.

This is my home, the sentry thought. *We should have killed them all, as our kind has always done in the past.* He thought of his own troop and remembered what happened last season. *My mate, my children, my home— all gone. Now I run without a fight. I should fight. it's my responsibility. If I knew where these creatures come from, I'd kill them all.*

The camera crew got started at dawn. Cage just finished his shift and watched the thin men jackass their equipment into the back of a Jeep. He smelled breakfast and walked to the mess hall, but when he reached the door, Schroder yelled at him from the office.

"Cage! We got VIPs today, so eat fast; you're working the day shift too."

Cage forced a smile, gave him a thumbs-up, and went inside.

Cage didn't notice he was the only one in the room until he'd piled his plate with bacon and eggs.

"Morning, everyone," Cage said. "Sleep well? That's great. Looking forward to another wonderful day?"

"Hell yes," a voice answered, and Cage spun around. "Frank Baldridge, PhD. You work here?"

"Yeah."

"Can you give me a lift to the platform?"

"Sure. I was just about to have breakfast, but—"

"Me too. I'm starving. I'll join you." Baldridge stuck his head out the door and whistled at the camera crew. "You boys go get set up. I'll meet you there in a bit."

Baldridge grabbed a plate, scooped up half a spoonful of eggs and all the bacon left in the tray. He shoved one piece in his mouth, walked over to Cage's table, and plopped down.

"So, what's your story?" Baldridge asked.

"Too long to tell."

"Me too," Baldrige replied, then stuffed another piece of bacon in his mouth. "You stationed here, or just here for the big show?"

"I've only been here a couple of days, but as far as I know this is my address for a while."

The small talk ceased for three minutes, the amount of time it took Baldridge to finish breakfast. Cage took his time and listened to Baldridge tell a forgettable story, interrupted regularly by a belch and waft of bacon across the table.

Cage put down his fork.

"Ready?" Baldridge asked.

"Sure. I'll grab a Jeep and be back for you in a minute."

Cage picked Baldridge up at the steps. At the platform, Baldridge got out and checked progress, while Cage stretched out behind the wheel and rested his eyes.

The camera was stabilized, the film was loaded, and they were ready to roll.

Baldridge checked his watch. "We've got about an hour and a half before the show starts, so go get some breakfast. The eggs are pretty good, but they ran out of bacon. Pick me up at my tent in an hour."

Cage received orders to watch the office, which he didn't quite understand, and Brice and Schroder headed for the platform.

Skinner pulled up and stopped in front of the office a few minutes later with his whole team crammed in a Jeep. Cage gave him a nod from his seat on the steps, and Skinner smiled.

"Damn, son," Skinner said. "Looks like you got stuck holding down the fort. You're gonna miss the whole show from back here."

"The new guy always pulls the best duty."

"Yeah, but hey, at least you're not cleaning the shitters. You be careful guarding those steps, and I'll catch up with ya later."

Skinner drove off, and Cage went inside to look for a pair of binoculars and was surprised to find one sitting right on Brice's desk.

Cage walked back outside, stood on the top step, and watched Skinner stop at the platform. He got out, and the rest of his team drove up the valley toward the waterfall.

Twenty minutes later Cage saw something flash on the opposite side of the valley and raised the binoculars again. It was the windshield of the Jeep. There were only two men left, and both got out.

The helicopter showed up right on time. The deep rumble in the distance announced it, and Cage watched it clear the cliff at the southern end of the valley. It descended out of sight, but the noise echoed off the cliff walls as it moved north. It emerged mid-valley and turned toward camp.

It landed at the far end of the runway at the top of the cliff, and before the engines wound down a line of people spilled out. They made their way along the cliff, onto the platform, and Cage lowered his binoculars. At the platform, the VIPs took turns looking over the edge; then a tall man in a gray suit stepped up onto a small wooden crate.

He smiled, outstretched his arms in a welcoming embrace, and took a deep breath.

"Good morning, gentlemen. First of all, I'd like to thank all the members of the US and UK armed forces for making the trip down here to witness this test, as well as the members of the Brazilian government who provided such a perfect site. On a personal note, I'd also like to thank the Brazilian air force for being such a gracious host. Thank you. By now you've had a chance to talk with the folks who developed ASH and know all about its wide range of civilian and military applications. In Manaus, you were treated to a series of films these fine gentlemen made of the process at their testing facility in the United States. What you'll see today, however, is a full-scale test that will demonstrate the capability of the world's only instant defoliant.

"You'll also be treated to a display of three new military aircraft, one of which you're already familiar with, the beautiful dual-rotor beast that brought you here today. The other two aircraft will be joining us in a few minutes, the F4-Phantom and the F-86 Sabre. Even though you navy boys in Brazil have pretty much settled on the P-2 Neptune, we couldn't resist showing off the latest versions of these two state-of-the-art warbirds one more time." The speaker looked at his watch, then gave a nod to a man crouched down next to him with a radio. "That said, it looks like it's time to get this show on the road, or more precisely, in the air. Let's start with a demonstration of unbridled speed. When you need to get there fast, hit hard, and get out, few planes can keep up with these two."

The speaker pointed to the south, and the audience looked down the valley. A moment later, the first aircraft appeared as a tiny silhouette that dropped down from a line of clouds. Spellbound and silent, they watched it grow, and with it the noise of its engines. It raced by in less than a second, and a sonic boom followed. The noise was deafening. Everyone who'd never been in combat covered their ears.

"That was the Neptune, but don't lower your hands just yet. It looks like the Phantom is hot on its tail."

Heads turned back to the south, and another aircraft roared their way. Unlike the last, this fighter had a muscular shape. The two jet engines on each side of the fuselage gave it mass, and the wings seemed to flex.

The pilot kicked in the afterburner, and the jet blasted by at twice the speed of the first, with twice the noise. It went nose up at the falls, flipped over, and headed back in the direction it came.

The roar of jet engines stopped the troop, and the sonic blast caused two creatures to lose their footing.

Agility kept them from falling, but they were shaken, as were the others. The children howled and clung to their mothers, and when the second jet passed, the whole troop picked up their pace.

Every bird fled the canopy, and in the flutter Katie listened to the noise of the jets reverberate through the valley. She kept her eyes to the south and expected to hear an explosion and see flames, but none came.

"Beyond the advantage of speed," the speaker said, "the vertical rate of climb separates the hunter from prey, and the only thing that will take a man higher faster is sitting on a launchpad in Florida."

The audience laughed, and the radioman looked for a cue. The speaker nodded, and the radioman called in the next run.

This time the F4 went first. It approached at a much slower speed than the last time, and the two seconds it spent in clear sight conveyed its power. Mid-valley, the plane turned straight up, and the afterburners engaged again. It rose just as the speaker said, like a rocket.

"Right now that pilot's experiencing the same g-forces astronauts feel when they blast into space. If you'll look to the south, here comes his pal. The Sabre."

The aircraft barrel-rolled into the valley, and at mid-valley it pulled up and took to the sky. It ascended, and in six seconds it was no more than a dot.

The troop heard the aircraft approach again, but this time they didn't stop. Most of the troop dropped what they were carrying, and the children wrapped both arms and legs around their parents. They raced through the treetops faster than even Katie could imagine.

The sentry brought up the rear so he could look after the elder if he needed help. Once more Katie looked for explosions, and when they didn't come she knew they were putting on a show.

Two passes, Katie thought, and looked over at the elder. *The next pass will probably be it. We'll never make it out in time.* She got the elder's attention, and when he looked back, she pointed at the trail up the cliff and shook her head. He didn't understand, so Katie raised her hand over her head for cover. The elder nodded, made two long howls and two sharp whistles.

The troop changed course and made for the cliff.

311

"These two exceptional aircraft would be my delivery method of choice for the real product you came here to see, so let's get this test underway. I'm excited to see what ASH can do, and I'm sure you all are too. For those of you without military training, keep in mind an enemy's best defense under attack is having a good place to hide. For enemies who depend on the jungle to provide that place, we're about to take that option away."

The speaker nodded once more to the radioman, and he tapped the cameraman on the shoulder. The cameraman flipped a switch, and the camera made a high-pitch whir as the film rolled.

"It might be a little late to ask," a man at the rail said, "but is it safe to be standing out here?"

"We should be far enough above the reaction, but be ready to run just in case."

"Run?"

"Don't worry," the speaker replied with a big smile. "Just kidding. We're perfectly safe."

The others had a good laugh, but the man who asked the question took two steps back from the rail.

"Remember, the valley was treated a couple of days ago, and the process has had plenty of time to spread

312

from the root to tip of every plant down there. When the aircraft drops the catalyst, you're in for a real treat, so don't blink."

The two aircraft approached, but this time they were side by side. They roared up to the southern end of the valley, and as soon as they passed the rubble, small bright objects spilled out of canisters on the wings.

The roar of engines returned, and through the odd break in the trees, Katie watched them approach. The first objects dropped just as the sentry leapt from the tree onto the cliff.

Katie almost lost her grip, but the sentry grabbed her. He crawled down the stone and swung into a narrow crevasse that widened at the ground. The rest of the troop was already huddled inside.

The observers watched the lights disappear into the canopy. There was a blinding flash at the southern end of the valley, followed by a roar and eruption of dirt, smoke, and stone like a volcano. The blast moved up the valley, and all of the spectators fled the platform and ran away from the edge.

Katie and the sentry peered around the opening of the crevasse and watched death consume the valley. Katie felt the impact coming.

It was an intense tremor, but the flames she expected to see never appeared. In two seconds, the eruption came into view. A second later, the world seemed to stop, except for the cloud as it approached. The ground vibrated. Katie could barely stand, and she saw the jungle floor rise like the earth itself was exploding.

Dirt and rocks shot into the air. She couldn't move. The sentry wrapped his arm around her waist and pulled her back. Her last glimpse of the valley was of the trees as those who stayed behind tried to reach the crevasse. One leapt and almost made it, but in an instant, all of them and everything beyond the entrance was gone.

The concussion of the blast threw Katie and the troop deeper into the crevasse and against the walls. Dust filled the air, and everything went black. Katie tried to open her eyes, but the dust forced her to keep them closed. She felt the bodies of creatures against her and heard them cough and moan. Arms and legs untangled themselves, and all of them gasped for air.

Katie felt an adult's head on her chest, but it didn't move; then she felt the tiny hands of a child on her face as it crawled off its mother's back. The little creature hugged Katie's neck and gasped. Katie lifted her shirt and covered the child's nose and mouth. It stopped gasping and took two deep breaths.

Masks, she thought. *They need masks*. She felt the sentry's arm against her leg and grabbed it. When she found his hand, he held hers. She squeezed back, then opened his hand and tapped on his claw. Katie worked her fingers underneath it and gently lifted it up. The creature extended it, and Katie patted his arm so he knew to keep it there. She rubbed the child's head, then moved the creature to her side and took off her shirt.

Katie felt her way back to the creature's claw and used it to cut and tear the shirt into pieces. The first piece she pressed against the child's face, and it reached up to hold it.

She did the same with the sentry, and she heard him take a deep breath. He understood what she was doing and helped.

Katie held a mask over the mouth of the adult resting on her chest, but it never took a breath. *I wasn't fast enough*, she thought, then felt something warm drip down her side. She ran her hand over the back of the adult creature's head and felt the open wound.

315

The creature's child nuzzled its face against Katie's neck, and she held the creature as if it were her own.

The onlookers reassembled into a group fifty feet from the edge and watched the gray cloud boil up and fill the entire valley. At the north end the waterfall disappeared into the dust, and to the south the cloud poured out of the valley over the giant stones.

Smith and Perez stood at the top of the trail until the dust rolled into the jungle. Neither man could see, so they retreated past the Jeep until they could. Skinner had backed off the platform as well and lost sight of the other side of the valley. He pulled out his radio and checked on his team.

"Skinner . . . Head count, over."

"Perez, over."

"Smith, over."

"Uri, over."

There was a long pause before Skinner called again.

"Gonzalez," Skinner said, "come back."

"Gonzalez here. Sorry. I can't see a goddamned thing. Pushing back, over."

"Roger. Visibility will clear. Stay sharp."

Katie and the creatures were the only life left in the valley. They huddled in the dark and struggled to breathe. Katie felt the sentry stand and listened to his hands move along the wall toward the opening. She heard him ascend the cliff wall but heard something else: the faint sound of clapping. Katie was ashamed.

The sentry returned twenty minutes later. He made his way back into the crevasse, felt around until he found Katie, and knelt down next to her. He took her hand and laid a strong vine in her palm, then pushed her hand in the direction of the others. Katie found the hand of the creature beside her and did the same.

The sentry waited until everyone had time to grab ahold and made a few muffled noises. Katie felt the vine rise, and she stood up. The child held tight, and Katie supported the child with one hand and held the vine with the other as the sentry led them out of the crevasse.

The ground under Katie's feet was soft like sand and rose as she reached the entrance. The consistency of the ground changed again. It was powdery on top, but below the powder was hard as cement. She still couldn't open her eyes, so she followed the sentry and listened. It was eerie. Katie heard the creature's footsteps and their nails and rough skin scrape along the stone wall. The only life she felt, however, was the little life clinging to her neck.

"I hope you fellas got that," Frank said as he slapped the camera operator on the back. "I expected a dust cloud, but holy shit, that was amazing."

"Yeah," the cameraman replied. "I got all of it. I can't wait to see how this new high-speed camera did. I followed the reaction from one end of the valley to the other, so you should be able to see what it looked like coming and going."

"Perfect. It doesn't look like the dust is going to settle anytime soon. Is there enough film left to shoot the valley after it does?"

"Hell yeah, Professor. We brought two extra rolls just in case, so we're good to go."

"Well, I talked these boys into giving me a ride back to town, but you guys stay here and get more footage. That Brazilian bush pilot will run you back to Ameia as soon as you're done. We've got some celebrating to do."

Frank caught up with the rest of the group, shook a few hands, and climbed into the Chinook with all the other smiling faces.

The rotors spun to a blur, and the downdraft became a storm. The giant helicopter rose, and the camera crew covered their ears and turned their backs. The helicopter turned north along the cliff, and the two men turned to watch.

It stayed low but well above the jungle. It turned west over the waterfall, and the downdraft kicked up a rainbow. Once across the river, the helicopter turned south and followed the opposite cliff wall toward the river. When it reached the end of the valley, the two men abandoned their equipment and headed back to the mess hall for a drink.

Brice and Schroder pulled up to the office, pushed past Cage, and disappeared inside. Cage stood there a moment, then looked through the binoculars at the platform. The cloud started to subside, and Skinner walked out to the rail.

"Hey!" Brice yelled from behind. "Are those mine?"

Cage spun around, and Brice pointed at the binoculars.

"Oh . . . yeah . . . I just borrowed them." Cage took them off, reached up to hand them to Brice, and he snatched them out of his hand. Brice scoffed, went back inside, and slammed the door.

Cage thought about stealing their Jeep but decided he could use a little exercise, so he walked out to see Skinner and whatever remained of the valley.

Katie and the troop heard the helicopter take off, listened as it circled the valley, and felt the downdraft as it passed overhead. Katie knew she was slowing their progress, but they never pushed.

It was a slow climb, particularly with her eyes closed. She kept one hand on the vine and the other on the cliff but never took her arm out from under the child.

Maintaining her footing was the hardest part. Blind, she slid her foot along the ledge, pressed down to make sure the ground was solid, then slid her other foot up the incline to move forward.

"See anything?" Cage asked Skinner as he stepped up on the platform.

"Besides a filthy cloud?"

"What do you think it's made of?"

"Who the hell knows? Scientists cook up some strange shit. I'm just trying not to breathe it."

"Did any of the creatures pop up?"

"Nah. The dust has just started to settle, but if I couldn't breathe up here, anything down there must be dead. I'll give it ten more minutes, then call it a day."

Katie tried to focus and keep her composure, but all the emotions were overwhelming: the destruction she just watched, the baby's mother dying beside her, her friends, the boat, and camp—she thought of all of them at once.

She wanted to cry, but she also wanted to kill everyone responsible. Hate and despair being equal but opposite emotions canceled each other out, and she maintained her focus on the ledge.

The cloudy remains of the valley continued to settle, and after fifteen minutes the darkness through her eyelids lightened. She felt the warmth of the sun and opened her eyes. The dust on her face forced her eyes shut, so she wiped it away with her hand. Sweat smeared it to a paste, but she wiped off enough to see.

Skinner turned his back to the valley and leaned against the rail. He propped his rifle up against the corner and looked down at his radio. Skinner changed frequencies and pressed the button on the side.

"Horsefly. Horsefly. Horsefly. Bravo, Tango, ready for extract."

"Horsefly. Roger. Echo, Tango, Alpha, two zero."

"Roger. Out."

Skinner changed the frequency once more and called his team in.

"So, what's the plan, Cage?" Skinner asked, and lit a cigarette.

"Plan? I'm doing it."

"Site security?"

"For now I guess so, but I always keep my eyes open for other opportunities," Cage replied, then noticed a small shadow move on the far cliff wall. Cage knew what it was, thought about the Otter Hound, and couldn't tell Skinner.

While Cage talked to Skinner, he made a point of looking off in other directions, but he always glanced over Skinner's shoulder.

"Not sure what they'll have us do next," Skinner said, "but I'm short a man. You interested?"

Cage wasn't listening to the conversation, but his brain registered the last bit.

"Interested?"

"Hell yeah, brother!" Skinner said, and slapped Cage on the arm. "You wanna be on the bag team and do more than guard shovels for a living?"

Cage thought about it, but Skinner wasn't one to wait.

"Tell you what," Skinner said, "take all the time you need. Our ride gets here in a few minutes. If you want the job, get on it."

"What about th— ?"

"Them?" Skinner asked as he slung his rifle strap over his shoulder and threw a dismissive wave at the construction site. "Fuck them. You just come with me and let Uncle Sam sort that out."

Skinner smiled and walked off the platform, then looked back at Cage. "Well, don't just stand there. Go get your shit."

Tears cleared Katie's vision, and she could finally see. With her face pressed against the cliff, she couldn't see the valley, and part of her didn't want to turn and look, but she had to.

A filthy cloud stretched out in a coffin of stone. For the rest of the climb, she and the troop had plenty of tears to wash away the dust.

The sentry was almost at the top when he heard the Jeep start and signaled for everyone to stop. He waited until it drove away, and they moved on. When they reached the top of the cliff, the troop went into the jungle and used anything they could find to brush off the dust.

Katie grabbed a small leafy branch herself, knelt down, and cleaned off the child. The branch took off the bulk, but Katie finished it off by fluffing its fur with her hand. In the process she discovered her passenger was a little girl.

One by one the creatures gathered together, and Katie was surprised none of the females came over to take charge of the baby. By now they knew who lived and who died, so they knew the child was an orphan, but none of them wanted anything to do with her.

"Alright," Katie said. "Looks like you're stuck with me, so you'll need a name."

The child liked the sound of her voice and touched Katie's mouth.

Katie tried to think of a name, and the dust reminded her of digging. That thought led her to archaeology, then anthropology, and she remembered the find in Africa. Katie had it.

324

"I'm sure your mother gave you a name, but I doubt I could pronounce it, so I'll call you Lucy. Is that okay?"

Katie picked up the child and walked over to the alpha and sentry. Unlike the other creatures, who stared down into the valley, they stared straight across to the camp on the other side. Katie looked as well and noticed Caio's plane. *There's no way he was a part of this*, she thought, then remembered the letter she left on the bed. "He came to get me."

The alpha and sentry both turned and looked at her; then the alpha motioned toward the waterfall, then at the camp. The creatures climbed up into the trees and headed toward the end of the valley. Katie stayed on the ground with Lucy, and she caught up with the rest of the troop at the falls.

A small cargo plane buzzed the treetops from the northwest, crossed the valley, and touched down at the airstrip. The bag team had already assembled next to the mess hall and was on its way to the runway when Cage walked up. Brice and Schroder came out to see them off, then saw Cage.

"What the hell's going on?" Schroder yelled. "You just got here!"

"Sorry, chief," Skinner said. "Cage is needed else-where, but I'm sure you'll find another mindless grunt to take his place."

"You work for me, goddamn it, and you're staying right here!"

The aircraft rolled to a stop, and the cargo ramp in the rear of the plane lowered. Skinner raised the rifle in his hand and gave it a curious look, then looked at Schroder.

"You're kidding, right?"

The rest of the team laughed, and they all got on the plane.

Katie rejoined the troop along the river, not far from the falls. She noticed a place along the bank where a huge boulder created a pool of water, and looked at herself. She was filthy, sweaty, pasty, and her clothes were full of grit.

"I could use a break. How about you, Lucy?"

The rest of the troop rested in the trees above, but they all stopped and watched Katie sit down at the edge of the water, take off her boots, and dip her feet. Katie noticed the water concerned Lucy, but the creature sat down in the grass next to Katie.

Katie leaned forward, cupped her hands, and washed her face. The water felt amazing, and the urge to get in was irresistible. She touched Lucy on the leg to reassure her and slipped in. With her whole body submerged, she ran her fingers through her hair and scrubbed her face. When she came up, Lucy was pacing, and the whole troop seemed concerned.

The pool was chest deep, so she slipped off her bra and shorts and rinsed them out. She twisted out the water, pitched them on the bank, and dunked herself again. Underwater, she looked up at the surface and saw Lucy's hand reaching in. Katie popped back up and watched the creature sit down on the edge and dip her legs in.

"You're a brave little girl," Katie said, and Lucy smiled.

One of the adults above made a noise, and Lucy looked up. As she did, the wet bank caused her to slide in. Lucy went under, but Katie grabbed her under the arms and pulled her up. Lucy wrapped her arms around Katie's neck and shook the water off her head.

Lucy looked down at the surface and realized half of her body was underwater. She watched her hair float and patted the surface. Katie scooped up handfuls of water and rinsed off the remaining dirt from Lucy's hair. She looked at the child and noticed every inch. For a moment she forgot where she was.

A breeze rustled through the trees, and Katie looked up. The alpha's mate said something to him, pointed at the valley, then at Katie, and climbed down from the tree with her child. The female sat down at the edge of the pool and dipped her feet in as well. The female smiled, and her little one stuck his hand in the water.

Katie looked at the female and could see she wanted to tell her something. The female pointed at the valley and tilted her head as if to ask why. Katie sighed; she didn't have an answer.

18
Vengeance

Caio pounded on the storage room door, and the wound on his head did the same to his skull.

"Open this door!" Caio shouted.

Brice sat behind his desk and smiled at Schroder. "Sounds like our guest is awake," Brice said, and Schroder shook his head.

"Want me to let him out?" Schroder asked.

"Open the damn door!" Caio shouted, and banged on the door again.

"Nah," Brice replied. "Better let him cool off a bit."

Schroder walked up to the door. "Knock it off," he said, then kicked the door. "We'll let you out when you calm down."

"Calm down! You son of a bitch. I'll calm down after I wring your neck."

Schroder smiled and Brice laughed.

"Real funny," Caio said. "I think you split my head open."

"Don't worry, Caio," Brice said. "After that stunt you pulled last night, there's obviously nothing in there that's going to fall out."

"Where's Katie?"

"Gone," Schroder replied. "And that's one pain in my ass I won't miss."

"Gone? Open the damn door."

"You just stay in there awhile."

Caio punched the door, sighed, and rested his forehead against it. "At least give me some aspirin. My head's killing me."

Brice looked at Schroder, grinned, and took a bottle out of the desk drawer. He emptied a few in his hand and threw them under the door.

"Son of a bitch," Caio replied.

Just then the front door of the office opened, and Holloway walked in.

"Hey, fellas. You mind if me and the boys borrow a Jeep? The dust has nearly settled, and we need to shoot a bit more film."

"Just take it," Brice said, and dismissed him with an irritated wave of his hand.

"Hey!" Caio yelled. "Let me out of here."

Holloway stopped and turned back. "What the hell's going on?"

"Nothing you need to worry about," Schroder replied, and rested his hand on the pistol strapped to his belt.

Holloway had dealt with his type before, so he shrugged and walked out the door. He waved at Gary and Vickers, then pointed at the Jeep next to the office.

"The sooner we get this done, the sooner we can get outta here."

Vickers got behind the wheel. Holloway took shotgun, and Gary hopped into the back seat.

"Take the runway," Holloway said.

Vickers turned right at the end of camp, drove to the runway, and hung a left toward the cliff.

Gary yawned, stretched, and opened a soda. "No wonder your wife moved back in with her mother. Your snoring kept me up—"

Gary yelled, and Vickers thought Gary had fallen out of the car. He slammed on the brakes, and he and Holloway looked back over their shoulders. Gary was on his back, and the sentry had him by the throat.

"Gary!" Vickers yelled, and started to get out of the car, but Holloway pulled him back in. The two men

331

watched the creature run the long claw on its other hand into Gary's torso, then raise him off the ground.

"Drive! Drive! Drive! Drive! Drive!" Holloway shouted.

Vickers shoved the gas pedal to the floor. The tires spun, then spun again when he shifted into second. They hit fifty miles per hour in no time and barreled down the runway toward the valley. Neither Vickers nor Holloway thought about the direction; they just wanted to get away.

"What the hell?" Holloway shouted, and they felt a thump.

Vickers looked in the rearview and saw two large eyes, surrounded by hair, then saw teeth. Vickers screamed. Holloway was too terrified to move, and the alpha leaned forward between them. Vickers screamed again and tried to jump out, but the alpha grabbed them both by the neck.

The creature's claws pierced Holloway's skin, and blood sprayed the windshield. Vickers struggled to get free, but the alpha cut his spinal cord just above the shoulders.

Paralyzed, Vickers watched the edge of the cliff get closer, and a hundred feet away the alpha leapt out. The alpha watched the Jeep disappear over the edge and, a moment later, heard it explode. The noise echoed up, and Brice and Schroder ran out of the office.

Brice stayed near the door, but Schroder eased along the trailer and looked toward the runway. He watched a thin plume of black smoke rise from the valley, then noticed someone standing at the edge. He couldn't tell who it was from the back, but when it turned and looked in his direction, he saw that it wasn't some*one* at all.

The sentry raced out from around the last tent in the camp and ran for Schroder on all fours. The creature was incredibly fast, but it only took a second for Schroder to raise his rifle and slip his finger on the trigger.

Katie jumped onto Schroder from the side, and the rifle went off. Schroder staggered but didn't fall, and Katie held on. Katie wrapped her left arm around his neck and punched with her right. She didn't care where the punches landed: head, ribs, arms, it didn't matter. She just kept swinging.

Schroder was more irritated than hurt, and he slammed Katie against the wall of the trailer. The punching stopped, but he slammed her against the wall again. Katie's left arm slipped off his neck, and she scratched across his eyes and face as she fell. She hit the ground, and Schroder dropped to his knees.

Schroder got back up and was furious. It wasn't just the pain; he couldn't see.

"Where are you, goddamn it?" he yelled, and waved his hands in front of him. "When I get my hands on you, I'm gonna—" He grabbed a handful of hair. "There you are, you little bitch." He pulled the pistol from his belt.

He raised it, and another hand wrapped around his. It wasn't the hand of a woman. He tried to pull free but couldn't, and the grip tightened.

The bones in Schroder's fingers broke, and he screamed. The jagged bits of broken bones pierced nerves and flesh as Schroder was dragged away.

Katie got up and noticed Brice at the foot of the steps. She ran for him, and he ran back inside. Brice slammed the door, but before he could turn the dead-bolt, Katie forced it open.

Brice rushed around his desk, yanked open the top-left drawer, and reached for his gun. A shot filled the room with a deafening blast, and a bullet tore through Brice's shoulder. He fell back against the wall and looked up at Katie and the barrel of Grover's gun.

With a steady hand, she stepped toward him.

"Hey!" Caio yelled. "What the hell's going on out there? Let me outta here!"

Katie looked at the door and smiled, then took Brice's gun out of the drawer and pitched it across the room.

"You're going to pay for this, bitch," Brice said as Katie unlocked the door and let Caio out.

"Katie! Thank God. I thought you were dead," Caio said, and gave her a hug. "We found your letter and I came up here to get you, but these two assholes knocked me out and locked me in the—oh shit!"

The alpha stepped into the office. Caio tried to pull Katie into the storage room to get away from the creature, but she pulled him out.

"It's okay," Katie said, but Caio's terrified expression never changed.

Two more creatures appeared in the doorway, and Katie smiled. They looked at Caio and hissed, but Katie held out her hand. "He's not one of them."

Katie looked down at Brice, and he crawled under his desk.

The alpha heard Brice, and Katie gave him a nod. The alpha shoved the desk out of the way like an empty box. Brice looked up just enough to see the creature and muttered something under his breath over and over again. When the alpha reached for him, Brice mustered enough courage to go for the gun.

The other two creatures were on him before he ever got close and pulled him outside by his ankles.

The alpha left with them, and Katie and Caio sat on the steps. They didn't speak for a while and watched the troop tear apart everything they could find. The tents were shredded, the walls of the mess hall were bashed in, and clothes were thrown everywhere.

Caio broke the silence. "Maybe you can find a shirt out there that fits."

Katie looked down and realized she was sitting there in her bra. She laughed, then put her arm around Caio, leaned over, and cried. He put his arms around her, and once again time passed without words.

The riot ran its course, and the creatures assembled in front of the office. A female came out from around the office with all the children, and Katie saw Lucy in her arms. Lucy saw Katie and urged the female to put her down. She did, and Lucy raced toward the steps. She bounced off Caio's lap and hopped into Katie's arms. Katie waved at the female, then stroked the back of Lucy's head.

The alpha, sentry, and two other males returned, and Katie didn't have enough feeling for either of the men to wonder what the creatures had done. The alpha walked up to Caio and reached out as if to greet him, but shoved him off the stairs instead.

Caio looked up from the dirt a bit dumbfounded, then grinned a Katie.

"I think he likes you," Katie said.

"I'm just glad he didn't cut my throat."

The sentry made his way toward the stairs, and Katie stepped out of the way. The other creatures followed, and the whole troop went in and had a look around.

Katie helped Caio up, and they walked off toward the remains of the tents. Lucy's arms relaxed a bit, and Katie knew her little girl needed a nap, but Katie kept looking for a suitable shirt.

Caio retrieved an unopened suitcase from one of the piles, opened it, and Katie found a shirt that was still neatly folded. She handed Lucy to Caio, put on the tartan button-down shirt, and tied a knot in the tail to take up the girth. Caio handed Lucy back, and Katie was right: she was asleep.

They walked over and checked on Caio's plane next, and with the exception of a few scratches on the fuselage and part of a tent draped over one wing, it was fine.

When they got back to the office, only the alpha and sentry were still inside. Katie walked in and stood next to the alpha, who stared at a drawing of the finished project on the wall.

The sentry was focused on a large topographical map on the other wall. The valley was circled, but other locations were circled as well, only they had been crossed out.

The alpha moved to the topographical map and got everyone's attention. All three looked at the map, and the sentry put his finger on the valley. He pointed toward the actual valley, then back at the map again. He said something to the alpha and pointed at each of the other red circles, but stopped on the farthest one. The sentry patted himself on the chest and tapped on the circle again. He repeated the same gesture for each of the circles and stopped at the one around the valley.

He moved his finger back to the first one, pressed the claw on his index finger into the center, and ripped the paper from one circle to the next. He punched himself on the chest, and Katie grabbed his arm.

Katie shook her head, but she could see the sentry was overwrought with guilt. He pulled his arm free, turned back to the map, and raked his hand across it with his claws. He stepped away from the map, threw the desk against the other wall, and rushed out the door.

The alpha turned to go as well, but Katie stopped him.

"Wait a minute," Katie said, and held up her hand. "Caio!"

Caio came up the steps and stuck his head around the door. "You okay?"

"I'm fine. Remember when I asked you how far your plane can go?"

"Yeah, like I said, it'll go as far as I need it to go, as long as I can stop for gas and oil along the way. Why?" As soon as he asked, he knew what she was thinking. "Hold on!"

"Just hear me out," Katie said. "I found out yesterday there were more of these creatures in the Amazon, but the same people who did this already killed them. This troop has no place to go."

"Can't they just start over in some other part of the jungle?"

"For a while, but I'm sure these people will find them, and I can't take that chance."

Caio sighed, and the pain suddenly returned to the back of his head. "Do you have a place in mind?"

Katie smiled and looked at the alpha, who was as puzzled as Caio.

"Help me find a map of North America," Katie said.

The alpha and Caio watched Katie rifle through the desk, then Caio grinned.

He hurried into the storage room, and long, rolled-up sheets of paper soon flew out the door.

"Got it!" Caio shouted, and came out with the right one.

The wall map was too big for the desk, so he unrolled it on the floor. It showed the entire western hemisphere.

"This is perfect," Katie said, and carefully got down on her knees. She tugged on the alpha's arm, and he crouched down as well. Katie found where they were in the Amazon and held the alpha's finger on it until he didn't try to move.

She moved her finger from his, out of South America, through Central America, into North America along the Rockies and tapped her finger. She made a small circle and looked at the alpha, then Caio.

"My family owns a lot of land right here. Do you think you can make it this far?"

"Not legally."

"Good, because our friends would never make it through customs. Is your plane gassed up?"

"You want to leave now?"

"Tomorrow will be too late."

"That's a long way. Do you think they'll understand?"

"I hope so. You go get the plane ready, and I'll explain it to them."

Caio got up and left, and Katie started to gesture an explanation, but the alpha stopped her. He patted himself on the chest and pointed at the area she circled. She took his hand and smiled, and he stood up. He took one last look at the map of the Amazon on the wall and left.

Katie got up and walked to the door. Lucy played with Katie's ear, and Katie smiled, but when she looked outside the rest of the troop was gone. She watched the alpha as he made his way toward the valley, then noticed the rest of the creatures along the edge of the cliff.

She touched Lucy's back and felt her warm body. *How could it come to this?* Katie thought. Then she remembered something Sid said. *I wonder if these people even considered all the what-ifs before they started. I suppose if they never have to see the damage done, they don't have to care.*

As Katie walked toward the plane, she watched the troop and some of their gestures.

"Are they coming?" Caio asked as he pulled the tent off the wing.

"They're discussing it. Can I give you a hand with the plane?"

"Actually, if we go north, we'll need cash or something to trade. The airfields aren't on the map, if you know what I mean. Would you go see what you can find? There's probably a cash box in the office."

"Sure," Katie replied. She took a few steps, stopped, and turned back. "Other than money, what else should I look for?"

"Guns and alcohol, but if you find any portable generators, those are great for bartering too."

"Got it."

"And don't forget the ammo."

"Yes sir, *capitán*," Katie replied with a smile, and hurried off to scavenge.

The office was the obvious first stop. When she walked in, she noticed the blood spray on the wall from the gunshot. *Strange,* she thought. *All the time I was in here, and this is the first time I noticed it.* That reminded her: Brice's gun was still in the corner, so she picked it up and set it on the desk, then stopped to think. *There was a security team, and all of them had guns, but I doubt they took them to Ameia when they left.*

Katie walked in the storage room and smiled. There were two steel gun cabinets with double doors, and three cases of booze stacked up beside. She carried the liquor out first.

Lucy was no help, but Katie managed to convince her to ride on her back, so at least that freed up her hands. Katie stacked the boxes next to the steps, then tried to open steel cabinets. They were locked.

"Shit." *Brice and Schroder probably have the key in their pockets*, Katie thought, and hoped Brice kept a spare in his desk. Katie searched each drawer, and the third one was the winner.

As she turned away from the desk, she stepped on something uneven; it was a clipboard. She almost ignored it, but the name of her university caught her eye, so she picked it up.

It was a list of names and where they were from. Most of the names were associated with the government or military offices, but among them was Francis (Frank) Baldridge PhD, ASH chemist. Katie pulled the page off the clipboard, stuffed it in her pocket, and went back to work.

She opened the gun cabinets and found two dozen rifles lined up on their butts, and wooden cases stamped AMMO on the shelves beneath. Katie grabbed three of the guns and carried them like firewood to the bottom of the steps, where she left the liquor. They were a lot heavier than she expected, and she thought about how she'd get everything to the plane.

There's got to be a Jeep around here, Katie thought, and walked over to the motor pool. Sure enough, one was sitting there. She put Lucy in the passenger seat, drove back to the office, and parked in front of the steps.

It took some time to load everything, and she had to drag the boxes of ammo along a board from the doorway to the back of the Jeep, but she got it done.

Caio was in the cargo bay when Katie drove up, and he froze when he saw what she'd found.

"Holy shit."

"Did I do alright?"

"If you ever want to change careers and go into the business with me, just let me know."

Katie got out and passed everything up, except the ammo boxes. She and Caio loaded them together, and Lucy supervised. When they were done, Lucy hopped back on Katie, and Caio got on the plane to tie down the cargo.

"Think this will be enough?" Katie asked. "I can go back and see what else I can find."

"This will be plenty," Caio replied, then stopped and looked toward the valley. "I don't see your friends. If we're going to make the first leg before dark, we need to get going."

Katie walked away from the plane and looked down the runway, then scanned the tree line. *Come on*, Katie thought. *Come with me.*

Ten minutes passed, and Katie stood vigil; then Lucy pointed at the trees. Katie didn't see them at first, but as the creatures stepped out of the jungle, she could see why: each had an armload of leafy branches.

Katie walked them to the plane. They were reluctant at first, but after the alpha's mate and child jumped in and laid down a nest, the rest did the same. The alpha, sentry, and three other males brought up the rear, and none of them carried branches. Katie motioned for them to get onboard, and the alpha climbed in.

The sentry and three other creatures stayed on the ground. The sentry patted himself on the chest, pointed at the other three, then pointed at the jungle.

"No. No. All of you need to leave. It's not safe for you here."

The alpha looked down at his friends, and the sentry touched Katie on the head. She looked at him and

345

teared up; then the sentry motioned for her to get in the plane as well.

Katie's heart sank, but she understood. *Maybe Sid was wrong*, Katie thought. *Maybe the military hadn't found all the creatures. If they hadn't, the sentry would surely find them.*

She tried to smile, and the creatures turned to go. Katie grabbed the sentry, and he turned around.

"I don't know if you hug," Katie said, "but I'm giving you one anyway." She wrapped her arms around him.

Lucy reached over her shoulder and grabbed the sentry's ear, and the two parted.

"Take care of yourself."

The sentry smiled, and all four males raced off into the jungle.

Katie watched them disappear, and the alpha nudged her on the back. He opened his hand. Katie took it, and he pulled her up.

Ten minutes later the wheels came off the ground, and every creature's face was pressed against the windows. As the plane passed over the valley, only the engines made a sound. Even the children were quiet.

The valley looked like the surface of the moon.

19

Home

Katie pushed open the rusty screen door, and the screws holding the top hinge pulled free from the rotten frame. Iced tea splashed over the rim of her glass, soaked her hand, and pattered on the porch. Without a grumble, she nudged the door back in the frame and sat down in a wicker chair.

She propped her feet up on the coffee table and rested the glass on her belly. In five months it had become the perfect tray.

The old door was on her list, and it was becoming hard to ignore. *No wonder farmers have so many kids*, Katie thought. *As soon as I fix one thing, two more things break. Sometimes I envy the troop.* They settled in right away; then she remembered the winter. *Amara would have laughed her ass off if she had seen all of us living under one roof.*

When spring came, they couldn't wait to get outside,

and Katie looked out at the trees. Leaves had already started to appear.

Katie's thoughts drifted back to the night they arrived. *This is one creepy house. I wouldn't have walked into this place on a dare by myself. Funny how having friends around makes things a lot less frightening. Of course, if there had been monsters, they wouldn't have stood a chance.* Katie smiled.

The exterior was weather-beaten and tired, but the house felt strong. Every day she noticed a new detail of its life or the lives of the people who had lived in it.

The Winston family farm was managed by the local bank, and when Katie arrived she questioned the expenses charged for upkeep. No one else in the family had any interest in the farm or property, and she thought the bank manager would have a stroke when she told him the family signed it all over to her.

Art Sutter and his wife sure make a cute couple, Katie thought. *One of these days they'll own that Co-op. That wife of his. She's a sweetheart. They remind me of a young version of the Bakers. I wonder if I'll ever feel lonely living way out here. The troop is always around, and I've just started to consider all the work I need to do. As long as I don't get bored, I doubt I'll ever feel lonely; besides, I'm not alone.*

Katie listened to the last of the snow drip from the eves and the waking limbs shake off the cold. The migrating birds hadn't returned, but the locals seemed happy.

She reached over and picked up the small hard-backed book called *King Solomon's Ring* from the end table next to her and put the drink down. *The weird little guy on the cover reminds me of Joao Pedro*, she thought, and smiled.

She hadn't had the book long, and she remembered having to drive into town to pick it up from the post office. Dr. Powel thought she'd like it.

Katie thumbed her way back to the beginning of chapter eight. She'd read it several times, but it hadn't gotten old. *Dr. Powel.*

She thought of Amara again and looked at the other book on the table. *If you didn't know it was a veterinary manual*, Katie thought, *you'd swear that was a miniature version of the Bible*. She reached over, thumbed through the pages, and saw all of Amara's notes. *No wonder she's such a great vet.*

The chains of the porch swing sang as a breeze sat down, and Katie clicked the button on her Parker Jotter as she read. When a thought was sparked, however, the clicking stopped and she stroked the clip instead.

Katie reached the end of the chapter and finished her drink. She stretched, looked over at *The Merck Manual*, and got up to get more tea. Merck wasn't as fun to read as Lorenz, and she knew she'd need more caffeine.

She stood up and carefully opened the screen door, but she heard a car engine in the distance and stopped. The land was posted and posted multiple times along the road. Signs warned visitors to call before crossing the bridge, and the swinging cattle gate was chained, so the sudden appearance of a car caught her off guard.

The creatures knew to hide, and even the smallest of the children obeyed, but Katie still worried.

A black Chevy sedan appeared through the trees, drove around the circular gravel drive, and stopped at the steps. She couldn't see the driver, but he wasn't a local. The car was too clean, and it wasn't a truck.

Katie only saw the lower half of the man through the passenger window and watched him turn off the engine, then open the door. A man in a white fedora stepped out with his back to her, and as he took it off, he turned around. The instant Katie saw his face, her stomach muscles tightened and the tiny hairs on the back of her neck stood up. Her grip tightened on the door, and her fingers pushed through the screen.

"Good morning, Katie," Sid said, and walked around the front of the car.

Without a word, Katie went into the house. When Sid reached the bottom step, he saw Katie's silhouette moving down the hall toward the front door. Three steps from the top, the screen door flew open, and none of the screws held. The old door tore free and crashed to the floor.

Katie followed, met him at the edge of the porch, and pressed the barrel of Grover's .38 against his forehead.

Sid stopped and smiled. "You killed me once already. Don't you think that's enough?"

Katie thumb-cocked the pistol but didn't say a word.

"I'm sorry," Sid said. "Okay? I'm sorry. I tried to talk them out of it, but I have to follow orders too. It's not like I had a choice."

Katie stared into his eyes without the slightest change in expression, and when she slid her finger from the trigger guard onto the trigger, his eyes followed.

"Alright. Let's try this another way," Sid said. "They know I'm here. They sent me, and if I don't come back, they'll send someone else and keep sending people until they get the answers they want."

Katie didn't move or speak. In the few seconds it took her to get the gun, she already knew what she'd do with his body and the car, but if he was telling the truth, she knew he was right.

She pulled the gun back and pointed at the porch swing. Sid stepped around her, walked over, and sat down. Katie returned to her chair, crossed her leg over her thigh, and rested the pistol on her calf. She released the hammer but kept the barrel pointed right at him.

"If it makes any difference," Sid said, "none of this was supposed to happen. You were never supposed to go down in the valley. If you had just done what you were told, you never would have known about these monkeys, and your friends would still be alive."

"It's my fault?" Katie yelled. "Is that what you're saying?"

"Well, in a way."

"If this is your way of convincing me not to put a bullet in your head, it's not working."

"No. I admit it. It's my fault. They already paid Joao Pedro to look the other way, but I thought we needed an outsider to agree. I didn't have time to find someone I could pay off, so I found someone who wouldn't know what to do. It should have been a field trip for you. Fly up, look down, and fly away. I made a mess of it."

Sid set his hat on the coffee table and rubbed his forehead. Katie sat quietly and watched.

"They found the bodies. Well, they found the film crew. They think they found Brice and Schroder, but the bodies were in so many pieces . . . Well, I just hope they didn't suffer."

"I'm sure they did," Katie said, and Sid looked at her.

They both sat quietly and gazed off across the yard at the trees. Sid broke the silence.

"They know you left Brazil."

Katie turned and looked at him. "Caio was only a contractor, but the Agency monitors all of its assets whether they own them or not. He flew for us, and we always knew where he was. Honestly, Katie, the camp was destroyed and men were killed after the test, so they knew the creatures survived. When you and Caio disappeared for three days, they tracked the flight. They know you brought the survivors here. They can't allow those creatures to live."

"Is that why you're here?"

"Katie, they have to be destroyed. They're too dangerous. Can you imagine what would happen if they ever came in contact with people? Besides, what happens when they start breeding? If they decide they need more land, they'll just take it."

Katie laughed and shook her head. "They probably said the same thing about us!"

"Oh come on, Katie. We're not talking about people, they're monkeys. They might be as smart as a dog, but they're just monkeys. I read some of the reports, and there was nothing remarkable about them. Monkeys, gorillas, or orangutan, they're not people."

Katie's brow dropped and she tilted her head.

"What?" Sid asked.

"You've never seen one, have you?"

"I've seen the blurry pictures and seen the damage they can do."

"But you've never seen one?"

"No."

"As much as I hate the thought of it, do you have kids?"

"Excuse me?"

"Kids, Sid. Do you have kids? Do you have a family you go home to when you're not doing terrible things no one knows about?"

"Well, I wouldn't put it that way. I just—"

"Do you!"

"Yeah, to be honest with you, I do."

"Good. Now imagine this: a bunch of people show up at your house, destroy it, then kill your wife and kids right in front of you. How mad would you be? What would you do to those people if you ever got ahold of them? That's exactly what you and your friends did to them, and you're damn lucky most of the workers in camp were gone."

"You just made my case," Sid replied. "These animals are killers, like wolves and bears, and we'd all be safer without them running around."

"Jesus, Sid. If you believe that, you really do have problems."

"I'm just saying we've got enough unpredictable killers on this planet. At least human beings can reason with each other."

Katie laughed. "You really are crazy. Maybe before you take sides, you should know what you're talking about."

"Katie, they're dangerous."

"Who? Your friends or mine?"

Sid shook his head and smiled. "I swear, Katie, you are the most hardheaded woman I've ever met."

"Maybe, but before you decide to exterminate a species, you should meet them first."

"Oh," Sid said, then chuckled. "You're suggesting I take a walk in the woods so I'll end up like Brice and Schroder?"

Katie smiled, took a deep breath, and thought for a moment. "Lucy! Come here please. There's someone I want you to meet."

Sid straightened up and looked off at the trees. Katie watched him tug at his pant leg and grinned. A floorboard creaked, and Sid spun back around toward the door. He didn't notice the fingers along the doorframe until they moved, and Sid leaned forward. Lucy peeked around the frame, then ducked back inside.

"It's okay, sweetheart," Katie said, and the child stuck her head out again. Her big eyes looked at Sid, then Katie, then back at Sid. "Lucy, come out and say hello."

Lucy stepped out onto the porch and looked at Katie again.

"I keep them out of sight of people, so she's a little nervous," Katie said, and Lucy smiled. "What have you got there?" The child held up a box of crayons, then pulled a coloring book out from under her arm. "Lucy discovered her artistic side this winter. She loves to color, and this jungle coloring book is her favorite."

Sid couldn't speak but thought of his own son and surviving the terrible twos. *That kid never stopped coloring at the edge of a page*, Sid thought. *Lynn and I spent all night painting the hallway before the realtor's open house, and the next morning that boy had illustrated* The Wizard of Oz *from one end to the other. Now, that kid had talent.* Then he remembered his own childhood. *Why clean the grout when you can just add some color?* Sid couldn't help but smile.

Lucy walked over to the swing, grabbed Sid's knee, and leapt into a seated position beside him. She crossed her legs Indian-style, opened the book to the picture she had been working on, and took a dark-green crayon from the box.

To his surprise, she took his arm, raised it over her head, and laid it on the back of the bench. She twisted around just enough to lean back against his side and handed him the box of crayons. When her strange little hand touched his, he felt the coarseness of her fingers, fine hair, and curved claws. She gave him one last look, then focused on her picture.

Sid watched her add color to the page. She was careful to stay within the lines, but whenever she crossed one she'd grunt with disappointment. He looked at Katie, and when she saw his expression, she moved the pistol from her leg to the table next to her.

"Winter must have been tough," Sid said. "I don't imagine they'd ever seen snow."

"It's a big house, and there's a barn, so they only got cold when they wanted to, but the snow was a new experience for them. The older ones were apprehensive, but the little ones loved it."

"So Lucy's parents are here as well?"

Katie's smile fell flat and she looked away.

"Sorry . . . that was a stupid thing to ask."

There was a long, uncomfortable pause, but Lucy continued coloring.

"So, what's your plan?" Sid asked, and Katie looked at him. "Shit, I can't say anything right. I mean, what do you hope to do?"

"The same thing I wanted to do the first time I saw them: keep them safe."

Sid looked down at Lucy and gently touched the top of her head. He watched her color, and whenever she wanted a different crayon, she'd look up at him, and he'd hold out the box.

Finally, Sid looked at Katie, then at his car. He rubbed the back of his neck and shook his head.

"You know, Katie, it really is a damn shame none of the creatures survived the winter."

Katie's jaw nearly dropped.

"I guess they are like people: one gets the flu and pretty soon everyone has it. They probably didn't have the antibodies to fight it. After everything they've been through, well, that's just terrible."

Sid picked up his hat, put it on, and began to stand up, but Lucy grabbed his arm. He stopped, looked down, and tore the page out of her coloring book. She handed it to him with a smile, and Sid's eyes teared up.

Katie walked him to the steps. He took two steps down, then turned and extended his hand. After everything he'd done, he didn't think she'd take it and was surprised when she did.

The End

The End

About the Author

The son of a soldier, William grew up in many different places, so as he would say, he's from everywhere. If he had to pick, he'd simply say he's an American. He earned a bachelor's degree in English at the University of Washington, in Seattle, and a master's in education at the University of Maryland, Baltimore County. He has lived in several states since then, but for nearly a decade the Philadelphia area has been his home.

Aside from writing, William enjoys photography and the creative visual outlet it provides. In his youth, he was an avid woodworker, carver, and even created a series of pen-and-ink prints.

Learn more about the author Online at:
www.williamjdavisbooks.com

www.ingramcontent.com/pod-product-compliance
Lightning Source LLC
Chambersburg PA
CBHW011457170626
46814CB00008B/2938